Praise for Shiloh Walker's *Always Yours*

"...Readers looking for a fast paced, suspenseful plot filled with a white-hot romance should not miss the highly enjoyable ALWAYS YOURS."

~ Holly, Romance Reviews Today

"...Always Yours is one hot read that will have the reader fanning themselves for relief. Kristen and Dylan's relationship will have the readers begging for more."

~ Sonya, Fallen Angel Reviews

"...Full of intrigue, adventure, romance and passionate love making, ALWAYS YOURS is definitely a hit for Shiloh Walker."

~ Amanda, Romance Junkies

D1556982

Always Yours

Shiloh Walker

A SAMHAIN PUBLISHING, LTD. publication.

Samhain Publishing, Ltd.
512 Forest Lake Drive
Warner Robins, GA 31093
www.samhainpublishing.com

Always Yours
Copyright © 2007 by Shiloh Walker
Print ISBN: 1-59998-722-8
Digital ISBN: 1-59998-498-9

Editing by Jessica Bimberg
Cover by Scott Carpenter

First Samhain Publishing, Ltd. electronic publication: May 2007
First Samhain Publishing, Ltd. print publication: September 2007

Chapter One

If there was one thing about Max Delacourte that Kris would change...it was his hair.

Something about hair that short on a man, well, she just didn't like it. Kris imagined, if he grew it out long enough, those wavy golden brown tresses would curl over her fingers just so.

Leaning over the table, she smiled at him as he poured more wine into her glass and teased, "So...am I going to be invited to spend the night?"

She quirked a brow. "You're leaving on a plane in three hours, soldier. What good would it do?" she said.

"Well, then I could take a raincheck," he answered with a grin.

"Where you flying off to this time?" she asked. She bit back a sigh when he arched his straight brown brows at her. He never told her where he went. He was never able to.

"Sorry—terminal nosiness," she said glibly, lifting one shoulder. Kris took her wineglass and sipped, licking a drop from her lip before she set it down. "You military boys can never tell us civilians much of anything."

He cocked his head, studying her. "You sound as if you've known a couple of military boys," he murmured.

She shrugged and said softly, "Only one. A friend's brother." She pushed thoughts of him out of her head and focused on the man in front of her. "So...can you tell me when you have to leave? How long you'll be gone?"

He laughed. "Damn, you're nosy. Leaving next week. Flying down to see my family before I head out. And no...I can't say how long I'll be gone," he responded.

She stuck her tongue out at him.

His response to that was to lean over and catch it with his own, tangling his hand in her hair and kissing her hungrily. She sighed and leaned into him, thoughts of that other military boy fading into the back of her mind.

ങ്കരുങ്കരു

Later that night, Kris lay in bed, her sheets tangled around her body, soaked with sweat while her heart pounded in slow, torturous beats within her chest. Outside her window, the lights of New York City drowned out the stars overhead and the ever mad rush of life pulsed on.

Within her dream, she was as far away from the glam and glitz of New York City and her nice little condo as she was likely to get. Kris stood in the corners of a primitive hut made of sticks and mud bricks, hay stuffed between the cracks. *Man... People really live like this...* It wasn't the important thing to be dwelling on. She knew that. But it was better than the alternative.

There was death in the air tonight.

Betrayal.

Evil of the worst kind. The kind that knew it was evil and just plain didn't care. As she stood in the corner, her hands closed into fists so tight, her nails biting painful little circles into her flesh, Kris could see him moving through the hut. He wore army fatigues, some kind of heavy combat gear. She couldn't see a damn thing to distinguish him, but she sensed he was a deadly bastard.

All she could see were his pale colorless eyes. Those eyes were soulless.

His gaze passed over the corner she stood in and she shivered, feeling her heart stop in her chest.

Who are you... What meaning do you have in my life? she wanted to ask him.

But then she knew, because the man who passed in front of her this time was one she knew. She knew him well, since he had been all of fifteen and she had been twenty-two and fresh out of college. An eager beaver junior editor, she had a job she had bullied her way into, using all her family's connections and all her sass, then worked to prove that she was more than her father's daughter and that she could damn well succeed on her own, away from him.

It was Dylan Kline, his face as familiar to her as her own, even under the grime of his face paint, and the fine coat of sweat. His mouth twisted with hate as he moved through her, towards the man who stood behind them.

Kris felt a ghostly chill race through her and she turned, staring at them, just in time to see somebody from outside the shack lift a gun. She screamed out Dylan's name.

But he couldn't hear her. As the gun fired, Kris jerked out of her dream with a scream and stumbled out of the bed, her eyes wide, her hair damp with sweat, and her thin camisole clinging to her.

Nausea roiled in her belly and she fought to push the nasty dream out of her head.

But it wasn't going any place.

She knew why.

It wasn't a dream. It was fact. Or at least, it would be. If she couldn't do something to stop it. She rubbed at her gritty eyes with hands that shook. Her legs wobbled as she made her way out of her bedroom and into her office. She had his phone number. Or at least an old one. She'd get in touch with him. Kris didn't care if she had to stay up the rest of the night.

It took an hour and a half, and numerous phone calls.

But she had come to accept one simple fact—it didn't matter if she did stay up all night. She could call everybody from Fort Bragg to the Pentagon, and it would be a waste of time. She was not family.

They were not going to get a fucking message to Dylan Kline for her, no can do, sorry, ma'am.

Well, that was okay, Kris thought with a tight smile. She knew who was family.

ଔଔଔଔ

Dylan was having sweet dreams.

Very sweet dreams.

There had been one time...only once, but it had been close enough for him to pretend there was something in Kris's eyes beside aloofness.

That one time had fueled his dreams for years and tonight wasn't much different. He was dreaming about her again. It had been a picnic, Labor Day weekend, at Nikki's cabin, when it started pouring down rain and they were caught under the trees by the lake, waiting for the rain to let up. Either that or make a dash for it.

Her eyes had met his and lingered...just for a minute. They were both wet from the rain, and he had been studying the front of her T-shirt. "I didn't know rich girls wore T-shirts," he drawled.

"Well, I gave the maid a few days off and I haven't done laundry, slick," she said, lifting a brow at him before returning her gaze back to the rain and sighing, a movement that made that miraculous chest rise and fall, drawing his attention to her hard, pebbled little nipples.

"Gasp...you know the 'L' word?"

"Bite me," she said, rolling her eyes.

He surprised her when he crossed the grass and asked softly, "Can I? Where?"

Her lids flickered and he watched as her tongue slid out, wetting her lips. "It's a saying, babe. You know, a sarcastic one, basically telling you to—"

The rest of her words were muffled against his mouth as he lowered his head and pressed his lips against her petal-soft mouth, very curious to see how she would taste. Damn, he'd been dying for a taste for years. The heat and the sun and a couple of beers, watching her all day was enough to weaken his resolve.

And that was where the dream differed from reality. In his bed, Dylan rolled onto his back, his hand resting on his belly, while in his dream, his hands came in and framed her face, holding her still. In reality, her lips had parted under his for a second, one sweet, brief second...and then the moment had been ruined as thunder cracked and the wind started to whip around them.

But in his dream...he backed her up against the tree and he never even questioned how it somehow became a bed. Or how her jean shorts and damp shirt were replaced by black silk.

Clichéd, maybe, but there was something about a long, slim woman wearing black silk.

Just as he was peeling the black silk off of her, her lips parted—ringing erupted from them.

His eyes flew open on a vicious curse and Dylan jackknifed out of bed, wide-awake and hornier than hell. He grabbed the pager and stared at the unknown number. Unknown, no emergency code, so he tossed the pager down and rolled over, going back to sleep.

It had actually been a pretty sweet dream, almost—it *almost* felt real. One day, he'd love to have that kiss followed by something more than his dreams.

ՑՀՖՑՀՖ

Kris was pulling her hair by sunrise. He hadn't called back. She didn't give a flying fuck if he didn't know the number. Did he have the decency to actually have a *voicemail* option?

Of course not.

The urgency in her gut grew—she had to talk him. Soon. Reaching for the phone, she called Nikki again and prayed she wouldn't get her head ripped off.

ՑՀՖՑՀՖ

Dylan growled into the phone this time as Nikki said in lieu of greeting, "You know, the reason you carry a pager, is so when somebody pages you, you can call them *back*."

"No, really?"

"Smart ass," she said. "Somebody called you this morning. She's waiting for you to call her back. I'd appreciate it if you'd call her so she'd leave me alone."

"I don't return calls I don't know," he said dryly. "My big sister told me never to talk to strangers."

"It's not a stranger. It's Kris Everett," Nikki said shortly. "She sounds pretty...urgent. Call her. Got the number?"

"Why in the hell does she want to call me? I'm not one of her hotshot writers. I'm tired. I want to go back to sleep." He wouldn't, though. No matter how tired he was. Just thinking about Kris was enough to clear the fog of sleep from his brain.

"I don't know what she wants," Nikki said. Her tone was sharp and annoyed and starting to rise as she repeated, "Do you have the number?"

Dylan rolled his eyes. "Yes, mother. I have the number. Now can I go back to sleep?"

"Not until after you call her." Her voice softened. "Take care of yourself, little brother."

Dylan grunted into the phone before dropping it back into the cradle. He'd call Kris later. Sleep wasn't going to come any time soon, but he couldn't talk to Kris so close on the heels of the dream he'd had.

The phone rang again and he grabbed it. "What?" he demanded, exasperated.

"Call her," Nikki repeated. Then the line went dead.

"Brat," he muttered. He scrubbed a hand over his eyes and started to put the phone down again. But if he did, his sister would just call again. How she'd know that he hadn't called Kris, Dylan wasn't sure. But she'd know.

Kicking away from the sheets, he sat up on the edge of the bed and stared at the phone's keypad for a long minute. "I sure as hell won't be getting back to sleep now," he muttered. No, after talking to Kris, he'd end up in the shower. A cold shower. Jacking off while he remembered how she had looked in a wet T-shirt.

Finally, he punched in the number from memory and when her soft, husky voice came on the line, it was like a punch to the solar plexus.

"So what has you calling my sister to track me down?"

"Dylan," she said, and there was something odd in her voice that sounded like relief.

"You wanted to talk me," he said.

"I have to talk to you."

Her voice was shaking. Dylan frowned and sat up straighter. "Kris, what's up? You don't sound good," he said quietly.

"Listen, this is going to sound absolutely crazy, but... shit. Dylan, are you going out on a job or whatever in the hell you guys call it soon?"

"A job," he repeated levelly, a grin tugging at his mouth.

"Yeah, a job, a mission, an op, whatever the term is," she snapped.

He could almost see her, too. She'd be pushing her hand through her hair, that tumbled, deep red hair, her green eyes snapping with irritation. The smooth ivory of her skin would be flushed pink with temper. Dylan had to smother a groan, just thinking about it.

"Why are you asking?"

For the longest moment she said nothing. And then, "Because whatever it is, you can't go," she said in a rush. "I know this is going to sound like I'm nuts. But I have dreams, crazy, insane dreams that sometimes make no sense, and last night I had one and you were in a hut in some primitive place, like a jungle or something. There's a man in the corner, and then I see you and—"

"Kris, sweetie," Dylan interrupted. "Why in the hell would you be having a dream about me?"

"It wasn't a dream, Dylan," she said softly. "Right before I woke up, somebody shot you. There's people, too many of them and hardly any of them are on your team. Gunshots and shouting and—"

Her voice was getting higher and sounding panicked. "Okay, okay, Kris. Listen, take a deep breath. Let's say this is real—"

"Damn it, it *is* real. Or it will be. My parents were supposed to get on a plane to France two years ago and I had a dream a week before. I threw such a fucking fit that they cancelled their plans. Well, that plane crashed outside Paris and half the passengers died, you jackass," Kris shouted in his ear.

Dylan winced, pulling the phone away from his ear.

"You need to ask Nikki why she cancelled her plans to take the family to Carlsbad last summer, slick," she railed.

"Okay. Okay," Dylan said. "I hear you." This was nuts. Absolutely nuts. But she wasn't going to calm down, either. At least not until she said whatever she had to say. "Maybe there is something going on then. Listen to me, I need to know everything about the dream, everything you can think of, okay?"

"Is there something coming up? Something in a jungle?"

A chill raced down his spine as he thought of the op coming up in Brazil. Lucky guess. He shook his head and sighed. "Rich girl, I can't tell you that."

"I take it that means yes," she said softly. "Dylan, you can't go."

13

"Just tell me about the dream, Kris. Okay?"

ରୟେରୟେ

She hung up the phone nearly an hour later, feeling drained and shaken. And totally useless. Because he was still going.

Kris couldn't help but wonder if she'd ever see him again.

Damn it. Covering her face with her hands, Kris leaned forward, bracing her elbows on her knees, and prayed.

Damn it. Damn it. Damn it. Damn it.

Oh, God. Please, keep him safe.

Dylan, damn his stubborn hide, was a damn near permanent fixture in her life and had been for the past eight years. Ever since she had stumbled upon the manuscript his sister had written and she had done everything but walk on hot coals to get Nicole Kline to write for Barnes and McNeel.

That sulky teenager, more man than boy, had grown into a man that set her heart to flaming even just hearing his voice.

If he had the nerve to let anything happen to him...

Kris breathed out a sigh. She had to stop thinking about him like this.

She actually had a man in her life again. A good one. One who made her heart quiver when he kissed her. So what if it didn't outright stop?

But that had only happened once.

That rainy day when Dylan had kissed her. Kris had waited for years for him to do it again, and had even thought about trying it herself. But time passed. Years actually. And she just never...did. She never forgot it, though. Pressing her lips together, she remembered the taste of him, that hot, unique male taste—oh, damn.

It was sad.

She couldn't remember how Max tasted—and he had just kissed her last night.

That was pretty pitiful.

CRCSCRCS

Dylan was pretty damned certain that if he got out of this mess he'd drop to his knees and kiss Kris's feet.

They had lived through the ambush only because he had been edgy, thanks to her weird phone call and he had turned at the last second, thinking for some odd reason he had heard her voice. That was when he had seen the signal flash between two of the hidden guerillas.

His desperate *"Drop!"* had saved most of the team.

The word *most* was bitter, but hell, at least they still had a team. Only two of their number lay dead on the field behind them and of the ten remaining, none had any serious injuries.

Big problem now—they were trapped.

Cornered.

They had walked into a trap, and the guilt ran gut deep, because he had been warned. They may not make it back home.

Behind him, he heard swears, a whispered prayer. That would be Nick Antonelli, Dylan thought, and he could see the Italian American reaching up to cross himself.

Nobody spoke. Jerry Sears was thinking furiously, trying to figure a way out of this mess. Dom was whistling tunelessly under his breath, the way he did when he was thinking, and thinking hard. From the corner of his eye, Dylan could see Dally Conroy and he wondered if his friends were seeing their lives flash in front of their eyes.

Dylan sure as hell was. Weird little blips. The day he came home from school and found his sister sitting next to their mom's lifeless body. Nikki's car wreck. Kris showing up in their lives, out of the blue, when he was fifteen. The picnic. The kiss. He'd wanted to kiss her again—and a hell of a lot more than that, but it didn't look like that was going to happen now. If he'd known he'd probably die this time out, he would have spent the past few weeks a little differently.

Dylan was just thankful that Max Blessett had stayed behind with the chopper. Max, with his new wife and baby, needed to stay alive.

At first Dylan thought he was hearing things, when he heard Max's voice come out of the darkness. Then he started swearing silently, certain whoever had had sold them out had revealed Max's position as well. Certain he had been captured and their one possible hope for escape was gone.

That was when he realized.

It was Max.

Max had sold them out.

Through the blur that followed, when a bullet took out Nick Antonelli, Max stood there, expressionless.

As Dylan lunged for the bastard who had shot his best friend, he felt an icy hot pain explode through his back. *A bullet*—he hadn't ever been shot before but he knew that was what that pain was. He collapsed to the ground, staring up at Max with hatred and fury.

There wasn't any sign of remorse in those friendly, easy blue eyes. When Dally raised his weapon to take out the bastard, Max had grinned.

16

"You sonovabitch, it was you," Dally whispered, shaking his head, his pale green eyes narrowed and angry. "It was *you*."

"Yeah, that little voice of yours led ya astray this time, didn't it?" Max smirked. "It had me a little worried for a while. You've had too many lucky hits there, but not this time. Your luck has run out, cowboy."

As Dylan lay there, trying to drag himself to Nick, Max turned around and walked away from the gun in his face. He never once looked back, not even when somebody shot Dally in the back.

Those laughing brilliant green eyes went forever dull and a scream started to build in Dylan's throat.

Chapter Two

January

Every muscle in his body hurt—his legs and lower back were on fire. "Son of a fucking bitch," he swore, sweating, as he shifted his body and pulled himself up to the rails until he could swing his legs and hips into the wheelchair. His dark blond hair was straggly, longer than it had been in years, and hanging in damp curls that clung to his unshaven face. The hollows and angles of it were planed down all skin and bone, giving him a hawkish look.

"You're pushing too hard, kid," Jerry Sears said from across the room, one shoulder propped against the door jamb.

Dylan ignored him as he rolled the chair in the direction of the counter. Snagging a water bottle, he emptied half of it before pointedly staring out the window. His breath came in ragged gasps and his chest burned while the muscles in his legs quivered and that only made the impotent anger rise.

He'd once been able to run for miles, swim endlessly, lift nearly double his own body weight. Months ago only, mere weeks, really.

And now, he could barely do the physical therapy exercises that had been ordered by a platoon of doctors.

"You want hurt to yourself, mess your body up even worse?" Jerry asked. "How badly are you trying to fuck yourself over?"

"Go to hell," Dylan panted, reaching for the wheels and setting the chair in motion. "You're not my doctor."

"No. I'm your commanding officer." Silence followed and then Jerry sighed, and added, "I'm your friend." He turned around to stare out the window over the grounds. "Your friend. And as such...ahh...you... I thought you should know that they are watching Kirsten Everett."

Dylan lowered the water bottle slowly. "Watching her for what?" For what? He had a sinking suspicion he knew. He studied his CO through narrowed eyes and hoped he was wrong. He wasn't though. He knew he wasn't. Kris was being investigated.

"To see if Blessett tries to contact her," Jerry said quietly, turning around to look at Dylan.

"Why would he contact her?" Dylan asked stonily.

"She's been dating Max off and on for more than a year," Jerry said quietly.

Okay, so that wasn't something Dylan had been expecting to hear. He squeezed his eyes closed tight and wondered if this was another seriously fucked up dream. He'd been having nightmares from hell ever since—well, for months now. But when he opened his eyes, Jerry was still standing there and he still had that tight, grim look on his face. "What in the hell did you just say?"

In a flat, level tone, Jerry said, "You know what I just said, buddy."

Dylan shook his head, once. Then again. "No." His eyes narrowed and he said it louder, "No. He's married. Damn it, he's got a wife and new baby."

"That doesn't matter to some." Jerry's lip curled in a snarl and his eyes darkened with the same rage that Dylan felt any time he thought about Max. "And Intelligence is watching Cassie Blessett as well."

"How do you know this shit?" Dylan asked.

"It's my job to know." He sighed and scrubbed his hands over his eyes. "Apparently Intelligence has been watching him, closely, for a while. But there's a file on him. And on her."

"Fuck. *Fuck!*" Dylan clenched his hands around the armrests of his wheelchair and slammed his head back, staring up at the ceiling. "Damn it, do they have anything besides seeing them together?"

"On Max? Hell, yes. What I want to know is why they left him in my unit for as long as they did. I lost five men. *Five* of my *friends*... On Kris Everett? There's a file of pictures of them together. A year's worth. Doesn't add up to much, because he only had sporadic leave time and he spent most of it with Cassie. But no proof on her—until now. What she told you is plenty of proof," Jerry said.

"Proof?" Dylan said bitterly, his gut churning. *No.* Just...*no.*

Then he slumped in the chair, brooding. He had to ask. He didn't want—seriously *did not* want—to ask. But Dylan knew he had to know. Softly, the words feeling like jagged glass in his throat, he asked, "Does she know he's married?"

Jerry started to laugh. "She's most likely guilty of treason. But that's what seems to have you the most upset."

"Fuck you."

CRCBCRCB

Kris jumped when the pounding started. It was pitch black, her head ached, and it was... Two-thirty-two a.m. Whoever it was had better have a damn good reason for waking her up. Otherwise, they might need an ambulance. Two a.m., for crying out loud.

Stumbling out of bed, she grabbed her robe off the edge of the bed by feel before walking down the hall, flicking on the switch and wincing at the light. Kris had to cup her hand over the peephole to look out, her eyes still far too sensitive to see. And she couldn't see a damn thing. The hallway looked empty.

She was getting ready to go back to bed, mumbling under her breath when the door shook under a pounding again.

She yelped and jumped back, startled. When the pounding came again, she flipped the locks open, leaving the chain in place, looking through the narrow slot.

What she saw froze her heart.

Dylan...in a wheelchair.

"Oh, shit..."

She slammed the door shut long enough to undo the chain and then she threw it open. Tears stung her eyes as she stared at him. "Dylan, oh, my God—"

"How long have you been doing Max Blessett?" he growled.

Her mouth opened.

It closed.

She blinked, tearing her eyes away from the chair he sat in and lifting her gaze to meet his. "Max who?" she finally asked, feeling somewhat numb just from the shock of seeing him in the chair.

He wheeled inside and reached out with his hand to slam the door shut. "Max Blessett. You forget him already?" Dylan asked, a mean smile on his face. "You just saw him the night

21

you called me. My height—when I could stand. Brown hair, blue eyes."

"His name is Max Delacourte," Kris said, her voice faint. The cold look in his eyes finally started to penetrate the fog in her brain and her belly went tight with nerves and apprehension and a hundred other nasty emotions that she couldn't name.

"No. It's Blessett," Dylan said flatly as he crossed his arms over his chest and stared at her. "Since he neglected to mention his real name, what about his wife and kid? Did he mention that?"

At that, Kris's legs buckled and she collapsed on the floor.

"Wife?" she repeated.

"Yeah, wife. You going to tell me you didn't know?" Dylan asked. His eyes were so damned hot with fury, they almost glowed with it and he stared at her with disgust.

"*What?*"

"How about the crap you told me on the phone? How I shouldn't go on the last op? Where did you come up with that information, Kris? When did you discover he and I were on the same team and that he was going to sell us? How did you find out he was setting us up? How did you find out what was going on?" He kept firing off one question after another without giving her a chance to even absorb what he was asking.

When she finally did get it—rage pumped through her, dancing hand in hand with the misery. The worst, though, was the pain. He believed that... What exactly did he believe?

"What in the hell are you talking about?" she demanded. She wasn't going to cry. Damn it to hell, she would *not* cry over this. Slowly, she took a deep breath and held it, hoped it would steady her, even just a little. It didn't. Her voice shook as she said, "I told you, I had a fucking dream. I have them. A lot.

Sometimes in time. Sometimes not. Sometimes they make sense. Sometimes they don't. If I can figure them out, then I do what I can. I'm usually too late..." Hot tears burned her eyes and clouded her vision. Desperate, she blinked them away until she could see a little better. She swallowed against the knot in her throat and just hoped she could keep from crying.

She wasn't going to bet on it, though. It was too much—way too much. Dylan was in a wheelchair. It had been months since he had gotten back, so it wasn't likely he was waiting for a busted leg to heal.

He continued to glare at her like she was the one who had put him there—maybe she had. She'd tried to warn him, but she hadn't gotten through. Maybe it was her fault. "What happened to you?" *God, please...Dylan, in a damned chair...*

A quiet, gentle voice whispered, *At least he's not dead...sometimes they don't come in time.*

"Because," he snarled, leaning down and grabbing her arm, snagging it and using it to drag her to her knees. "Half of my friends are dead. And your boyfriend is the reason why. We'd all be dead if it wasn't for your fucking phone call and I just don't believe in coincidences."

Kris felt the blood drain from her face, nausea roiling in her belly.

She couldn't deny the truth any longer. Not any more. Max was apparently some sort of traitor. That was bad enough. Sickening enough. She'd liked him. She'd almost slept with him. Yeah, finding out she'd been dating a *married* bastard who had betrayed his friends was enough to have vomit burning its way up her throat.

But the worst part was Dylan thought she was involved. Somehow. How could this be real?

The iron hand wrapped around her upper arm was the only thing that kept her from wilting back to the floor in a boneless puddle. "You son of a bitch," she whispered hoarsely. "You actually believe I could do something like that..." Her voice trailed away.

Fury churned inside her gut as she stared at him, looking for some sign that she was wrong. That she'd misunderstood. "How long have you known me, Dylan? Huh? Nearly ten years. And you still think I could do something like that. Thanks, pal. Thanks a lot."

Her tongue felt thick in her mouth as she spoke and her face was starting to feel hot. She couldn't breathe. This wasn't happening.

It couldn't be.

Dylan didn't actually think that.

Did he?

"Well, rich girl, I'm alive, and so are four other men, and none of us should be," Dylan drawled. His eyes trailed down her face and then he looked at her arm, where her skin was going white from where his fingers bit into her flesh. A frown passed across his face and slowly, his fingers unwrapped from her arm.

She sank back, falling to her bottom and scooting away. Bracing her back to the wall, she stared at him, her eyes wide and dark. "You believe that, Dylan? Do you really believe that?"

Kris watched as he sighed and sat back, scrubbing his hand over his face. "Hell, I don't know. I can't think straight, Kris. I took a fucking bullet in my back, but if it hadn't been for you, we would have been gunned down, shot in the back and all of us would have died. You could have warned me because you felt guilty—it would make sense."

"No," she said, her voice thick with tears. "No, it wouldn't. Because I'd no sooner be party to any kind of random killing than you would. Any more than I'd date a married man. Any more than you'd date a married woman."

For the longest time, Dylan was silent. He stared at her, his intense eyes burning a hole inside her. Then his lashes drooped and he blew out a harsh, ragged breath. When he looked back at her, his face didn't look quite as grim.

"Max Blessett is a traitor to the United States," Dylan said quietly. "Did you know anything?"

Kris smiled bitterly. "Anything?" she repeated. Dear God, this pain was awful. It was like something had crawled inside her chest and was eating away at her. She couldn't keep looking at him. It made the pain that much worse. "I didn't even know his real name."

Dylan accepted that with a tiny nod. Some of the knotting in her gut eased a little. He believed her. He was still pissed, still angry, but that fury was no longer directed solely at her.

"Army Intelligence is looking for him. Don't be surprised if they come looking for you, wanting to ask you questions," he said softly, before he wheeled his chair around and headed for the door.

"What?"

Dylan opened the door and then looked back at her. The dim lights in the hallway fell around him, gleaming on his shaggy hair like muted gold. "You can't really think that they won't want to talk to you, do you?"

Her eyes widened. "How in the hell can this be happening?" she whispered.

His only answer was a cynical smile. Kris followed him into the hallway, staring at the chair.

"Dylan?"

As he leaned forward to punch the down button, he shot her a look.

"Your...ah... Are you going to be able to walk again?" she asked, her eyes burning as she studied the sight of his long powerful body confined to that chair.

His brows lowered over his eyes. As the elevator doors slid open, he started to roll through it. Over his shoulder, he said, "Nobody knows. Nobody fucking knows."

CRCBCRCB

"I can't believe you went there, Dylan," Jerry said, pacing the room.

"She didn't know, Jerry." Air burned in and out of his lungs as he lifted his body up to the bars, up and down, up and down, before walking his body back to the chair, using only his hands.

"That was fucking stupid, boy, and you damn well know it!" Jerry shouted.

Dylan grunted as he swung his weight into the chair. He mopped the sweat from his face with a discarded T-shirt and reached for a bottle of water. He took a drink and then studied his commander as he twisted the cap back on the bottle. Then he said, "She didn't know anything, Jerry. Okay? She didn't know. Look, Dally—" His throat tightened as he thought of the slow-talking Texan he'd never see again. "Dally told you things. He had dreams, or feelings that nobody could explain. But that didn't stop you from acting on them."

"That's beside the point," Jerry bellowed, whirling around and slamming his fist into the wall. "This could make it look like *you* had something to do with it."

"Not once she's found innocent," Dylan said quietly.

"Aw, fuck." Jerry reached up, scrubbing his hands over his face, and Dylan saw the exhaustion in his eyes. And the worry.

Quietly, Jerry said, "I'm your commanding officer, but what I say means shit." Lowering himself into a chair, he studied Dylan closely. "Look, just...don't go there again. Okay? I'm asking you, as a friend. And I'm ordering you, as your commanding officer. Do not go down there again."

"I wasn't planning on it," Dylan said flatly. "Damn it, I'm not a total fool."

"Can't tell by me," Jerry snapped, shaking his head, skimming a hand over his head. "Just make this make sense to me. Okay? Explain to me why you'd risk ruining a damn fine career in the military, having this mark. Because don't tell me you didn't know how this could look to Intelligence."

Dylan's mouth twitched. Make it make sense?

He didn't know if he could. But it just hadn't seemed right.

Kris had too much...class. The kind somebody had to be born with, not something that could ever be learned or imitated. He could still remember how Kris had looked sliding out of that slick little Benz she had rented when she had come trolling for Nikki all those years ago. She hadn't gotten all that money from editing. Hell, she had been born with money, born with class.

Something else, a fire inside of her. Polish. Decency. Honor.

How in the hell had he forgotten that?

No way in hell would she have fucked around with a married man, not knowingly.

Beyond that, there was no way would she have sold out her country. She'd sooner slit her wrists with her credit cards. He heard a muttered curse and glanced up. Jerry was staring at him with hard eyes and Dylan just shrugged. "She's my sister's best friend."

"More than that," Jerry said, his eyes shrewd. "So when were you two together?"

Dylan laughed harshly. "In my dreams."

Jerry arched a black brow and asked, "You never struck me as the type to look but not touch."

Dylan said, "You haven't ever seen Kris. She's out of my league." That sure as hell didn't keep him from thinking about her all the damned time though. She hadn't seemed to mind him kissing her that one time. His eyes heated at the memory and his body tensed, his hands clenching into fists.

A few feet away, Jerry chuckled. "Ya know, for somebody who claims that a lady is out of his league, you look awful fixated on her. Maybe you ought to think about going and talking to her about this...fixation. Once she's cleared, that is. You talk to her again before that, I'm gonna kick your ass and I don't care if you are in that damn chair. And that's an order from a superior officer, got that, Sergeant Kline?"

Dylan bristled a little and he scowled. "I'm going to be a civilian in a few more weeks, Jerry."

Jerry saw the helpless rage in Dylan's eyes and it hit him like a sucker punch, because he could sense the pain and the fear that hid behind it. "Dylan, you don't have to retire. You know that."

"Yes, I do."

Dylan battled down the futile anger that rose every time he thought about it. No way was he going to continue trying to recover on a military base, and no way was he going to take a desk job.

In a few more weeks, he wouldn't be a sergeant in the US Army, wouldn't be an Army Ranger, wouldn't be doing the one thing that brought him respect. Wouldn't be flying airplanes, wouldn't be parachuting into countries no sane soul would walk in.

In a few more weeks, he was likely to be earning disability, back home in Monticello, Kentucky, unable to even work in his brother's construction company.

In a few more weeks, he'd be nobody. Again.

"I spoke with Dr. Clary. Everybody's sure you're going to walk again. You were right, damn it. Once the inflammation settles down, you'll walk. You're not going to be stuck in a wheelchair, Dylan. That ought to mean something," Jerry snapped.

His throat felt tight and the words sounded hollow, even to his own ears. "It does mean something. It means I'm going to be living a civilian life, dealing with a bum back the rest of my life while the traitor that did this to me walks around on two legs in prison for a few years." That was the worst of it; the man he had called a friend had sold him out, sold out the whole unit, and had walked away from it, leaving five dead and another in a wheelchair.

And he touched Kris, kissed her...probably took her to bed and made love to her...touched that sweet body, held her...

A growl started to build in his throat and he thought of everything else Max had cost him. Dally, and Nick...the others. And Dom—shit, Dom was paralyzed. He wouldn't ever walk again.

Yeah, Dylan would walk all right, but his buddy wouldn't. Dom was stuck in a chair. Paralyzed. He'd never have sex with a woman again, never be able to walk across the street, or even stand up and walk to the bathroom to piss.

29

"He won't be out in a few years, Dylan," Jerry said on a sigh. "You know it as well as I do. This is the Army. Not the outside. He is going to pay for what he did."

"The only price steep enough is if we can kill him ourselves," Dylan muttered. His mouth twisted with fury and his eyes narrowed. "Let us take care of it. That would be vindication."

"You think I don't feel the same way?" Jerry asked softly. His eyes heated and his hands clenched. "I'd like nothing more than to gut him, rip him apart with my bare hands. But I can't."

Slowly, the words coming like broken glass through his throat, Dylan said, "If we had listened to Dally... Damn it, if I had just listened to Kris. Between the two of them, that should have told us something was wrong. I didn't even tell you about her."

Jerry's eyes closed and he turned away. "Yes. I'll hate myself for the rest of my life for *not* listening to Dally. He knew. Somewhere in his gut, a part of him knew something was off with that last op. How many of our ops went smoother because of little things he told us? Him and that little voice of his..." A sad little smile crossed Jerry's face and when he turned back around, his eyes were bitter, far too bright, full of rage.

Great. Stupid fuck. "Jerry, don't blame yourself. This is none of our faults. It's Max's. May the bastard rot in hell." He bared his teeth in a semblance of a smile as he added, "Now, if I could just help send him there."

"If that ain't the pot calling the kettle black," Jerry murmured. "You think I don't know how guilty you feel? You saved five lives, Dylan. You and her. If you say she didn't know, that she wasn't involved, then she wasn't. I've never doubted you—no reason to start now. Which means she saved us. *You* saved us, five of us are still alive because of you," Jerry said, walking over and crouching in front of Dylan, waiting until Dylan's hazel eyes met his dark navy ones. "He's fucked our lives up enough, Dylan. I want that bastard found and dealt with and then I don't ever want to hear another thing about him. He's taken enough already. You'd be smart to do the same."

"Since when you did you take up armchair psychology?" Dylan asked with a ghost of smile.

Jerry quirked a brow. "Since I stopped being able to sleep at night. But I'm not wrong, am I?"

A listless shrug was Dylan's only answer and with that, his eyes closed and his head fell back against the top of the chair.

The damn chair.

Four damn months. He had been in this chair four damn months, scared to death he'd never get out of it, scared the swelling in his spinal cord would go down and the paralysis would still be there, scared he'd find out he'd never walk again, never have any feeling in his lower body. Scared he'd never make love to a woman again, never be able to sink his cock into a woman's satin wet heat and ride her until she screamed out his name.

One morning, barely a month ago, he lay in that bed in the quiet hours before dawn, telling himself he could move the appendages below his waist, the legs he couldn't even feel. He could do it.

Then he did. His right foot had twitched, shifted just a scant inch. It had done it again five minutes later, after he had worked up the nerve to try again. When the doctors came in, he was able to move that foot at the ankle, just barely. But he had done it.

After a battalion of tests, the doctors determined the swelling in his spinal cord caused his paralysis.

31

Would he walk again?

Only time will tell, son, he'd been told. More times than he could count.

Just this week, the doctors had told him it was very likely he would walk again. But walking was about the extent of it. He wouldn't run, wouldn't slink through the jungle again.

He would never be the man he had been just months ago.

Screw what they said. Dylan would run, he would swim. He'd be more than they thought. He wouldn't accept anything less.

But not a Ranger. Never again.

A hard, calloused hand came down to rest on his shoulder. "I know it sucks, man. And I swear to God, if I could change it, I would. But life ain't fair. Hell, kid, you oughta know that by now."

Dylan didn't say anything, staring out the window in stony silence.

"You don't have to retire, Dylan."

"Yeah, I do." Lifting his head, Dylan said grimly, "I have to. I need to get the hell out of here and get home. As long as I'm here, I'm going to be reminded of what happened, what I can't have. Hell, what I would still have, if I had listened to a phone call." He rubbed at a scratch on the armrest of his chair with his fingernail and added, "I'll keep feeling sorry for myself."

"You think going home to your family is going to help? You think your sister isn't going to coddle you and baby you and remind you of what you can't do?"

For the first time in days, maybe weeks, Dylan laughed. Nikki, coddling? Did she even know the meaning of the word? "That reminds me, Jerry. You never did meet my sister," he said, his head falling back, a tired smile on his face.

Turning his head, he met Jerry's eyes and said, "I've been so sure what I was going to do with my life. For the past six years, I've known who I was, who I was going to be. That's changed now. I need to go back home and figure it out again."

Jerry sighed, resigned himself that Dylan wasn't going to be around. He'd made up his mind. It was written there in those flat, hazel eyes, in the grim lines of his lean, tired face. "You gotta do what's right for you." He rubbed his hands over his face, feeling as tired and angry as Dylan Kline looked. "You mind if I grab one of those beers Hobbes brought in for you?"

Dylan shrugged. "Go ahead." He'd barely touched the one he had bothered to open.

"So, have you made plans to go home?" Jerry asked, popping the top and tipping the bottle back.

"I'm going to a rehab clinic first. I need to find out exactly what I'm...what I'm capable of before I go making any plans for the future," Dylan said bitterly.

God, he didn't even know where to begin. Since he was eighteen, he'd decided he would go into the Army. Before that, he had been heading for jail, or an early grave. His only goals had been to avoid both as long as possible.

He'd never taken the time to think about what in hell he would do with his life.

Now he had to start over again.

Chapter Three

April

Kris glanced at the time on the clock and thought longingly of her bed, a glass of wine, maybe a nice long hot bubble bath first. But she needed to stop by the office. Blowing a tired sigh out, she tried to figure out exactly why it was so damn urgent she stop by there tonight.

No major crises had come up during the week. In the world of writing and publishing, there was always a minor crisis. Minor ones could wait until morning.

But Kris knew damn good and well she wasn't going to sleep until she went by the office and got those damn papers. That nagging little voice in her head would see to it. Her lips curved up in a slight smile and she decided since she was out at ten p.m. doing business, she might as well make the most of it.

Not that she was sleeping much anyway.

Her dreams were getting...out of control. She didn't know how to handle it. Dreams of screaming and sobbing and crying...little children, broken women and young girls.

Her lack of sleep showed in her face. But the bits and fragments of dreams that she remembered weren't enough for her to do anything about. There weren't even faces. Just vague echoes she could barely remember upon wakening.

"Damn it, stop," she muttered, reaching up and pressing her fingers to her brow. "You told yourself you were going to stop thinking about this so much. And not during the day. Work. Think about work."

Nikki had missed her deadline. Kris might as well call her and jibe at her a little. Maybe, just maybe, she had heard from Dylan. Nikki still didn't know a damned thing about Dylan being in a wheelchair. Last Kris had heard, Nikki hadn't talked to Dylan since the past fall.

The unassuming, squat building that housed Barnes and McNeel looked even more unassuming in the dim light as she parked on the street. The garage was likely to be mostly empty and Kris had recently decided that she and dark places weren't very good friends.

Not that she was scared of the dark, mind you. But the last time she had come down here at night alone had been four months ago, and some bastard had come up on her, looming over her with a knife and demanding her purse. The purse hadn't been enough to make him happy and when he had grabbed at her, she had given him a palm strike to the nose before she had really even realized it.

The rage in his voice still lingered with her as well as the gut certain fear that he would kill her if he could. Which was why she had kneed him in the balls so hard he might be joining the women's chorus.

Kris had been glassy-eyed with shock while the onsite security guard cuffed the bastard and he had patted her back soothingly as he placed the phone call to the cops. Thankfully, by the time the police had arrived on scene, she had stopped feeling so hysterical. Years of karate training had risen when she had needed them, just like her legendary cool had slid back into place by the time professionals had arrived. Now if she just could stop the infrequent nightmares...

The guard looked up at her from his desk, blinking a few times. "Ms. Everett, rather...odd seeing you here so late," he said, standing. His gaze flashed to her face and he asked, "Is everything all right?"

Kris smiled as she smoothed a stray lock of hair back behind her ear. "Everything is fine, Bill. I just left a few things here that I need. Quiet night, I hope," she teased him. "Any more excitement going on?"

"Uh, well, not yet," he said. He opened his mouth again and looked as through he were ready to ask her something and then he sighed. "You've been rather quiet of late, Ms. Everett. It's not the attack, is it?"

Kris smiled gently. Bill had known her from the first day she had bullied her way into a job here. The older gentleman had been furious over the attack and had called her several times after to check on her. He was, without a doubt, one of the sweetest souls she had ever met.

He didn't like bullshit. Since she couldn't exactly lie to the man, she said, "Bill, have you ever felt like something was totally wrong with your life and you just didn't know what?"

Faded green eyes narrowed a bit. "I've felt like that a time or two, yes." Then he just smiled, that wise old smile that only those who have lived a while can ever seem to manage.

"Girl, if things aren't as they need to be, just...let go. What is meant to be will just happen, if you let it." He walked her to the elevator and pushed the button, smiling and then tipping his hat at her.

The silence of evening suddenly seemed a little too oppressive and Kris started to wish she had just gone on home. Damn it, there was nothing here that really had to be taken care of *now*, was there? Rubbing her temple, she scowled as she stepped out of the elevator and walked down the hall to her office, so caught up in her own thinking that she didn't even see the light coming from her office until she was standing in the doorway.

She blinked.

Then the rage started to seethe through her.

"You bastard, what the fuck are you doing in my office?"

Max Delacourte looked up at her and smiled. "I'm glad it's you, and not somebody else. Of course, if it had been somebody else, I would have just killed them. But you can be useful," he said as he continued to work at her computer.

"Get the hell out of my office," she snapped.

"I've got some business I need to finish up and then I will. I'm a bit pressed for time—I've got people all over my ass lately."

"They ought to just shoot it," she said flatly. "Get out."

He lifted his head. Cold, emotionless eyes stared out of his handsome face and he said gently, "Are you sure you want to give me orders, Kirsten? I'm a dangerous man—haven't you heard?"

"Go fuck yourself," she said sweetly. She walked over to her coat rack and hung her purse up, nonchalantly hitting the on button on her cell phone. The thin plastic shield over the keypad faced away from the desk and she just hoped he wouldn't see the faint glow of the screen.

She slid her jacket off and managed to hit the auto dial for Nikki as she hung her jacket up. *Please...* "So, what exactly are you wanted for? Murder? Treachery? Backstabbing? Oh...what about adultery?"

He grinned at her, that boyish, sexy grin that had caught her eye. "That might touch the tip of the iceberg. Why don't you make yourself useful? I'd like come coffee."

She flipped him off and stayed close to the door, to the phone. Praying so hard.

Angelically, she said, "You don't want anything from me. I'd slip cyanide in it. I keep it on hand to give to authors who give me a hard time..."

He winced playfully and said, "You realize that you ought to be really nice to me right now, don't you?"

She quirked a brow at him. "No, I don't. You don't have any reason to let me live anyway, now do you, Max? Tell me something... Are you aware of the fact that I know Dylan Kline? I've known him for years. You damn near got him killed. You're responsible for killing half his team. You son of a bitch, I was questioned by Army Intelligence!"

He ran his tongue over his lips and nodded slowly, pushing back away from the desk. "I am curious about why they were so intent on questioning you. I had planned on coming to hide out with you for a while. I worked damned hard building a good, solid trust with you, and then when I came looking to hide out, you had a tag everywhere I turned. Why is that?"

She blinked. "A tag?" she asked, glancing down at her clothes, puzzled.

"A tail, somebody watching you everywhere you go. A tag," Max clarified.

She smiled and winked. "You've got your secrets. I got mine," she said, lowering her gaze to her nails.

It was more to hide the fear in her eyes than anything else.

She'd be damned if she let him see how damn scared she was.

From under the veil of her lashes, she slid a sideways glance at the phone and saw it was still on and it had been answered.

CRCRCRCB

Jerry Sears ran his tongue around his teeth as the agent on the other end of the line briefed him. He'd never make it to New York City in time, but there were other people already moving in. Kris was no longer under suspicion, officially, but they were still keeping an eye on her. It probably had something to do with the fact that Max Blessett had yet to be found.

Until now.

The woman was apparently trapped with the treacherous bastard and she had dialed her friend's number. Nikki had called her emergency contact number for Dylan. And Dylan in turn had called Jerry and every authority known to man.

Poor Max probably didn't even know hell was about to open up under his feet.

There was no way to warn Kris either, but she had known what she was doing, or she had some clue when she had called Nikki. She must have. Surely she hadn't been expecting Nikki just to call nine-one-one.

No. She wasn't expecting the local cops to come busting through that door.

Jerry just wished to hell and back that he was close enough to be there.

When his cell rang, he already knew who was on it. "I don't know anything yet. I'll call you as soon as I do," he said.

Dylan said softly, "If he hurts her, I'm going to kill him. You need to know that. Now I want to know what in the hell he is doing in her office."

"Not sure yet, but he's been using it for a little while. I was able to get that much information. The reason she still had her tag was because they were waiting for him to try and contact her. He never did, but he did get into her office. Regularly. So they tapped her lines, and he apparently never had a clue," Jerry said flatly.

"Why?"

"Well, because incredibly intelligent people also possess an incredible amount of arrogance," Jerry said with a grin.

"I meant why was he using her PC? Why her phone lines?"

Jerry laughed. "He's trying to get his money," he said, once he stopped chuckling. "I guess it never dawned on him that he might get discovered and his assets would be frozen. He moved some outside to Switzerland, and there are a few things that we can't touch, *yet*, but we will. He's banging his head against the wall trying to get to his money and he's doing everything short of blackmail to get more money out of the bastard he teamed up with. But he's no good to them now."

Jerry scratched his head, the tumbled jet curls tangling around his fingers. "He's up to something else, but he's got a smokescreen up, which means he's not totally stupid. He'll be getting more money in. Sooner or later. We just don't know how."

"Are you going to New York?"

"By the time I got there it would be over," Jerry said, shaking his head.

"I want you there. Damn it, I want somebody I know there," Dylan said roughly.

Jerry heard the unspoken words. Dylan wanted to be there. "Evan Hobbes is from Queens," he said quietly. "He may be around there somewhere. Want me to look him up?"

In the ensuing silence, Jerry laughed and said, "I guess that was just a dumb question, wasn't it? I'll call him and tell him to keep us both updated. But they aren't likely to just let an unknown waltz in."

"Then I guess it's a good thing he's good at not being seen or heard, isn't it?" Dylan asked neutrally.

Jerry muttered, "Smart ass," under his breath and jammed the disconnect button before dialing Hobbes. If he wasn't in the area, Dylan was likely to have his ass.

CRCBCRCB

Dylan hadn't ever felt so helpless in his life.

He couldn't do a damn thing.

As he walked to the window, leaning heavily on his cane, he had visions, glorious ones, of using that cane to bludgeon Max Blessett bloody.

No. That wouldn't satisfy him.

He wanted to use his own hands.

But his legs wouldn't cooperate.

Even though he had been walking for a month, first with crutches, and now with a cane, he couldn't do it on his own, and he could do no more than a few hundred yards at a time. It got a little farther every day, and he got stronger every day.

But Dylan couldn't take Max on his own.

Well, he thought, reevaluating, he could always put a bullet in him. Maybe in his back, like Dylan had taken. Even the field a little.

But Dylan couldn't take Max on his own.

He had to rely on friends, on colleagues. He was in the dark.

Was this how his family had felt when he'd disappear for months on end?

Yes, it was.

Swearing, he walked over to his desk and collapsed onto his chair, hooking his cane over the back of it and booting up the computer. So Max's assets were frozen. He was trying to get to money in other ways.

What other ways...

Dylan may be left in the dark when it came to action, but he had other ways to see.

ନ୍ତେ୨୍ତେ୨

Kris's breath froze in her lungs. Something had caught Max's attention and now his eyes were cold and emotionless, locked on her face, his head cocked as though he was listening to something she didn't hear.

"You've done something," Max said softly.

"Done what?" she asked, lifting one flame red brow at him.

He smiled, a snake's smile, cold and reptilian. "Don't play with me, bitch. You're good, very good. You're a piece of work, I'll give you that—cold as ice. But I'm better." He tapped a finger to his chin. "I'd like to know—how did you know I was going to be here?"

She rolled her eyes. Okay, so maybe he was just paranoid. "I didn't know you were going to be here. I came to pick up some work I forgot to take home," she said calmly. But there was still a frigid fear closing around her heart.

"Hmmm."

He moved too fast. No man should be able to move that fast. She screamed and threw herself to the floor but he caught her, pinning her to the floor and shoving her wrist high between her shoulder blades. "Now...the truth. How did you know I was here? Who is coming?"

Kris shrieked out, "I don't know," as her arm and shoulder screamed in agony. Then she lowered her voice and coldly said, "But I hope they kill your ass."

He stilled and released her arm, rolling her over. "So somebody is coming," he said, arching his brows questioningly. She tried to slap him and he caught her hand, first one, then the other, pinning them over her head.

"I sure as hell hope so," she said, keeping her voice level, blanking her eyes.

Max sighed, a forced sound as though she was trying his patience. "Kirsten, Kirsten, Kirsten...darling. You are making this so hard on yourself. Let's make it easy. Did you or did you not know I was here?"

She smiled brilliantly. "No. And that's too bad. Because I would have tried to think of a way to burn the building down. That's the best a traitor like you deserves," she said sweetly.

He hit her with the back of his hand. Then he licked the blood away from his knuckles. "Okay, that was a good start."

He sat down on her belly, forcing the air of her in a rush, smiling as she paled. "Now, why don't you tell me who is coming? How you managed it?" He ran a hand down the front of her chest, groped her roughly, smiling obscenely as he ripped

43

her shirt open. "Are you wired? Did somebody shove a bug up your ass?"

She spat at him.

When he hit her again, she prayed this time she'd black out. Because there were a few things that Kris just didn't tolerate very well. Being terrorized was one of them. Her breath started to burn in her lungs as her throat locked tight. Kris had been terrorized, once before. At the mercy of somebody else and she just didn't think she could handle it again.

His eyes narrowed, gaze thoughtful as he studied her face. "Hmmm...I think I see some real fear here," he murmured. Max leaned down, stretching her arms painfully high as he put his face right against hers.

That emotionless stare drilled into her and he smiled as he gazed into her wide terrified stare. "You *are* terrified—why is that? You were so cool, so cocky, just a minute ago. What happened?" Then he grinned, a quick, playful grin, as though they were playing a game. He licked a wet trail down her cheek and he bit her ear hard.

"I know what happened. You're pinned down," Max whispered. "A shrink would just love to get a hold of me, Kris. I'm such a paranoid bastard. I heard about how the little rich girl was kidnapped from school, held for ransom. How one of the kidnappers was a pedophile, and almost slipped his leash...damn shame, what nearly happened to you."

A sob tripped out of her as Max levered his body over hers, pumping his groin against her body. "Mommy and Daddy moved away from Los Angeles, moved to New York City after that happened. Poor baby, only eleven years old, almost raped. The man who saved you was the man who put you in that place to begin with," he crooned.

She jerked her head away when he lowered his mouth to kiss her streaming eyes. Against her belly, she could feel his throbbing erection and she felt like she was going to puke. He was turned on by this, by her fear, by what had happened to her as a child.

Something that should have repulsed him aroused him.

"What in the hell is wrong with you?" she gasped out. "If you're so sure somebody is after you, why aren't you running?"

He rose up onto his knees and smiled. "Because you're the bitch that led them to me. The military hates a traitor, Kris. They'd just as soon kill me as look at me. It's too late to try and slip away. They're already here. I want a shield."

Kris froze as he jerked her up by her arms so he could snarl into her face. "And if you try to *help* them—I'll make what nearly happened to that sweet kid you used to be seem like a weekend at the spa."

She bit back the sob that threatened to spill out.

When he jerked her to her feet, she went along, forcing her mind to calm and to focus. Damned bastard. No, she wouldn't *try* to help them. She *would* help them.

No sooner had she made that decision when the soft hum of electricity tripped. Lights flickered and then died.

Max swore softly and jerked her against him and Kris went, biding her time. Now wasn't the time. She'd wait...until he was certain she'd lost all her fight, until he was certain she was too caught up in her own fear to even think of fighting.

Kris wasn't sure what to expect, but it sure as hell wasn't for Max to bellow out, "You might as well get the hell out of your hiding places, guys. I know you're out there. You know I've got a civilian in here with me. Stalemate."

An easy, southern drawl said, "Not exactly. We know she's been helping you out from day one, Sergeant Blessett. We're not too concerned with her safety. We've secured the building and the night guard is out of harm's way. You want to just get this over with, easy like?"

Kris squeaked, "Helping him?"

Another voice laughed, "Don't bother denying it, Miss Everett." It had come from somewhere else, another direction. "Fortunately for you, the court may buy the bullshit you hand them. But Blessett, well, he gets a court martial. That jury won't be so easily fooled. You aren't my problem."

Kris's face flushed red and her entire body quivered with rage. *Damn it, they lied to me!* All these months, thinking the fear of being investigated was behind her...and then her mind kicked in.

The phone, damn it. She had called Nikki.

She had gotten through to Nikki. Nikki had gotten through to Dylan.

Kris was letting her mind interfere with common sense. These guys were here for him, not her. Kris closed her eyes tightly. She just had to focus on that, and she had to remember that. *Play along...buy time.*

"Damn it, I didn't do anything," she said, whining. The whine wasn't even faked. She was entitled to whine a little bit here. And pout, and sulk. Hell, Kris figured she was entitled to a full-blown tantrum at this point and if she made it out of this alive, she was going to give into the urge to scream and cry for a few minutes.

"They don't seem to believe you, babe," Max whispered when a dry laugh was the only answer that came.

"Let go of me," she shrieked when one hand came up and stroked over her breast.

46

He chuckled. "Better get used to it. Sounds like they seem to think you belong in jail...and a pretty thing like you? Some bitch in jail is going to want to have you for her own."

Her belly rolled. *Oh, no. I'm not listening to this,* she thought. She drove her elbow back and stomped on his foot, grinding the spike of her heel on his toe. The suddenness of her attack when Kris had just been whimpering was just enough to give her that start of surprise she needed to throw herself away from him, into the darkest corner of her office.

"Bitch!" he shouted.

That was when the world exploded.

Her door flew open and men swarmed in, the dark shadows of their bodies barely visible in the darkness. Kris clapped her hand over her mouth, smothering her scream. Keeping her back against the wall, she started to creep toward the door, away from the men who were taking Max struggling down to the floor.

Light came on and she flinched as somebody lifted her up, holding her back against a hard body. "Be still," a harsh Queens-accented voice said. "This isn't over. Not—"

That was when gunfire erupted and Max came off the ground. Two men fell dead. Max lunged for Kris, only to come up short when the man holding Kris lifted a gun and pointed it at Max. "Head another direction, man," her savior said. "You look at me for more than five seconds and you're dead."

"Hobbes...you lucky bastard. Don't you know you're supposed to be dead?" Max asked, a cold grin curving his mouth up as he walked sideways to the door, keeping the gun aimed toward Kris. Somebody started to edge toward him. He said, "Don't. I'll kill the bitch and don't try giving me that shit that you think she's guilty."

The agent lowered his weapon and backed off, his lips peeled back from his teeth, his eyes glinting with hate.

47

Shiloh Walker

Hobbes squeezed Kris's shoulder reassuringly. Then he focused his eyes back on Max as he asked, "Don't you know I'm coming after you?"

Max laughed. "You won't find me. I was right there, next to you, for months. And you never saw me then."

Hobbes laughed. "I never had a reason." Then he squeezed the trigger.

Kris screamed.

Max's eyes widened and his fingers tensed on the trigger of his own weapon, but Hobbes had already taken her to the floor.

CRCECRC3

Dylan walked across the room, his sweat-soaked hair lying in damp curls against his neck. Jerry lifted his gaze from the beer he had been drinking and smiled half-heartedly. "Hobbes got him. We know that. He took a bullet in the gut, left a blood trail as he ran off. Maybe Hobbes saw it wrong and it caught his dick and he'll get gangrene—they'll have to amputate," he said wickedly.

Dylan said quietly, "He knows too much about Kris. She'll be in danger now."

Jerry sighed. "She's been in danger since she had the bad luck to run in with him," he responded, shaking his head. "The Army won't leave her unprotected. I don't know what they'll do, but they won't let her get hurt because of their screw up. They've already got a tag on her, and this time they won't mess up. She's ours now."

Dylan collapsed into his chair, closed his hand into a loose fist and pounded it onto the arm of his chair. *She's ours now...*

48

Well, not mine. He wasn't going to be active military anymore. "You aren't going to shut me out, are you?" he asked softly.

Jerry slid Dylan a glance. "Anybody ever told you that you have some serious trust issues? Even after three years with us, you have to ask if I'm going to cut you out. Shit, Dylan, you're still one of us, whether you leave or not. Have you forgotten that?"

A sheepish grin crossed his face and he shrugged. "Well, I dunno if I forgot exactly. Maybe I just have trouble adjusting to what's coming."

Jerry arched a brow. "It's still your choice, man," he said quietly. "And you know I wish you wouldn't."

Dylan was silent. A long moment passed and then he just shoved the subject aside by changing it, pushing his monitor around, showing the screen to Jerry. "For some odd reason, Max has developed an unusual interest in teenage gab groups," Dylan said. "I broke through the wall he had on Kris's computer. He was hiding this."

"You're such a subtle bastard, Kline," Jerry drawled. "I've always admired that quality about you." Then he leaned around the desk and craned his neck to see what was on the computer screen and a straight black brow lifted at what he saw. It was the familiar *AOL* screen.

Jerry scowled. "How in the hell did you get through?" he demanded, striding around the desk and crowding behind Dylan, staring at the screen with a confused scowl. He reached for the mouse and scrolled through chat rooms. "Damn it, how in the hell did you figure out where he's been hitting?"

Dylan just stared at Jerry.

Jerry shook his head, and muttered, "Dumb question, shoot me. Damn it, these are kids' groups."

"Nothing but," Dylan agreed.

"Maybe he just likes them young," Jerry said, his mouth twisting in a snarl. "Damned prick already proved he was a traitor. Maybe he's even worse than we thought."

Dylan rested his chin on his fist.

"No. It's more than that," he muttered. "But there's nothing else for me to find. He hasn't done anything on her PC but try to get his money and chat in some rooms."

"Why use hers? Why not just find an internet café?" Jerry asked, scratching his head. He ran his hand over his hair, tugged on his ear.

"Could be a couple of reasons. Maybe he didn't figure we'd look for him here. Or maybe he's toying with us," Dylan said. "I don't know." He shut his computer down and sighed, scrubbing his face with his hands. He was so damned tired. "Can you find out what's going to happen with her? Who's going to be tagging her? I'm having the hardest time finding out anything in here. You'd think I was already discharged."

Jerry grinned. "Classified. But don't feel bad. They ain't telling me much either. I have to remind them of what happened and I'm not listening to the classified shit. When that doesn't work, I just get mean." A black lock of hair fell into his dark blue eyes as he smiled a particularly wolfish smile.

Yeah, Dylan could see where Jerry getting mean could accomplish something.

"Well, go snarl at somebody and see if you can get me walking any faster," Dylan said, spinning his cane in his hand.

Jerry turned and rested a hip on the desk. He leveled a patient look at Dylan and said, "Buddy, you are walking. You seen Dom? No, you haven't. The man is in a wheelchair. A wheelchair. For good. He's not as bitter you are. Hell, he's already gone home. He's planning on going back to college in the fall. Says he's planning on being a lawyer."

Dylan closed his eyes and let his head drop back against the padded headrest on the chair. "Dom's a better man than me," he said quietly. "He's got a focus. Hell, I don't even know what I want to do with my life and he's going to college. Shit."

Jerry opened his mouth, but whatever he had been about to say died as he stared at Dylan. Finally, he just sighed and clapped his hand on Dylan's shoulder and he walked away.

Chapter Four

May

Shoving her carry-on back up on her shoulder, Kirsten Everett took a deep breath and asked, "Any idea when my luggage will get back from Sri Lanka?"

She was not having a good day.

But why should that surprise her any after the past few months? Lately, her good days had been outnumbered by her bad days three to one. After the past two weeks? She should be feeling lucky *she* hadn't ended up in Sri Lanka.

But that was okay—because she was away from New York. The nightmares had grown to unmanageable proportions after that night. She heard gunshots in her sleep, and she couldn't turn a corner without seeing Max.

It had taken two months to work up the nerve to quit her job, two months to decide she was leaving, and where on earth she was going to go. For two months, her plans were uncertain.

But then she had flipped open *The New York Times* and seen the ad.

Her sanity had been questioned and her financial security was definitely going to be at risk. Well, not exactly. Her mama and daddy were rich, after all, and Dad was a financial genius, who had in turn raised a woman who knew how to treat her money.

She had a small fortune tucked away, and more than enough for a rainy day. But investing in a small, unknown publishing company in Kentucky, of all places...and moving to Kentucky...of all places... Yes, some people were sure she needed to have her head examined.

The investment was going to eat up some of her money.

If it didn't work out, well, she wasn't sure where she was going to end up.

But this felt right.

Besides, it was closer to someplace important.

Louisville was just three or so hours away from Nik, instead of a pain in the ass flight every time she wanted to see her friend.

"It went to Las Vegas," the airline attendant replied cheerfully, Kirsten's sarcasm floating right over her empty blonde head. Those heavily mascared lashes batted over her purple eyes and the ditz just continued to smile and chirped, "We should be able to have it here by tomorrow evening."

Great. She didn't have anything more than her make-up, her laptop, a book and her purse. But Kris could handle this. Taking a deep breath, she counted to ten and said, "I'll call, then, tomorrow. Who should I call?"

The attendant, Stacey, according to her crooked nametag, pursed her lips, which were almost as purple as her eyes, and looked thoughtful. "Hmm. I really don't know. Would you like me to check?"

She managed to say, "Yes," without gritting her teeth. As Space-cadet Stacey wandered away, Kris glanced at her watch and cursed under her breath. "Damn it." Already late. She had less than thirty minutes to get her rental and make it to the hotel where she was supposed to be meeting up with her new partner.

Wasn't this just swell...

"Wonders never cease," a soft voice drawled.

Kris froze. Her eyes closed and her breath shuddered out of her lungs. She swiped her tongue across her lips before she turned slowly and met those sultry hazel eyes, the heat of them penetrating her through and through.

"Dylan," she said quietly.

"Miz Everett," he drawled, inclining his head. In one hand, he held a cane, but he didn't rest on it—he stood.

Kris's knees wobbled and her lips trembled. "Oh, dear God," she whispered, one fisted hand pressed to her lips. "Thank You."

Dylan's mouth quirked. "Sounds like you've been saying some prayers over my sorry tail," he said, one straight brow lifting as he studied her face. "Thank—"

The rest of his words were murmured against her hair as she moved against him and wrapped her arms around him. "I've worried myself sick about you," she whispered. "I couldn't ask Nikki, couldn't ask anybody. I'm so glad to see you."

A big, rough hand stroked down the back of her head, his chest rumbling as he laughed. "Damn, rich girl. I didn't realize you cared," he teased.

She moved away, staring up at him. "Are you going home?"

"Yes," Dylan said, his eyes darkening. "Gotta face the music."

"You never told them how bad you were hurt, did you?" she asked.

He arched a brow. "I'm standing here, aren't I? Nikki finds out, she's likely to put me back in the hospital," he said, running a hand through his hair.

She watched as the dark gold and brown curls twisted around his fingers, then forced herself to focus on his words. "Now...she's not likely to react *that* bad," she said.

He cocked a brow. "You do remember Nik, right? Short, mouthy, reddish-brown hair?" he asked. He nodded toward the counter. "You got somebody looking for you, rich girl."

Kris rolled her eyes, staring pointedly at the smiling man standing with his shoulder against the wall. She was sure the military had some cool name to call this man who followed her everywhere she went. She just called him the pain in her ass. "I keep hoping I'll lose him."

Dylan laughed, glancing at the man who made no attempt to hide himself. "Now, Kris. You don't want to do that. Besides, you couldn't do it anyway. He knows where you are all the time," Dylan said levelly. Then his eyes grew serious. "Make sure it stays that way. He keeps that butt of yours safe."

"Yes, sir," Kris said, snapping a salute.

He grinned at how she placed her hand, with the back of her hand against her forehead. "You'd make a terrible soldier. That's a Navy salute, not an Army salute, rich girl." He gestured to the desk. "But that's who I was talking about. She's looking for you."

Kris looked over as Stacey wandered back over to the desk, smiling vacuously. "If she had been in New York manning the counter, I think I would have been too afraid to get on the plane."

Dylan smirked a little. "You on your way to Nikki's?"

"I've got some business stuff I need to attend to first. But I'll be around."

55

Dylan nodded. "I'm setting up in Wagner, sooner or later. So, if I don't see you, take care of yourself." His eyes lingered on her face and he started to walk off. Then he turned back, his steps slow, but steady. He stared down at her face as he murmured, "There are two things I never told you. I should have." Dylan looked down, staring at his big feet like they fascinated them. Finally, he looked back up at her and softly said, "I'm sorry. And thank you."

Then he was gone, moving through the throng of people, his tall, lean frame moving slowly, easily. Watching him walk was a beautiful thing. Even if she was watching him walk away.

"He's cute!" Stacey whispered.

Kris closed her eyes and shook her head.

Cute didn't even begin to touch what Dylan Kline was.

CRCRCRCR

Sheets tangled around his body as he slept. The air cranked out of the hotel air conditioner, cooling the room as Dylan slept, trapped in a dream that haunted him nearly every night.

He was back in that hut, staring at Max.

"You sonovabitch, it was you," Dally whispered, shaking his head, his pale green eyes narrowed and angry. "It was *you.*"

"Yeah, that little voice of yours led ya astray this time, didn't it?" Max smirked. "It had me a little worried for a while. You've had too many lucky hits there, but not this time. Your luck has run out, cowboy."

And as Dylan lay there, trying to drag himself to Nick, Max had turned around and walked away from the gun in his face, not even turning when somebody had shot Dally in the back.

Those laughing brilliant green eyes went forever dull and a scream started to build in Dylan's throat.

Only this time, it was worse...because Max suddenly had Kris. And as the bullet exploded through Dylan's body, Max was jerking her around, reaching for the back of her dress with one hand, his other hand holding the gun he had at her neck—not just pointing, but shoved against it, the metal biting into the soft, pale flesh.

Her soft sobs tore at his heart, but he couldn't get out of the wheelchair to do a damned thing... *Wheelchair... I'm not in a wheelchair here.*

Dylan came to full wakefulness in the blink of an eye, jerking himself out of the dream, away from the rage, the misery such a betrayal had caused.

Slowly, Dylan sat up in bed and swung his legs over the side, planting his large naked feet on the cool tile floor. He could feel that cool, hard tile, just as he could feel the fullness in his bladder, the stiffness of his joints. He wasn't paralyzed.

Flexing his feet, he lifted his eyes skyward and whispered, "Thank You, God."

In the past five months since retiring from the Army, those had been the first words out of his mouth, each and every day. Even though some days he questioned whether or not he believed in an Almighty Power. It had started when he had left the base and gone out to Arlington, to see Nick's grave.

Dallas Conroy, the son of a Texas millionaire, had been buried on a family plot just outside of Mesquite. Only fitting for a Texan to rest eternally in Texas, Dylan remembered thinking. Dally, with his odd feelings and even odder dreams had saved their tails so many times—if they had only listened this last time. Maybe...just maybe.

Dylan had sat in his wheelchair, staring down at the green grass, remembering Nick and his sheer love of life. *You gotta be thankful every day, man. For whatever you have, be thankful.*

Some of us don't have so much to be thankful for, Dylan had said once.

Hell, you better not be talking about yourself, slick. You got brains, you got guts. You're an American, able to think and do and say what you please. That's more than some sorry bastards have.

That had been a few years ago. Before Max. At the time, Dylan had still been able to stand up, able to walk on his own. He hadn't paid much attention to Nick's words, not then. Now, though? Now he thought about them a lot.

Even if he did have to use that cane to walk, even if he never did manage more than a slow walk, he'd been thankful. He *could* walk. That wasn't the case for Dom Salvatore. Poor bastard was paralyzed, for sure and certain, from the waist down.

Yeah, Dylan had more than a little to be thankful for. So, every day, he said thanks. Since Nick wasn't here to do it.

Slowly, he stood. Without looking at the clock, he knew what time it was. The impersonal feel of the hotel room made him even more anxious to get home. It was time to leave. Time to get on the road.

In a handful of hours, he'd be back in Monticello.

What he was going to do with his life, he still didn't know.

Well, that wasn't completely true. The first thing he was going to have to do was figure out how to deal with Nik. Out of everything he had done in the past few years, all the lines he had crossed when he was a teen, all the battles he had fought, Nicole Kline Lightfoot was one of the few things on God's green earth that could still strike fear into his heart.

58

Not that he'd ever let her know that.

She was going to be royally pissed once she found out just why he had been in a hospital, why he was accepting an early retirement. She'd be royally pissed at him for not bothering to let her know before now.

"Like she doesn't have enough on her hands," he mumbled to himself as he walked over to the tiny little coffee pot and set about fixing a cup before he got dressed.

Between the kids and her writing, not to mention the college courses she had decided to take, the last thing she needed to deal with was a damn handicapped bastard who sat around for hours at a time, feeling sorry for himself.

Now, he just had to find a way to make Nikki understand his side of things.

Like the fact that seeing her upset and in tears while he was flat on his back was just a little more than he could have handled. Taking a cup of black coffee, he headed for the shower.

He'd figure out how to handle Nikki in a couple of hours.

Hell, he'd disarmed live bombs.

Surely he could handle one short redhead with a big mouth and a bad attitude.

CRCRCRCR

Then again, maybe not, Dylan thought warily as he waited for Nikki to react. His stomach started to rumble. He'd bypassed the meal on the flight, figuring they could stop and get some food on the way back to Monticello, but Nikki had mentioned pot roast. No way was he going to choose the golden arches over a pot roast.

But sitting at the kitchen table, surrounded by three pairs of censuring eyes, Dylan realized there was a distinct possibility he'd be wearing the pot roast, not eating it.

Jack Kline wanted a beer, Dylan could tell simply by the look on his face. It had been easily a decade since he had taken a drink, but the craving, the need for it would never completely fade. That was what being an alcoholic did to you.

He was getting old, Dylan realized with a start, and it was starting to show. The lines of his face had never seemed so heavy and his eyes looked unbelievably weary.

Jack pushed back from the table and stood, staring at his son with unreadable eyes. "You okay now, boy?" There was so much more Jack wanted to say, but he sometimes wondered if he had the right. Nikki had done more to raise these boys than he had.

"I'm fine, sir. No longer fit for active duty, but everything is in working order. I'm walking fine. Don't even need the cane all the time. I'll be able to do more as time goes by. How much more, I don't know."

Jack's eyebrows quirked at the "sir", but he made no comment. "I reckon you had your reasons for keeping yourself away from those who care about you while you were hurting. So I won't be asking why you did it, but I do think it was the wrong choice." His large, rawboned hands clenched briefly around the chair as he pushed it back in place. "Nik, I think I'll go have that cigarette now."

Shawn's eyes were turbulent, flashing sparks of green fire as he waited with a clenched jaw for the door to shut. "Always have to handle things on your lonesome, don't you, man?" he said, fighting to keep his voice low. "You stupid bastard, if you'd been paralyzed, would have bothered to call and let us know?"

"Shawn—"

But the younger man had already stormed out of the kitchen, the glass in the door pane rattling behind him as he slammed it shut.

Well, he'd totally managed to alienate two of them. They weren't even the worst, he thought, turning to meet Nikki's hazel eyes. His fingers had started to beat a tattoo on his thigh and he closed his fist, clenched it, then relaxed it as he waited.

"Why?" Nikki asked simply.

Her voice was thick with tears and her eyes gleamed with them.

"I had to," he said gruffly. "I had to. I'm sorry. Seeing you standing over me, while I was doing my damnedest to get back on my feet—" he broke off and blew out a breath. "You've always been there, always. You always will be. I know that. But I had to know what I was going to be able to do. I had to."

"We would have helped," she said flatly, rising from the table and slamming her glass down before stalking away from him.

He caught up with her, catching her arm. "You would have tried. I know that. But...you know how you wake up at night after a bad dream, and any time you go to talk about it, it just sticks in your throat, and you can't say anything? Talking about it always seems to make it more real. I had to deal with this on my own, in my own way," he whispered, staring into her eyes.

Her lashes lowered and she nodded, slowly. "That may well be," his sister said quietly. "Now I need to deal with this, in my own way."

Dylan felt his heart die a little at the look in his sister's eyes.

Fuck.

CRCBCRCB

"He was paralyzed, Wade," Nikki hissed, slamming down a plate. "And he didn't even bother to pick up the phone to say, 'Hey, I'm in the hospital.' The bastard."

"Nik, you know how Dylan is," Wade said, making sure he had the table between the two of them, and that the plates were all out of her hands. "You've got better luck getting news from a doorknob than him."

As if she hadn't even heard him, she muttered, "A hospital. Took a damn bullet in his back, and does he call? Did he even list a next of kin in case he took a bullet in the head?"

Wade laughed. "Nik, as hard as his head is, it would damage the bullet more than him," he said, walking around the table and wrapping his arms around her from behind.

Her mouth quirked up in a smile. "Well, there is that," she agreed, covering his hands with hers and squeezing.

The door opened and closed quietly as Nikki tipped her head back to study her husband. "I love you," she whispered.

She turned her head to see her father standing there and Nikki sighed. The grim look in Jack's eyes probably didn't mean anything good. "Shawn's looking to rumble. I think I need to head on home for the night. Want me to take him with me?"

She sighed and rested her brow for a minute against Wade's chest. "No. Nobody needs to go anywhere. I'm going to go talk to Dylan," she muttered, shaking her head.

CRCBCRCB

"You really are a jerk, Dylan. You know that?"

"Look, I need to get a room for the night," Dylan said without turning around. Staring into the coming twilight, he kept his hands tucked in his back pockets and his eyes away from Nikki. "I ought to be heading back into town, okay?"

"Oh, shove it, Sergeant," Nikki muttered, moving onto the porch and leaning against the rail. "I don't agree with what you did. Or any reasons you may have for doing it. But...it was your call."

"I was having a hard enough time handling it myself, Nik," Dylan said gruffly. "How could I keep focused on what I had to do with you folks around?"

"You were scared," Nikki said, her voice husky with surprise.

"Yeah."

"I didn't think you'd ever admit to something like that," Nikki said quietly. "You've never admitted to any other human reaction."

"I'm just as human as you are," Dylan muttered, pinching the bridge of his nose. Had he ever felt this tired? Maybe during training, when he had gone without food and sleep. When he had woken in hospital the day after they told him he would never walk again.

"Oh, I know that," Nikki said with a laugh. "I remember when Mom was trying to get you potty trained, for crying out loud. I remember when you were trying to learn to ride a bike; you kept falling off, busting your knees up and skinning your elbows. But you didn't cry. When we found Mom that day, you didn't cry. I know you're human, Dylan. But sometimes I think you've forgotten that."

"Nik, the last thing I need right now is an evaluation from an armchair shrink," he said, finally turning around to face her in the fading daylight.

"What do you need, Dylan? You've never told anybody what you need. Hell, I practically raised you and Shawn, and I don't think you ever told me that you needed anything. Or anyone."

"I needed to walk," he told her, folding his arms across his chest, the material spreading taut across his shoulders. "I needed to be able to stand up while I take shower. I needed to come back home and see you. See everybody."

"But only in your time," Nikki added as his voice fell silent. "You needed us, but only according to your time frame. Have you ever let go of that pride of yours long enough to really need somebody, Dylan? You don't need any of us, not really. Not because you don't love us. But because you don't let yourself."

His dark gold hair fell over his eyes and he tossed it back irritably. "I need you," he said, turning back around, bracing his hands against the smooth wood of the railing. A soft summer breeze drifted by, bringing the scent of grass, flowers and the pond. Dragging it into his lungs, he remembered how many times he wondered if he would ever be able to come back here, how many times he wondered if he'd ever see his nieces and nephew grow up.

"No. Dylan, you don't know what it's like to really need a person, so badly that that person is all you can think about, all you can see, all you can feel. You've never needed any of us so badly that the sole thought in your mind was getting back home to us alive," Nikki said, her voice barely loud enough to hear. "If you had, maybe you could understand why it bothers me so much that you never bothered to call, never bothered to let us know how badly you'd been hurt. Why you never understood how much we worried about you.

"I'm so proud of you, of what you've made of yourself," she continued. "So damn proud. But not a night goes by that I didn't think of you, hope you were safe, in one piece. If a late night phone call came, I panicked, almost too scared to answer it for fear of hearing something had happened to you.

"But I always did answer, because I thought if something had happened, you'd need us with you," she finished, shoving her hair back, holding it in a loose ponytail at the nape of her neck. "But when something did happen, you never even bothered to call. That hurts, Dylan. It hurt all of us."

"I'm sorry," was all he could say. Rubbing the heel of his hand against his chest, he pondered how easily she could make him feel the fool.

"Maybe next time something happens to you, you'll let us know. Even if you don't need us there, maybe we need to be there," she told him, moving close enough to lean up against his arm.

"I guess I should have done that to begin with," he said wearily, wrapping his arm around her. She felt tiny against him, something that never failed to surprise him. God knows he'd never admit to her, but she scared the hell out of him, always had. The way she loved so passionately, with everything inside her, the way she fought her way out of the slums they'd grown up in. "I just... I had this crazy feeling that talking about it would make it more real."

She smiled. "Just like if you looked for the monsters in your closet they would be there, but if you kept your head under the covers, you were safe," she said.

Dylan knew, without a doubt in his mind, if she hadn't succeeded and taken them away from Portland, he'd still be there. If she hadn't fought as hard as she had, proven that something good could come from them, he never would have tried.

So fierce, so loving and so damn gentle. Sometimes he wondered how in the hell she had come from their parents. He could see some of his father in both himself and in Shawn, but he could never see anything of Mom or Dad in his sister.

A gentle throat clearing had him looking down. The sly smile in her wide soft hazel eyes had him shoring up his defenses.

Fierce, gentle...yeah. But he'd forgotten devious. She was so damn devious.

"I talked to Kirsten earlier. She said she ran into you at the airport... Did you know she's moved to Louisville? Y'all are going to be practically neighbors," Nikki said, her voice, her face incredibly innocent.

"Kris has moved to Louisville...ah, no. She didn't mention she'd moved. Mentioned business, figured she was just there on...business," he finished lamely. Kris had moved to Louisville. Funny... Jerry hadn't given him that piece of information.

"Hmmm. Well, it is business related. She quit her job. Won't tell me what's up—keeps saying she'll tell me about when she gets down here. She looking good?" Nikki asked, batting her eyes.

"Like she always does," Dylan replied irritably. Elegant, beautiful, and totally beyond his reach.

Nikki smiled sunnily at him as though she could read his every thought. And then she said, "You're not going into town, Dylan. You'll stay here."

If she had told him that a year ago, he would have smirked at her and leaped over the fence, walked the thirty something miles just to prove her wrong. Even if it took half the night. But there was no way his back would let him walk that kind of distance. He was hard-pressed to walk a damn mile now.

As if she could read his mind, Nikki moved back to stand beside him. "You walk, Dylan. Maybe not as far as you like. And maybe you can't run. But you said it yourself—you are walking. You have friends that won't ever walk anywhere again. One is stuck in a wheelchair forever and he will never do so many of things you said you *needed.* Two of them will never see a sunset, or look at a pretty woman. Never see their families."

With that, she reached up, brushed his hair back before laying one hand against his cheek. After studying his face for a long moment, she smiled at him, then turned around and went back inside.

He blew out a breath and studied the sky overhead for a long time. She was too damn young to act like his mom.

Not that her age had ever stopped her before.

CRCSCRCS

It took a week of running around like a mad woman, and a lot of begging and pleading, but she got the long Memorial Day weekend she had been hoping for off. Actually, she got a bonus.

The owner of the little romance publishing company let her leave Thursday, though what it had taken to get out of there didn't set very well in Kris's belly.

Nikki was so not going to go for it.

But as Kacie had put it, *It can't hurt to ask, now can it?*

No. It wouldn't hurt Kacie for Kris to ask Nikki.

But Nikki would look at Kris and just give her that stare. Or she'd laugh.

It was going to be weird enough editing romances. But asking her best friend to think about writing one... Kris shook her head as she took the exit to the small two-lane highway.

It was bad enough she was going to have to come up with an explanation for why she had developed an unusual growth.

One shaped just like a man.

One who followed her everywhere she went, who dogged her every step, who checked out damn near any room she went into, one who had *tapped her damn phone lines*. She slid the car in her rearview mirror a look and sighed when Raintree just waved at her. He wasn't even subtle about following her.

She had asked him, "Damn it, don't you all *want* to catch Delacourte? Damn it, I mean Blessett?

"Yes, ma'am. But not by using you as bait." He had just smiled, that patient smile. She really hated that smile. She'd come to realize that smile meant she could argue with him until the world ended and it wouldn't change a damn thing. He was making her too damned nervous.

Kris just hoped Dylan had headed on out, because if he was around, it would only make matters worse.

Nikki had said he was planning on living in Wagner, finishing up his rehab there. Look for a job. That was fine. Anywhere away from Kris. She couldn't take seeing him—damn it, even thinking of him was enough to bring back nightmares she had fled New York to escape from. It was a downward spiral—she thought of him, then she thought of the time she saw him in the chair, and what he had accused her of, and then she thought of Max...and that night. The gun, pressed against her head, her own screams.

But she wasn't so desperate to avoid him that she was going to avoid her best friend. She needed to see Nikki. Damn it, she just needed to relax.

It still looked the same, Kris thought. She slid out of the car and stared up at the house that sprawled over the clearing. Honey gold wood, acres of sparkling glass. And very pitiful-looking flower beds. A smile crossed her face as she studied the flowers that tried to survive. Chances were the ones that made it were planted by the kids. Nikki had once planted the flowers upside down...

As the door opened, a pint-sized, ebony-haired version of Nikki shot outside. "Aunt Kris! Aunt Kris!"

Kris dropped to her knees to hug the child to her. "Mandy, you've gotten so big," she whispered, leaning back to brush the raven black hair out of dark brown eyes.

"I'm five," Mandy said, holding out a grubby hand, displaying five fingers. "Abby is thirteen and she likes boys. Taylor is seven and Mikey is two. His ears are sick." After giving Kris the run down, she stopped and, cocking her head, studied Kris with narrowed eyes. "You're sad."

Silent, Kris stared into the wise, young eyes. "What makes you think that, baby?" she asked softly, once she swallowed the knot in her throat. She could see Nikki in those eyes, the snapping intelligence, the easy perception.

With a shrug of her tiny shoulders, Mandy said simply, "Your eyes make me think that." Reaching out, she stroked one hand down Kris's cheek. "Your eyes aren't smiling."

No, Kris thought, *not much to smile about lately.*

Mandy looked over Kris's shoulder where Raintree was leaning against the door of his car, his arms hooked over the top of it, his chin resting there. Looking as peaceful and harmless as he could. Which wasn't very.

In a loud whisper, Mandy asked, "Who's he?"

Kris glanced back and said, "Well, I guess he's sort of a friend."

Shiloh Walker

Mandy arched her brows. "Sort of? Dontcha know?"

Kris lifted her eyes heavenward for a brief instant. "I haven't exactly decided yet. But he has to help me for a while. So I guess he ought to be my friend," she finally said.

Raintree called out, "I know your Uncle Dylan, Miss Mandy. I'm a friend of his. Does that help?"

Mandy shouted, "I'm not 'posed to talk to strangers. You have to stay there 'til you're not a stranger no more. Anybody could say they know him. How do I know you ain't a liar?"

The man tipped his face to the sun and laughed. "Damn it, she's just as cute as Dylan said she was. Just as precocious. Okay, Miss Mandy. I'll wait here. You let me know when I can move."

Kris chuckled. "Better be careful what you tell her, Raintree. She'll try to hold you to it," she said over her shoulder. "Come on, Mandy. Let's go get Mama and introduce you to your uncle's friend. Although *I* didn't know he was friends with Dylan."

Mandy chirped, "We can just find Uncle Dylan and ask him. He's still here."

Kris felt her stomach drop to her feet. *Wonderful. Just wonderful...*

Mandy glanced up. "Your eyes still aren't smiling. And you look awful nervous now," the little girl said.

"I'm not nervous." She wasn't. Not really. What Dylan made her feel went beyond nervous. "I'm—uh, I'm kinda tired. Long drive. You know, you're an awfully sweet little girl, I bet you can help me smile again, Miss Mandy," Kris said, following the child up the stairs and inside the blissfully cool house.

With a solemn nod, Mandy promised, "I'll try my best."

70

When she was sure nobody was watching, she wiped her damp palms off on her shorts. Then she wished she had a mirror. Too late now. She'd be damned if she ran back to the car just to fiddle with her hair. Kris had no more than taken five steps into that blissfully cool house when she walked headlong to Dylan, his hands tucked into his pockets, his cane nowhere in sight. His lids were low over his hazel eyes and his gaze roamed over her face.

It wasn't until that moment it dawned on Kris that he must know about that night in New York City. Not just a few vague details, like she had given Nikki, glossing over most of them.

He probably knew all of them, right down to how Max had damn near ripped her shirt off her and how she had been close to sobbing before the military boys had shown up.

Her breath locked in her lungs.

Damn it. The most terrifying night of her life. The most shameful and he knew.

"Hey, rich girl," he drawled, reaching out and catching the bag that had slid unnoticed down her arm.

She frowned and tried to jerk it back, but Dylan ignored her and slung it over his shoulder. Wade had come up behind them and was already halfway upstairs with her other case. Dylan lifted a brow and said, "I thought you were just staying for the holiday weekend. Not a month."

Nikki slid between them and smiled sweetly. "Females require a little more than a spare pair of underwear and a toothbrush, brother dear. And Kris requires even more than the average female," she said. "And you actually packed light this time, sweetie." A look of false concern on her face, she said, "You aren't sick, are you? You didn't bring the kitchen sink. That's not like you."

Kris forced a smile and just shook her head. "Hey, Nik. I've got...company...I kind of need to talk to you about," she said, forcing a light tone into her voice as she turned away from Dylan.

Dylan had already moved around them and glanced outside, a slight smile appearing on his face. "Company, huh? How come he looks frozen?"

Kris replied, "That's Mandy's doing. She said she's not supposed to talk to strangers and he has to stay there until he's not a stranger no more. He said he's a friend of yours but that's not good enough for her."

Dylan started to laugh. "Damn it, I love that kid."

As he headed outside, Kris looked at Nikki and forced a smile. "Ummm, I have a bodyguard...sort of."

Nikki lifted a brow, warning lights dancing in her eyes. "You think that's going to be good enough? I want a little more detail than that." With that, her best friend turned and headed upstairs.

Kris sighed. She wasn't surprised.

Dylan was here. Nikki wanted details.

She wondered if she shouldn't have just stayed in Louisville. Swam in the pool, shopped for a house, laid around the house. All of that. Any of that. It would have kept her away from Dylan.

And that was the smartest thing for her, staying away from Dylan.

That would be easier said than done. Because she figured out about twenty minutes later, Nikki had him in the room across from hers.

Nikki had given the room on the main floor, right below the stairs, to Kris's shadow. And *that* was where Dylan usually stayed.

But the two men had put their military minds together and decided that was where her shadow should stay. Damn it, Raintree was starting to make her claustrophobic. But with Dylan sleeping right across the hallway, she'd take the claustrophobia over what Dylan did to her any day of the week.

CRCBCRCB

Kris sat on the deck, studying the low-hanging stars. It was late, but she couldn't sleep; what else was new? If she got more than four hours of sleep a night, she was feeling lucky. But it wasn't insomnia keeping her awake tonight. When that plagued her, she felt incredibly tired, but couldn't sleep.

Tonight, she wasn't tired at all. Her mind was clear, her body revved. Restless and edgy, and she knew damn well why. The reason for it was sleeping in the bedroom across the hall from hers. Far too close for her to be able to clear him from her mind.

"Up kind of late, aren't you?" a low voice drawled from behind.

Her muffled shriek died in her throat as she wheeled around to stare at Dylan. "Are you trying to scare me to death?"

His shoulders, bare and gleaming in the bright white light cast by the full moon, lifted in a shrug. He lifted a bottle to his lips, drank, before moving farther out on the deck. "Guess you're used to staying up late in New York," he said as though she hadn't gone sheet white.

"What in the hell do they teach you in the Army? How to sneak up on women and scare them to death?" she muttered, willing her pounding heart to slow down. She hadn't even heard him, hadn't realized he was behind her. So much for self-awareness, she thought with disgust.

"Yep," Dylan replied, leaning his hips against the railing as he studied the moonlit sky. Her eyes went to those narrow hips, that flat belly and unwittingly, she licked her lips before she tore her eyes away as he continued.

"That, and how to totally disgust and disappoint our families."

She lifted a brow at him. "Did I miss something?"

He grinned wryly. "You missed the family show. I had to tell them all about what happened, why I was out of the Army. Of course, I left out how I nearly got you killed. I figured I should leave that part for you."

Kris sighed and said, "Dylan, that wasn't your fault. That was Max's, pure and simple. And it's not like you introduced us. I met him at a bar, for crying out loud. It's pure bad luck, or maybe good luck, that you two were on the same unit, or team, or whatever in the hell you call it. What if I didn't meet him? Would you and the guys you worked with have gotten out of that?"

Dylan softly said, "Looking for another thank you?"

She twirled her glass in her hands and said wryly, "No. I'm looking for reasons. I have dreams that haunt me all the time. They rarely make sense, and when they do, I can't always act in time to do anything, to make a difference." A weak smile curved her mouth and she whispered, "It felt—*good* to not be too late for once."

"You've had those dreams before?" he asked, his voice soft.

She could feel his intense stare on her face, but she wouldn't look at him. She thought about how many dreams she'd had. Too late. Sometimes she'd dream for days and days, always the same one, but it would never make sense and when she finally made sense of it, it was too late.

"Yes, I've had dreams before. I hear—voices in my head sometimes, even when I'm not asleep. A lot. Most of my life. But they rarely make any sense. And when they do, I can't always do anything to help," she said quietly. Lifting her eyes to his, she shrugged. "I wanted, just once, for it not be a waste."

"It's not a waste. It's amazing, Kris," Dylan said, his voice just a sigh on the night. "If you aren't able to do anything, it's because you weren't meant to. You saved lives with what you told me. I hope you already knew that, but if you didn't, well, now you do. I just wish I had listened a little better." His face hardened and his eyes glinted like broken glass as he swore roughly, "If *I* had listened, maybe nobody would have died."

"Nobody had any clue he was going to try what he did." Lifting her glass to her lips, she drank, wetting her dry throat and trying to still her rapidly beating heart. *Not too late...for once.*

"It's our job to know things like that. We should have known," Dylan said.

"Hell, Dylan," Kris snorted, shaking her head. "I didn't realize you were Superman." Then her eyes slid over to his and she cocked her head, resting her cheek on her fisted hand. "Why do you think they are disappointed in you?"

Dylan shifted against the railing and turned so that he could gaze out at the night. The wind blew his hair back from his face and he lifted one naked shoulder. "Why wouldn't they be? I let them down. When I did actually need them, when I *let* myself need them, I wouldn't let them come. I wouldn't even let myself call them." He lifted his beer to his lips and drank, draining half the bottle in one long pull.

Kris felt her heart twist at the despondency in his voice, in his face. Sighing, she set her glass down. "Dylan, they aren't disappointed in you. They are damned proud of you—they just hate how thick that skull of yours is. Ranger Dylan, he doesn't need anybody." Suddenly, she noticed the amber bottle he held. Her brows drew together and she demanded, "Where did the beer come from? I didn't notice any beer."

"Shawn brought it up with him when he got here a little while ago," Dylan answered, gesturing to the deck doors. "He just moved it into the fridge in the basement, if you want one, but you probably prefer your white wine."

She lifted her shoulders in a shrug. "I'm fine," she replied. Actually, she wanted that beer pretty bad, but getting up meant passing by Dylan. She wasn't sure she trusted herself just to walk by him yet.

Heaven, had he bothered her like this before? Of course, other than those few minutes months back when he'd come to her apartment, it had been a couple of years since she had seen him last. Kris liked it that way. Dylan had always bothered her, Kris was aware of that. He bothered her to the point that she tried to avoid seeing him whenever she could.

Something about the way he looked at her, that slow, almost lazy smile. Then there had been that kiss... Yeah, that had been disturbing.

Right now, disturbed didn't even cover it.

"How's life for the big editor going?" he asked when she remained in the lounge chair, her long legs drawn up against her chest, arms wrapped around them.

"At the moment, life sucks," Kris replied, startling herself. She hadn't really said that, had she?

"That night giving you some bad moments?"

Lowering her head, she pressed her brow to her knees and silently called herself ten different kinds of fool.

Dylan's voice was gentle as he said, "Baby, it's all right to be afraid. You saved your life that night. The man watching you that night hadn't been paying attention and by the time he caught up with you on his own..." His voice trailed off and Kris slowly lifted her head.

She stared at him coolly, her tone regal as she said, "I'm not afraid of something that is over with."

Dylan cocked a brow at her. "Doesn't bother you that somebody tails you everywhere you go, because he hasn't been caught yet? Raintree isn't making you nuts yet?"

She blinked. "Of course he's making me crazy. Having somebody watch you twenty-four seven would make anybody crazy," she said, gritting her teeth. "Where in the hell is he anyway?"

"He was watching you from the kitchen," Dylan said, flashing her a smile. "Trying to give you a little bit of peace. I told him I'd come out here and pester you. Well, I used the words keep an eye on you. He went on to bed. And I came out here. Would you rather me go get him so he can continue watching you?"

"You can be a royal ass," she said flatly.

"Yeah. So, what kind of lifestyle of the rich and famous are you up to these days?" he asked, jumping from one thing to the next with nary a blink.

She frowned, wetting her lips as she tried to follow his rapid change of subject. "Editing. Just switched companies," she replied.

"To someplace in Louisville?" he asked. "What are you editing? The *Courier*?"

Irritated, she rolled her eyes. "I'm tired," she said. rising off the lounge in one fluid motion. She was going to bed, damn it. Talking to him was too confusing. It made her head hurt. She was going to go to sleep and she wasn't going to dream of him, or think of him. Even if it meant beating her head against the wall to get him out of it.

"Before you go to sleep, rich girl, there's something I'd like to know," Dylan said, moving and barring her way with his body.

The heat from him reached her through her clothes and the smell of him filled her head while she waited, one brow arched, her bare foot tapping silently against the wood.

"What exactly is it you want to know, slick?" she asked, keeping her voice from shaking through sheer will power alone. *Could you die from unrequited lust?* she wondered. *Was it possible die from this kind of need?* If it was, then she was in serious trouble.

It heated her belly, pooled low there, like some kind of animal just waiting to be freed. Like a hot velvet glove, it stroked over her skin, keeping her on edge, waiting, yearning, needing... *Damn it, Kris, stop it!*

"Just this," he murmured, closing the distance between them with one step.

She felt him winding her hair around his hand, felt him lifting her head. His mouth brushed against hers briefly before he drew back. His face was shadowed, but she knew his eyes were on her. *Did he just kiss me?* she wondered. Had she fallen asleep and dreamed this?

Hell, she thought wildly, *if I am dreaming this, then I'd better make the most of it.*

Rising on her toes, she pressed her lips against his firm mouth, sliding her hands to his shoulders. His hands clamped around her waist, dragging her closer to his long, hard body. One arm went around her shoulders, his forearm arching her neck as he pivoted and pressed her body between his and the waist-high railing.

A tiny whimper rose and died in her throat as he tasted her, as she tasted him. He tasted of wheat, yeast and man. He pushed his tongue into her mouth, past the barrier of her lips and teeth, hungrily, almost as if he had been as hungry for her as she was for him, Kris thought with wonder.

Strawberry ice cream, Dylan thought. She tasted like strawberry ice cream, cool, creamy and of springtime. Her lithe body pressed up against his and he could feel her heart pounding. Ravenous, desperate, his hands raced down the length of her torso, slid under the hem of her cotton top, seeking the warm, bare skin beneath.

One hand closed over her breast, massaging it, tweaking the nipple until it peaked and crowned against his fingers then he moved his mouth away from hers and pressed a line of kisses down her neck as he shoved her shirt higher, baring her breasts.

Her slim palms skimmed up and down his sides, over his hips, and pulled him up against her. Heat against heat, he felt the tremor start from deep inside her body. *The hell with it,* he thought, his hands returning to her waist, her shirt falling back down as he boosted her body up so that her hips rested on the small ledge that ran down the length of the railing.

For the first time in weeks, in months, he didn't think of his injury, didn't think of the ragged line of twisted scar tissue that prevented him from active duty. He was only thinking of the woman he had pressed up against his body, the woman he had wanted from the first time he had laid eyes on her.

Running his hands up the length of her smooth, silken back, he drew her shirt up until it caught under her arms. Pulling back, he stared down at her, smiling as he took in the hot, dazed look of pleasure in her eyes. Her body shook, quivering all over, as she reached for him.

Catching her behind her shoulders, he bent her back, leaning over her and catching the hard, crested tip of one nipple in his mouth as her upper body hung free in the air. The soft sob that fell from her lips echoed in his ears, raced down his spine as he slid one hand down her side. Catching her hip, he dragged her forward and rocked his cock against her cleft, shuddering as the heat there seemed to scorch him.

Scraping his teeth roughly over the nipple, he suckled on her until he had her writhing against him, her hands clutching desperately at his shoulders, her hips undulating against his. He slid his palm under the edge of her brief shorts and found her cleft with his fingers, hot and wet. She was swollen and creamy, sobbing out his name as he pushed two fingers inside her slowly.

With a growl, he went for the waistband of her shorts, wanting her naked and open.

His blood ran even hotter when she gasped out his name, pressing herself up against him as he withdrew from her. Through slitted eyes, he watched as she lifted her hips to help ease the shorts down her legs. God, her legs. There had been times he had nearly driven himself insane thinking about those legs, the round curved hips.

As her shorts fell to the deck floor, he shifted back reaching for the buttons of his jeans, steadying her body with one hand. One step took him back between her spread legs. Taking her hips in his hands, he drew her closer. Her hands came up to grip his shoulders, those wide green eyes staring up at him with hunger and need.

"Dylan," she murmured, pressing her mouth against his as he pressed his length against her.

Slowly he started to penetrate, never taking his eyes from hers as he slid just the tip inside her, that hot, wet molten silk beckoning to him to just drive deep inside and never leave. He surged a few inches deeper and Kris clamped around him, her inner muscles twitching and shuddering, her body shaking minutely.

"Please," she whispered, pulling away from his restraining hands, trying to pull him deeper inside.

One second, his body tensed, ready to take. And then he was gone, his bare back presented to her while his hands dragged his jeans back up, his narrowed eyes on the silent house.

"Dylan?" Kris asked, her voice shaking. As he lifted one hand, a light on the second floor came on, followed by footsteps on the stairs just outside the kitchen. Kris froze, but Dylan turned, scooped up her shorts and tugged her off the edge, guiding her into the shadows, away from the window.

Damn it, he thought viciously, barely able to think he hurt so bad. If whoever in the hell was up had waited another ten minutes...

Aw, hell. Five. Bad as he hurt, bad as he wanted her.

His mind started to clear as a light came on in the kitchen, casting pale squares of light through the window. Arching his head, he saw Wade's profile as he took a glass from the counter and walked by the window, out of Dylan's line of sight.

Seconds later, the light went off and he could hear footsteps going back up the stairs. With her body pressed against his, he could feel how much Kris was shaking. Drawing back, he looked down at her in the pale light cast by the moon, at her wide, almost blind eyes. With one hand, he brushed her cheek, smiling slightly as she arched against his hand like a little cat.

What in the hell was he doing? he wondered, holding her body against his, stroking her back with his hand in long, soothing motions. Nikki would kill him. And in the morning, once her mind cleared, Kris likely would want him disemboweled.

He started to ease her away but she only burrowed against him, her hips rolling against his, her breath coming in soft, ragged little pants. He was really going to hate them both in a few minutes, he thought with disgust. But he couldn't leave her like that. He turned them, so that his back was braced against the wall, hers pressed up against his chest. Nudging her backside with his hips, he tortured himself a bit while he stroked her breasts. Easing one hand down the slope of her hip, he parted the curls between her thighs, slid against the hard little knot of nerves, dipping inside. Rotating his thumb against her, working her with his hand, Dylan gritted his teeth when she started to climax around his invading finger, her muscles squeezing around him. Roughly, he moved his hips against her bottom, seeking some relief. Lowering his head, he bit the curve between her neck and shoulder. With a soft scream, she flowed into his hand, her body sagging back against his.

While her breathing started to calm, Dylan, shifted, letting her weight go back against the wall while he knelt down to search for her shorts. His lower back screamed at him, on fire, and it protested twice as loud as he stood back up.

"Come on, darling," he murmured into her ear a moment later, once the tremors had passed from her body. "Let's go to bed."

Sleepy, sated, she smiled at him, a soft, "Hmm," escaping from her swollen mouth. Her arms came up around his neck, and Dylan cursed viciously. God, what he wouldn't give to be able to pick her up and carry her up those stairs, into her room where he could lay her down and love her all night.

Instead, he eased her back, drawing her twisted shirt back down until it covered her bare hips. And then he led her back inside the darkened house, up to her room where he eased her inside the door, kissed her lightly.

Then he closed the door and walked to his own room, where he planned to pace the floor until his weary body forced him into sleep.

CRCBCRCB

Kris awoke with a smile on her face. What a dream. Rolling over, her hand slid down the empty expanse of bed, searching for a warm body. When it encountered nothing but smooth linens, her eyes flew open.

She remembered the entire night. Her face flushed crimson, and mortified, she sat up, drawing her knees to her chest and pressing her face into them as she wished for a hole to open up and swallow her whole. Hot color stained her cheeks and nausea started to roll in her belly. God, she'd hidden it for years, years, and then to go and lose it like that.

All because he kissed her.

Turning into a whimpering, hot molten puddle of flesh from one kiss. Well, Kris thought with a tiny curve of her lips, one kiss didn't exactly describe the feel of Dylan's firm, sulky mouth pressed against hers as he ate at her mouth like he simply craved the taste of her.

A knock sounded on the door before Nikki's voice called out. Before the door could open, Kris flopped onto her belly and drew a pillow over her head, pretending to be oblivious.

The door swung open and Kris could hear Nikki's laugh through the pillow. "Cut the act," Nikki said cheerfully. "I know you're up; I heard you swearing a second ago." Then in a singsong voice, she said, "I've got coffee."

Not even for coffee was she willing to face reality yet. "Nikki, please leave me alone and let me die in peace," she pleaded desperately, her voice muffled by the pillows.

"Bad night?"

A pitiful whimper was all that escaped her and she cringed at Nikki's sympathetic chuckle. "What's up? You hung over?"

No, just not ready to face him yet. "Nik, I need to sleep," she mumbled.

"We're going to the lake for the day. Don't you want to come?"

"Who is 'we'?" The thought of getting out of bed and facing everybody was terrifying. But not as bad as the thought of being stuck in the house with Dylan.

"Everybody. Shawn's going to meet us at the marina. Dylan and Wade went into town already to get bait while everybody gets ready. The guys are going to pretend to fish and we can lay out and be lazy."

"I'll lay out and be lazy here," Kris muttered.

"I can't hear you with this thing over your face," Nikki said, jerking the pillow out of Kris's hands. "What's wrong with you?"

"I just don't feel like going to the lake," she said, jerking the sheet up over her eyes with a scowl.

The sheet was summarily jerked down and she was left to glare at Nikki with sleepy eyes and tangled hair, her torso bare to the world. "Do you mind? There are kids in the house."

"Nope," she said cheerfully. "Not right now. They are all in the garage looking for rafts, fishing poles, and the blow up thingies to put on Mandy and Mikey's arms. What's up with you?"

With narrowed eyes, she wrapped her hands around the sheet, jerked and succeeded in pulling it from Nikki. Once she had it, she tucked it up under her arms and said, "I don't feel like going out to the lake. Remember what happened last time? I ended up looking like a bloody lobster, and feeling about as well-cooked."

Nikki studied her with thoughtful eyes before lifting her sun-kissed shoulders in a shrug. The straps of her bathing suit peeped out from under her ragged tank top as she pushed off the bed. "Suit yourself, sleeping beauty," she drawled as she headed for the door.

As she closed the door behind her, Kris heard her say with a laugh, "Coward."

Absolutely, Kris thought, flopping back onto the bed and rearranging the sheet around her naked body. Hell, had it really happened?

Pressing her lips together, she could almost taste him. Every part of her body he had touched seemed to burn still and as she remembered, one long shudder racked her body and she murmured, "Yeah. It happened."

How in the world was she going to be able to look him in the eye again? She certainly couldn't stand being trapped on a boat with him for an entire day. Rolling over, she pressed her hot face back into the cool linens and prayed for oblivion. Once the family was out of the house, she'd figure something out.

CRCBCRCB

It was still early enough in the year that the water hadn't warmed yet and as Dylan dove in, it slid over his flesh like silk, cooling his overheated body. Why was it you never remembered just how hot and muggy a Kentucky summer could get? His abandoned pole remained on the boat as he swam through the water of Lake Cumberland, heading for the small island where Nikki and the kids had decided to land.

Shawn, Wade and Jack continued to pretend they were fishing. Shawn's current babe lay on the boat in a tiny thong and top, pretending she wasn't aware of the male attention being directed her way. Dylan figured it wasn't going to be much time before Shawn tired of her, especially when he realized just how many times she was aiming those baby blues at Wade, and every other guy within fifty feet.

Of course, if Nikki noticed... Dylan grinned as he cut through the water. Those pretty baby blues would widen with terror if Nikki decided to get upset about her flirting with her husband.

Reaching the shallows, he planted his feet on the bottom and waded through the water, sliding his hands through his hair. Low riding cut-offs molded to his lean hips, and just to the right of his navel, there was the ugly exit wound, red and puckered. The entry wound at his back was smaller, almost surgically neat, but it was surrounded by a series of long thin lines, scars from the repeated surgeries.

As he moved closer, he heard Nikki tell Mikey not to play with the bugs, her mouth curling in disgust, laughter in her eyes. Why hadn't he realized how much he had missed them? he wondered, absently, lowering his body to the warm sand.

The laughing, squealing kids, his brother and sister, his father. Hell, even the brother-in-law he had once wanted to pound into the dirt.

And Kris.

Not that he had ever seen her a hell of a lot, but before he had left, he'd seen her around once or twice a year, talked to her, however briefly, on the phone.

"So are you sleeping all right?" Nikki asked, interrupting his daydreams.

With a shrug, he drew his knees up, hiding his belly from the approaching kids, shifting so that the driftwood close by blocked his back from their eyes. "Yeah. I don't need much sleep."

"Of course not," Nikki replied, rolling her eyes. "Not the big tough Army Ranger. But how about my brother, the man who was shot, paralyzed for a while? Shouldn't he be taking care of himself?"

"I came home, didn't I?" he asked shortly.

"Several months after the fact," Nikki replied, reminding him she still hadn't let that go. Then she shrugged. "I was just asking. I thought I heard somebody up and moving around last night."

She hadn't heard him, Dylan thought.

"I figured it was Kris. She has trouble with insomnia, gets worse the more stressed out she is," Nikki continued, cupping sand in her hand and letting it run through her fingers. "I hope she isn't waking you up."

Dylan lifted his shoulders in a shrug, eyeing the cooler sitting a few feet away. "When are we going to eat?" he asked, glancing towards the kids. "That boy of yours eats any more bugs, he's likely to turn into one."

Nikki's lip curled slightly and she shuddered. "I don't know what it is about him and crawly things. The doctor assures me it won't hurt him." Dutifully, she turned her head and caught Mikey's eyes just as he squatted down and started to reach for another insect.

After the chubby little hand fell away from the bug and his lower lip started to quiver, Nikki sighed. "He looks like he lost his best friend, doesn't he?" she murmured, shaking her head and pushing up to her feet. Dusting her hands off on her hips, she went over and picked up the little guy, pressing kisses to his neck until he started to giggle.

Moments later, Dylan found his arms full of sleepy baby as Nikki told him, "See if you can enchant him as much as bugs do. I'll start putting the food together."

Dylan straightened away from the driftwood, eyeing the little person on his lap warily. He'd gotten so big. Mikey had been six months old the last time he'd been home. Now he was walking, running, talking...eating bugs. *Well,* Dylan figured. *I've eaten worse than that.* He shifted his legs so that he sat Indian style with Mikey settled in his lap.

Those big sober eyes stared at Dylan curiously before dropping to his shoulder. "Owie," Mikey said, lifting his dirty hand to a slender three-inch long scar on Dylan's right shoulder. His eyes started to sting when the boy lowered his mouth and pressed a smacking kiss to the old scar. "All better," Mikey said solemnly, his voice surprisingly clear.

"Thanks, fella," Dylan said roughly, stroking a hand down the sun-screened back. "I, ah, I think your mom wants me to keep you from eating any more bugs for a while."

When Mikey scrunched his nose up like that, he looked just like Nikki, Dylan thought. Mikey said, "Ucky bugs."

"Yeah, it's pretty gross. But you seem to like it."

With a decisive nod, he agreed, "Like it."

Dylan laughed. "I guess they have to watch what they say around you any more, don't they?"

Approaching from the back, Nikki lowered the small portable grill to the sand, securing its legs as she said, "You have no clue, bub. I dropped something a couple of months ago and said what's natural when you're aggravated. Then Wade comes home and I lied, telling him Mikey and I were teaching the dog to sit. 'He's saying sit, Wade, that's what's he's saying.' I think he even bought it."

"Good cover up," Dylan agreed, watching Mikey investigate the chain he still wore around his neck.

Mikey glanced up and chirped, "Cover up."

Dylan laughed and shifted the sturdy toddler. "They're all getting so big, Nik. Can you believe it?"

Glancing over at her youngest, who was turning Dylan's dog tags back and forth, Nikki shook her head. "No. I can't. You know, Abby's thirteen. She's crazy about boys, wanting to date. It seems like she was just five years old. You never realize how fast time goes by until it's already gone."

Mikey tired of the chain at Dylan's neck and took off after his sisters, squealing and laughing. Dylan's smile faded and he turned to Nikki. "What's going on with Kris?" he asked.

Nikki lifted her shoulders as she tore open a small bag of charcoal. "She's not talking to me much about anything. Don't think she slept good last night. She didn't feel like coming down here all day."

Behind his sister's back, Dylan's eyes rolled. After clearing the wide grin from his face, he said, "That's not what I mean." Even the faintest smile faded from his eyes as he added, "She's not acting like Kris. It's not like I see her a lot, but...well, something's bothering her." *Something* like almost dying. But he

89

wasn't going to go into that until he knew just what Nikki knew about that night.

"She's quit her job. Moved to Louisville. What's going on?"

With a sigh, Nikki shrugged and said, "I don't know." After setting the coals alight, she settled down on the sand within arm's length of the grill. "She just quit a very lucrative job to start one that could flop. She could just be worried about that. Could be she's still upset about what happened a few months ago. She's not really talking about things much right now." Nikki blinked innocently and gave him a sweet smile. "I don't suppose this Army friend of yours—and don't tell me he isn't Army...I won't buy it—I don't suppose he has told you why in the world Kris needs a bodyguard all the time, has he?"

Dylan shrugged. "He hasn't told me anything. Classified, that's all he says, and I'm not Army anymore," he said. And all without lying. Because he hadn't had to ask Ethan Raintree a damn thing. He already knew.

Nikki studied him through narrowed eyes, as though debating whether to believe him or not. Finally, she turned away.

Through lowered lids, Dylan focused his eyes on his sister. "Is she seeing anybody?"

With a lifted brow, Nikki asked, "Why? Do you ever plan on letting her know how crazy you are about her? I do know she isn't sleeping with tall, dark and sexy. I know, because I already asked."

"Who said I was crazy about her?" Dylan asked, returning her stare levelly.

"Dylan, I may not know everything there is to know about you, but I do know you. You've been crazy about her for years."

His skin started to feel a size too small, and he could feel the dull rush of blood to his face. Turning his head away, he said, "Hell, I don't have a chance with her. Shit, Nikki, can you actually see her wasting her time on me?" The sour feeling in his gut intensified as he imagined the kind of man she did spend her time with. Somebody smooth, polished—loaded.

"Why wouldn't she?" Nikki asked.

"Why would she?" he countered.

Lifting her brows, she said, "I dunno. Maybe because you're a great guy, you treat a lady well. You—"

"Spent the majority of my teenage years in and out of a detention center?" he asked bitterly, rising to his feet. "Could barely spell my name when I graduated? How about the fact that I have absolutely no clue what I'm going to do with myself now? Or that I'm going to be fighting a bum back the rest of my life?" He stalked up to the water's edge, staring out at the boat barely a hundred feet from shore. That swim had exhausted him. "Or how—"

"How about the fact that you got that injury defending your country?" Nikki interrupted. She marched up until she stood toe to toe with him, and jabbed him in the chest with her finger. "How about the fact that you not only figured out how to spell your damn name, but you made it into the Army Rangers? You think any idiot off the streets can do that?

"There's not a damn thing wrong with you, Dylan Jackson Kline. Not a damn thing. And you're good enough for anybody. But if you can't see that, fine. She's not going to hang around waiting forever. You don't wanna take a chance while she's here? Fine. But don't try to avoid it by calling her a snob. And damn it, her life hasn't been a cakewalk. She went through hell a few months ago. She won't tell what happened, but I know something did. She was in New York on 9/11, she saw what happened in person and she lost three friends. Then there was what happened..."

Nikki's words died away and she clammed up, turning away.

Dylan narrowed his eyes. "What happened?"

"Nothing. It's not my place to be talking about," she said, staring out at the river. "But she's not had the rich and pampered life you seem to think. She was only a block away from Ground Zero, did you know that? Two of her friends worked in one of the Towers, and another was a paramedic. All three of them died." Nikki tried to bat away Dylan's hand but finally glared up at him, her eyes bright and angry.

"What else happened? What aren't you telling me?" he repeated. "I can find out. You know I can. So why don't you just save me the trouble?"

Nikki scowled. "She was kidnapped when she was a kid. I think she was eleven. They did it for money—you know her parents are loaded. But that wasn't the bad part. One of the guys was a pedophile and while the head guy was out of the room, this guy came in, threw her on the floor and tried to rape her. He covered her mouth, tore her clothes off and almost got it done, but she bit his hand. He let go of her and screamed. The guy who was running the thing came in and jerked the guy off, beat the hell out of him. She said he went ballistic. He was really sorry, begged her not to hate him, he just needed the money, he really had no intention of her getting hurt. He took her away from there and finished the deal on his own."

"Her dad paid the guy and he wasn't ever caught—I don't think Kris really wanted him to be. After that, they moved away from California and settled in New York."

She jabbed Dylan again in the chest and said, "So don't act like she's never had it rough. She's got money, but that doesn't mean she's had it easy. She's perfect for you, damn it. She's always wanted you. But if you can't see that, fine. You just sit on your ass in your little apartment in Wagner, and she'll find somebody in Louisville and you can be miserable thinking about it. So if you don't want to take a chance, fine, so be it. But if you don't, you'll regret it your whole damn life and it will be your own damn fault. Because you're a damn coward."

Dylan stood there, watching her walk away. She'd tried to poke a damn hole in his chest. He rubbed at the spot. With a scowl, he muttered, "Well, you sure as hell are batting a thousand right now, slick."

Chapter Five

She's not going to hang waiting forever.

Nikki's words were still echoing in his mind as he climbed out of the Blazer hours later, his body pleasantly tired, his lower back stiff but not on fire. His mind was revving. *She's always wanted you.*

A chance with her? Hell, he wanted more than a chance. He wanted *everything* and all of it with her. Dylan rarely slept a night when he didn't dream of her, think of that long, pale body and ache to feel it against him. A single kiss with her, years earlier, had haunted him more than entire nights spent with other women. Hell, that one kiss had been more fulfilling than entire nights he'd spent with other women—up until last night.

Sometimes he felt like he had spent his entire life just waiting to touch her again.

But touching her wasn't enough.

He was flat out in love with her, and suspected he had been from the time he'd looked into those cool green eyes when she had strolled up to their apartment when he had been all of fifteen years old. Although if anybody had ever told him that he would have beaten the man bloody. Love at first sight was something that belonged in fairy tales, and a happy ending wasn't something he was looking for.

That didn't mean he didn't secretly hope for one.

Kris was out on the porch, working on her laptop. She had her long legs up, ankles propped on the railing, crossed neatly. She met his gaze over the distance and colored hotly before lowering her emerald eyes back to the screen.

Raintree glanced up from his perch at the other end of the porch, took one look at Dylan and disappeared with a mischievous grin.

Dylan didn't even spare him a glance as he studied Kris's face. Her eyes lifted and met his and they stared at each other. Her cheeks turned pink. He felt his cock swell and his lids drooped. The temperature of his blood seemed to shoot up about thirty degrees and his hands closed into fists. He could hardly think when he got this close to her, just barely able to keep her from seeing what was raging inside him.

You're good enough for anybody... Damn it, he wanted that woman.

Not just for one damn night, either, and it wasn't just her body he wanted. He wanted *her.* He wanted the stubborn arrogant proud woman who was crazy enough to track down an unknown nineteen-year-old kid from Kentucky and turn her into one of the bestselling fantasy writers in the country. He wanted the softhearted woman who stood by his sister as Nikki's world fell apart around her. He wanted the cool business woman he'd seen in the airport and he wanted the laughing woman who loved to cuddle her best friend's children.

All of her. Dylan wanted all of Kris, from her long, deep red hair to the soles of her feet and every smooth, pale inch in between, all intricacies of her complicated soul and sweet heart that she hid behind that sophisticated exterior.

He had wanted her since he was a mouthy punk running wild in west Louisville and he'd go to the grave wanting her. Her cool smile and appraising green eyes had driven him crazy for years.

He had seen all sorts of emotions in her eyes, everything from approval, to anger, to disdain, and disgust. But he hadn't ever seen that disgust in her eyes when she looked at him.

Why?

Her taste, the silk of her hair in his hands had haunted him for years. After last night, Dylan knew how she moaned and whimpered as she came, how wet the folds of her sex were under his fingertips while he touched her, and how silky soft she felt, how easily she was primed once he started to touch her.

Sweet hell...

Behind him, Nikki hummed under her breath. "She's blushing, Dylan. Why is she blushing?" He gave Nikki a narrow glance and she smiled at him, innocently. "Ah, so maybe there were two people up last night."

Wade chuckled and herded Nikki and the kids inside. Dylan moved slower, still staring at Kris.

Kris felt his eyes on her, the sultry hazel eyes that seemed to stare right through her. Why in the hell hadn't she taken Nikki's car and driven into town? The door closed behind the kids, Nikki and Wade—but Dylan was still out there. She couldn't hear him and unless she lifted her head, she couldn't see him. But she didn't have to see him or hear him.

Kris could feel him, that overwhelming presence, that life which seemed to drown out everything and everyone else when he was in the area. His silent footsteps closed the distance between them. Her skin prickled as he drew nearer, her nipples puckered and tightened, her breathing got more and more shallow.

Slowly, watching her hands to make sure they stayed steady, she shut down her laptop and closed it. As he drew near, Kris lifted her head, her gaze tracking over the bare tan belly, the rock hard muscle left bare by the sleeveless denim shirt he had pulled on over his denim cut offs. The light scattering of blond hair on his chest did little to hide the ridged wall of muscle there. His dog tags rested between his flat nipples, rising and falling with each steady breath.

She forced her eyes to meet his and saw he was watching her steadily, one sandy blond brow cocked.

"Any luck, hot shot?" she asked, sliding her laptop aside and propping one arm along the back of the chair. She rested her chin on her hand and stared at him with a cool smile.

He shrugged. "Didn't bother trying much."

His eyes were bland, and she couldn't detect any double meaning there—but with Dylan, you could never tell. Her cheeks started to burn but she fought not to let him see or hear any sign of her discomposure. "I don't like early mornings," she said evasively.

Bluntly he said, "Am I supposed to apologize for last night?"

Her face went flame red and all attempts at remaining distant went out the door. *Oh, hell...did he have to go and bring it up?*

"Why did you do it?" she asked slowly, forcing herself to meet his eyes.

Dylan didn't answer right away. Instead he sat down next to her.

Oh, man, he smelled good. Hot male and sunshine. Kris wanted to lean in and press her mouth to the bare skin of his chest. She looked away from his chest, blushing, but he wasn't looking in her eyes. He was staring at her mouth.

97

Kris felt her heart skitter to a stop when he reached over and traced his thumb across her lower lip, his big rough palm cupping her cheek. She gasped when he reached for her, his hands grasping her hips and dragging her across the glider. "I've been dying for another taste of you for years," he muttered, reaching up and burying one hand in her hair, the other arm going around her waist like a band. "That one kiss of you a couple of years ago wasn't near enough. Last night wasn't enough."

She arched a brow at him and coolly said, "Well, I have to say that your lines have improved." Of course, it was hard to be as arrogant as she was trying to be when she was pretty damn certain her face was almost as red as her hair.

Dylan's lips quirked, curving his mouth up in a rare smile. "Are you going to hold me accountable for what a punk kid said, over ten years ago?" he asked, laying a hand on her thigh and lazily stroking upward, giving her a chance to resist.

Her lids fluttered closed as the tips of his fingers breeched the edge of her shorts. "Ahh..." was about all she was able to articulate at that time. Forcing her eyes to open, she stared at him. He was just a breath away. So close she could feel the warmth of his breath on her face.

Kris inhaled slowly and tried to calm her racing heart. No good—all that deep breath had done was bring more of his scent inside her head and turned her into mush. That sulky mouth... It had made her wonder and burn for years. Now it was on hers again, his tongue pushing past her lips, as one big, warm hand settled on her side, the thumb rubbing the soft underside of her breast.

The other hand left the hem of her shorts and she whimpered when she felt it grip the curve of her ass. A moan rose and died in her throat as he lifted her, positioning her astride his lap. Automatically, she rocked forward to meet him. The thick ridge of his cock wedged between her thighs and she whimpered, rubbing up against him greedily. His hands cupped her ass, urging her on.

Kris cried out when his mouth left hers to trace a burning path of kisses down the line of her neck. "Dylan...we can't...do this here," she whispered as his mouth closed over the aching point of one nipple, drawing it into the wet cave of his mouth. Electric little shocks went darting through her system as he circled his tongue around her flesh.

"Hmmm," he murmured under his breath.

She threaded her fingers through his hair. To pull him away. Seriously. They were out in broad daylight, on a porch swing, with a house full of people just feet away. But instead of pulling him away, she urged him closer.

Oh, hell, that felt so good. He used his tongue and pushed her nipple against the roof of his mouth, sucking deep as he started to rock his hips against her as he pushed her down on him.

"You're sweet," he whispered as he pulled his mouth away, staring up at her through a fringe of lashes. "I thought maybe I'd imagined how sweet you tasted. No woman could taste that good, feel as good as you did. I must have imagined it. But you really do feel as amazing as I remember. Damn it, you drive me crazy."

His hazel eyes were slumberous, heavy lidded, the heavy fringe of black lashes at half-mast as he stared at her. There was a faint smile on his mouth. A sleepy, sexy smile so full of promise—damn, if he lived up to half the promise she saw in that smile, she might not live through it. Kris slid her hands down to rest them on his shoulders, her cheeks heating under his intense scrutiny. "I find it hard to believe that. You hardly speak two words to me."

A grin flashed like quicksilver across his lean, tanned face. "That's because any time I look at you I lose about fifty IQ points. Why in the fuck would you want to talk to me? I didn't exactly make the best first impression, did I?"

Heat raced through her at his words, her eyes dropping to his mouth. "Fifty IQ points, huh?" Then she smiled slowly. "You made a lasting first impression, I'll give you, that. You were a kid, Dylan. And what a sexy one you were, even then..." She lowered her hand, taking his dog tags in her hand and playing with them. Through her lashes, she watched his face as she admitted, "Maybe if you had been just a little older, I just might have taken you up on it."

A groan rumbled out of his chest and before Kris realized what he was doing, she was sitting on her ass, and he was stalking to the railing. "Shit, baby, don't go telling me things like that when we most likely have an audience." He leaned his hands on it and stared up at the sky, breathing raggedly while Kris smiled with hot female satisfaction at his obvious discomfort.

And all she had done was admit she had wanted him back then. Did he even realize, though, that back then his eyes had been every bit as haunted as Nikki's had been? If he had been older, she would have done almost anything to get that troubled look out of his eyes.

"What are we going to do about this?"

His quiet voice floated in and disturbed her reverie and she turned to see him staring at her, his arms folded over his chest, the powerful muscles in his arms bulging and catching her eye, distracting her. She traced her gaze over his body lingeringly, staring at the lean, powerful muscles, studying the way his hair curled over his forehead. She could stare at him for hours. God above knew she'd wanted to do just that for years. Finally, she looked into his eyes and found him staring at her with a focused, intent, *hungry* stare.

He was talking about wanting her.

She sure as hell wasn't going to pass up the opportunity to feel that sleek, powerful body moving over her, under her. "I can think of any number of things we can do. When should we get started?"

His sudden bark of laughter caught her by surprise. "I'm not just talking about finding a place to get you naked, sweet. I lost my taste for quick meaningless sex pretty fast, and I lost it years ago. I've had feelings for you for years, been damn near obsessed with you for years. A quick romp in the sack might get rid of a temporary problem, but it will make it worse in the long run."

But Kris had lost track of what he was saying after the words *I've had feelings for you for years...* Oh, boy. They really needed to learn to say things to each other from time to time, more than, *Been up to much lately, hot shot? Broken any hearts, rich girl?*

Dylan's lips were still moving but she couldn't quite hear him as she slid from the seat and moved to face him, staring at him. "Shut up a minute, Army boy. Okay? Just shut up a minute."

Shit, what in the hell did I say? That was why he didn't talk much. Dylan always ended up saying the wrong damn thing. Something had her eyes glittering like wet emeralds as she moved away from the glider to stand in front of him, staring up at him with wide, sparkling eyes.

But before he could ask her, she threw her arms around his neck, plunging her tongue deep inside his mouth, hungrily. Like she was ravenous, she arched her body against his and sucked his tongue deep inside her mouth, rubbing against him and whimpering deep in her throat. Kris's fingers dipped into his hair, clenching there. Dylan reached for her, wrapping his arms around that amazing, wonderful body, feeling those soft, lovely curves align against him, just like he had dreamed about a million times.

"Obsessed?" she murmured, pulling her sweet mouth away, moving to nibble at his chin as her fingers grazed his waistline, teasing him into forgetting that there were people, and some of them were very very *nosy*. "Obsessed, you say? I've been obsessed, had to fight with myself not to ask about you every time I talked to Nik. I look for you every time I come down here and I'm sad every time I don't see you. I hate not knowing where you are, and then I saw you in that damned chair and I hated myself. If I had tried, just a little harder, I could have stopped you. I could have kept you from getting hurt. I could have done *something*—"

"Shhh..." he murmured, brushing her hair back from her face and kissing her back into silence as her body started to stiffen. "Don't. Don't think about it." *Somebody had worried for me...* Pushing his tongue inside her mouth, he pivoted, bracing her back against a post, rocking his pelvis against the soft hollow between her thighs. Under his, her body relaxed and went pliable, as though she had been waiting for him to touch her, just like this.

A loud knock on the window caused him to pull his mouth back, though he didn't release her. Peering over his shoulder, he scowled at the raised eyebrows on Shawn's face through the glass. Dylan stroked his hands up and down Kris's arms in gentle, soothing motions.

"We've got an audience."

CRCBCRCB

Kris lifted the phone with a smile. "Hey, hot shot," she murmured. Wagner was too damned far away for her. But it gave her a hot little thrill in her belly every time she thought of him, which was often, and every time he called her, which was daily. He drove out to see her once a week, and she drove out to see him once a week.

It still wasn't enough.

"Hey, rich girl," he returned. That slow, sexy voice of his sent a quick shiver down her spine as she settled back in her chair in the small office Kacie had set up in her house in Old Louisville.

"I'm going to be finishing up a little earlier, I think." She crossed her fingers as she glanced at the pile of work on her desk. "I was going to head out your way—if that's okay with you."

She could almost hear the smile in his voice as he sighed. "Well, I was planning on hitting the night life down here. I guess I could hang around home and wait for you to get here instead. I've got an appointment with a damned therapist at three, and then an interview at four-thirty. What time were you planning on getting here?"

Kacie appeared in the door, arching a black brow. The ring pierced through it flashed in the light. And she was mouthing, "*Go now. Go now. Go now.*"

Kris smothered a laugh, and said, "Well, actually, I think I can leave now. I may stop on the way and pick up something to fix for dinner, if that's all right with you."

"Pass up my cooking, or a hamburger, in favor of a home-cooked meal? I think I can handle that," he said levelly.

"Smart ass," she returned. She stood and scooped up some discs and files, dumped them in her bag. She blew Kacie a kiss. "I'll see you soon, slick." She disconnected and looked at Kacie with a wide smile. "I love you."

"Just give me details. Those quiet ones just give me the shivers looking at them," Kacie said, shuddering dramatically and rolling her eyes. "You never did tell me what happened when you talked to Nikki Kline."

"Well, the time hasn't been right," Kris hedged.

"Chicken," Kacie called as Kris hotfooted it out of the cramped office.

The only thing that gave her a little bit of pause was the car she knew was waiting out in front.

Her tag.

He had been ever present since she had made the damned bad mistake of dating one Max Blessett aka Max Delacourte, supposedly single with a steadily rising, promising career in military intelligence.

But ever since Max's very narrow escape from the military authorities who had damned near caught him, Kris's tag was obvious. Normally it made her feel safer and she didn't mind.

But she'd rather he not be around when she was seducing Dylan.

She slid her tongue over her lips as she walked out to the car where the man she knew only as Raintree was leaning against the hood. He had a camera installed in her office and a tap on her phone line and he watched her like a mama hawk.

Well, maybe a mama hawk wasn't quite accurate. He was six feet five inches of dark Native American sex appeal, attitude, and just the right amount of mischievous charm thrown in, enough to make her laugh, and he was stubborn, smart and funny. Everything he needed to be to make this situation tolerable. He had gray eyes that watched you out of a dark face, eyes that were disconcertingly pale, and disconcertingly thorough in their appraisal. His hair was short and dense black, so black it had a bluish sheen to it in the light—and he was one of the most intimidating guys she had ever seen.

If it wasn't for that smile, Kris would probably be scared to death of him. But he had an amazing smile. It could be downright mischievous or playful, depending on what he was up to, or what mood he was trying to convince her out of.

The guy he shared his shifts with was his dead opposite, a silent, brooding bastard with cold, dark eyes. He had introduced himself as Luciano that first night and since then, she might have gotten a few grunts out of him. Other than that, she saw him come, she saw him disappear at the break of dawn when Raintree came on, and that was it. Luciano was not a man who seemed happy to be around her.

But that was okay—Luciano took the nights, so she rarely saw him. Raintree seemed to like her, and that was good, because he was more likely to give into her.

Or so she thought.

"No can do, darlin'," he said, shaking his head, tossing his keys up and down. He slid her a wicked look and asked, "So how come you want to ditch me? Got a hot date?"

"I'm just going to Wagner," she said, blowing a frustrated breath out. "I'm going to be with Dylan. I'll be perfectly safe."

"Uh-huh. And when Sergeant Kline sees you don't have your tag, he will have my career, my ass, and my head on a platter." Then Raintree's pale eyes softened and he smiled gently as he added, "Not to mention the fact that I've gotten to like you a little too much to let you go risking that nice neck of yours. Drive on to Wagner. Believe it or not, there's not a damn thing you can do there that I wouldn't know about. I don't exactly go writing your daily life up in a report. I'm here making sure you don't get killed. We messed up—that's why your life is in danger, ma'am. So until you're safe again, we're here to protect you. But we aren't going to interfere in your life either."

Kris resisted the urge to poke out her lip. Well, she hadn't gotten her way.

But he was such a sweet guy. It was hard to be mad at him about it.

CRCSCRCS

Kris studied her dress.

She wasn't waiting any damn longer.

They had been dating for three damn weeks.

This long-distance relationship, driving back and forth, an hour each way, was for the birds. It didn't help that Dylan was going out of his mind here. He tried to act like he was looking for a job, and she knew he was going to interviews, but the problem was he didn't know what he wanted to do.

He was overqualified for most jobs in the area. The one thing that *might* satisfy him, he couldn't do; he couldn't be a cop. Not with his back injury, he wouldn't get through the training just yet, even though he could still kick the asses of everybody on the force in hand to hand.

Stifling a sigh, she shook her head. What in the hell was he interviewing for? It was after seven.

She paced back and forth, rubbing a hand up and down her tense neck and worrying. He'd go slowly insane if he didn't find something to keep him busy, and *satisfied*. She just hoped it was around here. Kris wasn't sure she could stand to lose him when they had just now gotten started.

Being with him helped keep the nightmares at bay. And not just the nightmares of Max. But the other ones...man, the others. The screaming. Girls' faces. Young, broken and terrified. Their screams seemed to intrude even on her waking hours.

Those were getting worse. Sometimes, though, if she thought about him enough, focused on his face enough, daydreamed about him enough, by the time she fell asleep, she was so tired, the nightmares didn't really have the energy to attack her.

That didn't always work.

She had one last week. It had repeated itself, over and over, every night this past week.

A little girl. In a tiny little cabin by the muddy, flood-swollen Ohio, miles away from here, just shy of Louisville. Kris had even thought she recognized a gas station where the little girl had tried to run away.

Wide terrified eyes, round cheeks, white blonde hair.

A scar, jagged and ugly, on her back.

When she searched the web this morning, trying to find out if a girl that matched her description had gone missing, she had felt like ripping her hair out. Of course a girl that matched her description had gone missing. The question was...which one was she? When had she gone missing?

You're an editor, Kris. Not a private investigator. You've no clue how to handle this. And you couldn't handle it anyway. You'd go crazy, she said to herself, shaking her head. Hell. She *was* going crazy, trapped in the small house, waiting on Dylan. Nervous as hell.

She worried the choker of pearls at her neck and looked at the clock. "Come on, Dylan, where are you?" she muttered. Her mind wandered back to the dream. It pulled at her and she closed her eyes. The dream seemed to wrap around her and she started to feel cold. Icy cold.

She could hear people talking. Two voices. Familiar. She felt scared. Cold. Hungry.

Then there was a noise. Kris jumped and whirled around. For a second, she didn't know where she was and then recognized Dylan's apartment. She pressed her fingers against her temple and muttered, "You need to start sleeping a little more."

She hadn't come here to obsess over a dream she couldn't figure out. She had come here because of Dylan. *Dylan. I'm here to seduce his socks off. And a few other pieces of clothing.*

Speaking of clothing, she made her way into his bedroom and flipped on the light, standing in front of his mirror and studying herself.

The dress...

About the dress.

A smile curved her lips. It was black, of course, and went to the ankle. It had a slit from the ankle up to mid thigh, and she wore opaque black stockings under it, and a pair of lacy boy shorts. Nothing else. The dress had one of those nifty built in bras, which was good, since it dipped rather low in the back. So low, in fact, that if it went any lower, she would have to forgo underwear as well as a bra.

Tossing her copied key up and palming it, she smiled a cat's smile and looked around the little rental house. It was perched on a hill overlooking the river and it was as cozy as you could hope to find.

Dylan had better be home soon. She was getting as nervous as a cat and it wasn't just over the dreams that haunted her.

"Chill out, girl," she muttered as she wandered out of the bedroom and into the kitchen. "He'll be here."

He was going to find lasagna, his favorite meal, Nikki's recipe of course, some good wine, though he wouldn't appreciate it as much as Kris would, so she had put some beer in the fridge as well. There were candles she would light as soon as she heard his truck, and the music was already playing. Jazz, which she had discovered he had a fondness for, much to her surprise. The low, bluesy sound of saxophone playing in the background, and sultry female voices, a local group recorded by friends of Nikki's, played throughout the entire cottage.

She left the kitchen to check the living/dining area. It was roughly just a little bigger than a postage stamp but it had a fireplace and a window that looked out over the heavily forested riverfront. Outside the sky was leaden gray with the threat of rain. Judging by the looks of the thunderheads piling up, they might even get some storms. The thought of making love to Dylan while rain pounded down on the roof, thunder booming in the sky and a fire crackling away, was enough to make Kris groan in frustration.

"Where in the hell are you?" she muttered as she walked back into the bedroom to check it. Again. For the fourth time. Kris didn't believe in letting little details go unchecked. She'd had the dress, and the sheets, and the groceries that hadn't needed to be bought fresh in her trunk since this morning. The sheets were ivory cotton sateen. Silk was too blasé, in her opinion, and also too damn chilly. The red silk-velvet comforter topped the bed and she had pulled it back in invitation.

His navy comforter and sheets were bagged and in the closet.

Yep, when Kris staged a seduction, she went all out.

The silver ice bucket and two champagne flutes were already on the table by the bed, waiting for the ice and the wine that was chilling in the fridge.

Everything was ready. Now if Dylan would just show up. Kris turned and walked back into the living room and settled down on the couch to wait.

ભ્ય૪ભ્ય૪

The dim glow of light greeted him as he climbed out of his truck. Kris's car was in the driveway, and Dylan sighed, rubbing the back of his neck in frustration. He never should have done this. How in the hell could he have a relationship with this woman, when he didn't even know what in the hell to do with himself?

There was nothing here for him.

No work. No job. Wagner wasn't the smallest town on earth, but it wasn't booming with jobs either. It was a college town. Most of the decent jobs were related to the university and that was the last thing on earth he wanted, even if he had been qualified. Other than those jobs, anything decent was either taken or he had no interest in doing.

He supposed he could find a job sitting in front of a computer all day doing some kind of tech work. He had no idea the labeling that went with it, but he could do any damn thing with computers that he wanted to. Problem was, he had absolutely no desire to work with them and the monotony of it would drive him insane.

The only thing that had any kind of potential was being a cop but even that was months away. And he'd go braindead within months.

He needed to be doing something that felt *right*.

That *needed* him.

Kris seemed to be putting down roots in Louisville. Her job with the newly established publishing company was fast becoming a career and she was looking at houses to buy.

Gravel crunched under his boots as he headed up the driveway, his footsteps weary, heading first to the gray Ultima where David Luciano waited. The window went down and the first words out of the ex-Ranger's mouth were, "You are one lucky bastard, you know that? That woman has got legs up to her neck, I swear."

Dylan cracked a grin. "She doesn't like you. If you bothered to speak to her now and again, that might actually change. Of course, if it went anything behind mild friendship, I'd have to kill your ass," he said amicably.

David shrugged. "I'm not paid to talk to her, or for her to like me. I'm paid to make sure the cute little butt of hers stays safe if and when Blessett ever makes his move. I don't think he's going to. It's been more than four months. He's probably living the high life down in South America now," he said, blowing out a puff of air as he reached for a cigarette.

Dylan cocked a brow. "Thought you quit. Didn't you kick that habit back while we were training together?" he said as David lit a cigarette.

David shrugged and studied the glowing tip of the cigarette. "I quit because I didn't want anybody smelling smoke on me when I was supposed to be hiding in the jungle. I don't hide in jungles in my line of work any more."

"What line is it, anyway?" Dylan asked conversationally.

111

David slid him a look as he took a deep drag on the cigarette, his eyes narrowed with pleasure. "If you'd really wanted to know, you should have kept your ass in the Army, slick," he replied.

Dylan flipped him off.

David's gaze moved to the house. "Well, you're not exactly my type. Besides, I'm not sure, but I bet that's what the lady in the house has planned for the night."

Dylan muttered, "I'm not going to get my hopes up about that." He still couldn't figure out what in the hell she was doing here. She was wasting her time with him, and sooner or later, she was going to figure that out.

Pick a fight, send her away. Make her wonder why she ever wanted to be with you... You're wasting her time...

The scent of jasmine and vanilla wafted to him as he opened the door, and homemade lasagna, yeasty bread. And underneath it all, Kris, hot, sweet woman.

Seated on the couch, watching him, lifting a glass of wine in toast, she smiled a hot female smile. Dylan felt all the blood drain out of his head as she slowly rose from the couch, her long, curved form outlined in a sleek, body-hugging dress all in black.

"Hello, handsome," she murmured softly, moving in his direction. Drops of pearls hung at her ears and a triple stranded pearl choker wrapped around her neck, with a diamond pendant nestled in the hollow of her throat. Her hair, that dark, rich red hair, was piled on top of her head in artful curls, making him want to yank the pins free, just to see it spill around her shoulders.

Damn it, I'm in trouble.

"Are we celebrating?" he asked, keeping his voice casual through sheer will alone.

"No." That Mona Lisa smile remained on her slick red mouth and she shook her head. "Just having dinner."

"I think I'm underdressed."

Kris had no comment. Instead, she held out a hand and when he accepted, she turned into the kitchen. Dylan's gaze dropped to her back. "Oh, hell." Her whole damn back was bare, from the brief band at her neck that held her dress up, down to just above the swell of her ass. All that flesh was naked, soft, smooth and scented, just begging for his touch.

Kris glanced over her shoulder. "Of course, we can always start with dessert first."

Hardly able to think as he gazed at all the bare, ivory flesh, Dylan asked stupidly, "What's for dessert?"

Her laughter was low and husky. Dylan thought he'd hit the floor when she replied, "Me."

All the blood drained out his head. Within heartbeats, he was so damned hard he hurt from it. His ears were roaring and his heart pounded so hard, he could hardly breathe from it. Dylan narrowed his eyes and studied her face. "You sure about that, rich girl?"

She smiled slowly. "Hot shot, you're the one who has been slowing things down. I've been sure about it for quite a while." With a tug of his hand, she led him down the hall, and Dylan arched a brow at her as she opened the door to his room, toasty warm from a fire, ivory linens on his bed, a ruby red comforter, wineglasses, a bottle of wine in a silver ice bucket, ice chilling it. And in front of that, a pile of silver foil-wrapped packets.

"Lady, you do know how to set a scene, don't you?" Dylan mused, trailing his fingers down the bare skin of her back, lowering his mouth and kissing the smooth, soft skin of her neck.

"Hmmm. It's a skill I was taught early in life." Taking his hand, she led him into the room before turning and wrapping her arms around his neck. "I've been dying to know what it would be like to be with you, Dylan. For years and years, I've wondered. Don't make me wait anymore."

She didn't have to say another word. Dylan fisted a hand in her hair, burying it inside the thick knot. It fell down around her shoulders as he lowered his mouth to hers. He wrapped his arm around her waist, pressing his palm against the silken flesh of back. She was soft, smooth. Dylan didn't think he'd ever touched anything or anyone that felt like this.

The taste of her flooded his senses but it wasn't enough. He wanted more. Craved more. No more waiting. No more wondering, not for either of them. That hot, sexy little body was pressed up against his, the firm push of her breasts, the diamond hard touch of her nipples evident through her dress and his shirt, her soft tummy cradling his cock as she moved seductively against him.

Pulling back, Kris smiled up at him and reached behind her neck. Dylan felt his heart simply stop in his chest as her dress fell to her waist, revealing her breasts, full, proud and naked, topped with hard, rosy nipples. She worked the dress over her hips, bending down slowly, never taking her eyes off him, in a move that would have done any stripper proud as she slid the dress to her ankles.

When she stood, she was wearing a pair of lacy shorts that hugged her hips, dipped well below her navel and showcased those curvy hips to perfection. And her legs... Oh, damn her legs were encased in opaque black thigh highs. Lifting his eyes back to hers, Dylan couldn't stop the wicked grin that split his face. "Are you gonna leave the thigh highs on?"

She smiled a naughty smile as she turned around, treating him to the back view. Dylan groaned. The shorts rode high on the cheeks of her butt, showing him the firm, rounded curves. He wanted to lean over and just bite her right there as she moved to the middle of the bed and settled there, drawing her knees to her chest in a pseudo-modest pose as she studied him, smiling angelically.

"If you'll get out of those clothes, we can do whatever you want," she promised.

Reaching behind his head, he tugged the T-shirt he wore up and off, tossing it to the ground, never taking his eyes off the long, pale lines of her body, white against the black of her lingerie. He could just barely make out the upper curves of her breasts. Perfect breasts, round and full, and they lifted and fell with each breath. The rhythm of her breathing kicked up while she watched him.

He kicked off his shoes while he flipped open the buttons of his fly. In one movement, he shoved his jeans and boxer-style briefs down together, catching his socks on the way. Naked, he straightened and moved to the bed. He held her gaze with his as he crawled across the bed and hunkered over her.

She lifted her mouth as he lowered his. Their tongues met and tangled. The taste of her damn near blew his head off. Sweet and wild...honey and wine, he thought. He could have feasted on her for hours every day and for a hundred years and he'd still be hungry.

Kris arched under his hands and hummed a little, a low, sexy sound. He traced the line of her shoulders and spine and then closed one hand over the curve of her rump. He rocked forward and shuddered as he pressed against the soft, silken skin of her belly.

SHILOH WALKER

The smooth, satiny skin cuddled against his cock. Dylan groaned raggedly and urged her down onto her back. Her breasts pressed flat against his chest, the cushion of her tummy cradled his rigid cock, and her long, sleekly muscled legs came up to wrap around his hips.

Dylan buried one hand in her hair, fisting it there and arching her head back, pressing a line of hot, stinging kisses down her neck, along the line of her collarbone, to her breasts. The flesh there was smooth, softly scented and fragile. He could see the fine network of veins under the ivory skin. Capturing one swollen nipple in his mouth, he suckled deep and hard.

Kris fisted her hands in his hair, urging him on. Dylan needed very little guidance, though. He'd been dreaming of this for far too long. Working his way down her body, he kissed the hollow of her navel as he hooked his hands in her panties and stripped them down her thighs. He tossed them aside and laid his palms flat against the outer curves of her calves. As he stroked his hands back up her silk-enclosed legs, he stared at her.

Their gazes held as he lowered his head and pressed his mouth to her cleft. Kris shuddered and screamed as he pierced her folds with his tongue. She cried out his name. Here, she tasted darker, sweeter. Sweet and hot and so damned heady—it was like tasting liquid fire. Potent and powerful.

He circled the entrance of her sex with his tongue and then pushed inside. He listened as she moaned and screamed out his name. Working two fingers into her tight sheath, Dylan started to pump them in and out of her wet cleft, rolling his eyes up and staring up the length of her body as she started to sob out his name. Her hips lifted to meet his hand and she arched, convulsing and shattering when he lifted up slightly, flicking his tongue around the hard little pearl nestled atop her slit.

116

While she was still quivering, he moved up her body, reaching over and snagging one of the condoms. He tore it open with his teeth as he wedged his hips between her thighs. Rising to his knees, he quickly rolled it on, staring down at her, hungrily, hardly able to believe he was here, with *Kris*. Covering her, he cupped her head in his hands, watching that lovely face as he probed her depths, pushing slowly inside. Her lids fluttered open and she moved her hands up his chest, sliding them behind his neck as she lifted her hips to meet his, angling them to take him deeper.

"That was...mind-blowing."

Grinning down at her, he said, "That was just the appetizer. Now we'll start with the main course." Lowering his mouth to hers, he kissed her, feasting on her mouth, shuddering with pleasure when she didn't turn away from the taste of herself that lingered on his mouth. "You taste so damn good, like sex, and sin. I want more."

Dylan pulled out and surged back inside her, angling his hips so that he rubbed over the bed of nerves buried deep inside her, rolling against her. The walls of her cleft caressed him tightly, silkily. She was so wet, so tight, perfect... "You feel so good." Surging back inside her again, Dylan gritted his teeth as climax started to rush forward already. "Damnation, I can't make this last, baby. I've wanted you for too long."

Moving higher on her body, Dylan took her mouth in a rough kiss, using his body so that he was riding against her clit as he thrust into her. He held back until she tightened around him, until he could feel the muscles in her belly spasming under his as her sheath milked his cock with her climax.

Then he started pounding into her, tearing his mouth away from hers and burying his face against her neck as she started to scream out his name as she came. He came with a ragged cry, his eyes going dark for the briefest moment before he sank down, resting his head between her breasts.

Kris was fairly certain, that if she tried, she could move her body.

But she wasn't sure if she remembered how to try.

Breathing was natural. She didn't have to think that part through. But moving her arms and legs, that was going to take some thinking. She was sure of it. As her breath shuddered in and out of her lungs, she curled her fingers into the damp, thick silk of Dylan's hair and reveled in the sheer bliss of the moment.

Seven long years, she had wanted this.

Or had it been longer?

Sometimes, she felt like she had been born wanting this man. One large, calloused palm skimmed up her side and Kris's skin quivered in reaction, her heart jumping, skipping a beat.

"You smell fantastic," he murmured softly, nuzzling the skin between her breasts, stroking his thumb across the rounded outer edge of her breast.

"Ummm," Kris murmured. Her lips curled up in a cat's smile. She couldn't help it. She felt like her belly was full of cream, and she was downright smug and pleased with herself.

"If you don't quit looking like that, I'm gonna slide back inside you and fuck you again," he rasped, moving up and licking her nipple.

Opening her eyes, she felt heat scorch her belly, shoot through her veins at the look in his eyes. His lids were low, his gaze hooded and shadowed, as he stared down at her, possessively, hungrily. Her thighs parted easily as he pushed his knee between them, watching her. He smiled at her and said, "I think I'm going to do it anyway."

Kris licked her lips and opened her mouth. It took two tries, but she finally managed to put a couple of words together. "Sounds good."

His grin was wicked and wild. His eyes, dark and intent, could see clear through your soul, Kris thought. He thrust deep, so deep, her heart echoed with it. Lifting up, she caught his face in her hands and tugged his mouth to her and kissed him hungrily as he rocked against her. He moved so hard and deep inside her, his heartbeat pounding in tandem with her own.

"I want to hear you moan my name," he muttered against her lips, pulling back a little, sliding one hand down to lift her thigh, angling it up over his hip. "I want to hear it on your lips as you come, and later, I'll make you scream it."

With a twist of his hips, he shifted his angle so that he was riding against her clit rough enough to bring shattered, broken moans to her lips with the first thrust. She was gasping out his name with the second. She saw the gleam of triumph in his eyes as he pummeled into her and she went flying off into orgasm, her eyes blind, lungs screaming for air as he crushed his mouth to hers.

CRCRCRCR

The food had to be heated up.

Of course, that was the good thing about lasagna. It reheated well. Which was why she chose that meal.

Curled against his chest, she heartily ate her own while Dylan looked on with amusement. "Hungry?"

"I worked up an appetite," she replied loftily.

His plate, half-empty, he had set aside, watching her eat with obvious amusement.

"Aren't you hungry?"

"I prefer dessert."

She shivered at his husky whisper. His hand rested high on her thigh, moving up under the edge of his shirt. A smile curled his lips as he watched her nipples stiffen and press the plain white cloth.

Dylan was every bit as sexy a lover as she had imagined. Squirming on his lap, she jabbed him with her fork and muttered, "Stop it. I want to eat. I need my energy. I'm not as physically fit as you are." She eyed the muscles that shifted and played along his arms and shoulders and licked her lips. Lust curled in her belly and she squirmed again.

She remembered the feel of his muscles, his body against her, and wanted to whimper, strip off the shirt she had swiped from his closet and demand he do it all over again.

Kris forked another bite of lasagna into her mouth and asked, "So what did you do today? Anything interesting?"

Dylan head fell back against the couch. "Yeah, scads. I finally accepted a damn job offer. Sucks, but I'm going insane right now."

"What is it? You're not going back to Somerset and working with Shawn, are you?" she asked worriedly.

"No," he said shortly, his mouth tensing. "I told him to shut the hell up about it. I don't need a fucking job out of sympathy. I could have stayed in the Army for that."

"That wasn't sympathy." Kris set her plate aside and straddled his lap, staring into his eyes as she caught his face and forced him to look at her. "I don't know much about whatever the Army offered you as a job, but I know *you*. Your

120

intensity, your drive, your soul. You don't know a damn thing about quit. Whatever they would have given you would have been because it was something they wanted and needed you to do."

His mouth quirked up. "You sound like Jerry. Sure you haven't met him?"

"I think I'd recall meeting another sexy Ranger," she purred, leaning down and sinking her teeth into his lower lip. "Now what is the job?"

"Paramedic. For now. I'm a trained medic and it's something worthwhile at least. Wade suggested it while I was there over Memorial Day. It's part-time. I'm going to take some college classes for a while and try to find something that...fits."

Smoothing her hands in soothing circles on his chest, Kris kissed him gently. "You'll find it, Dylan. You will."

Chapter Six

It found him. Six months later, as he spent the weekend back home with his family.

With his camera bag slung over his shoulder, he moved through the woods, reveling in the quiet and peace. Kris and Kacie were in St. Louis for a fantasy convention, pushing their new publishing company, but there wasn't much pushing to do, because Kris had finally broken down and asked Nikki about writing a romance, only to discover Nikki had started a romantic fantasy a year or two earlier and just never finished it.

And *viola*, Kris had it in her hot little hands. Barnes and McNeel would frown upon the sweet little tale. But Escapade Publishing loved it. Needed it. Had to have it.

So everybody was happy.

Well, Dylan wasn't particularly happy. He was working a job he didn't particularly care for, and right now, his woman was in St. Louis—but, that was life, wasn't it?

At least he could walk without limping. He could actually run a mile or so, and farther every time.

Right now, he was in the silence of the forest, walking on his own two legs, and he had a pretty peaceful day. Later on, he'd join his family for a burger before he headed back to Lexington. So what if he had a job that didn't matter that much to him? It was a job that meant something to others—that ought to be enough for now.

In a few days, he would have Kris back in his bed.

In a few more weeks...he was going to talk to her about them moving in together. Granted, they lived nearly two hours away from each other but they could figure something out.

So, things shouldn't be that bad for him.

Lifting the camera, he framed the doe that he saw ahead of him in it. He captured her in the light and shadow and grinned as he caught the perfect picture just before she scented him.

He turned to head down a different trail when something caught his attention. Something out of place. Broken branches, the trail badly disturbed, leaves and plant life off to the side badly messed up...a faint scent that didn't belong. Moving off the trail, his booted feet stepping carefully, Dylan eyed the ground. It had been disturbed, badly, and pretty recently. He sniffed and caught the odor of something foul.

Something dead.

Backtracking, he stepped back onto the trail and reached for his cell phone, calling nine-one-one. He was still standing there an hour later when the county sheriff, his eyes blank, eyed the Kline boy standing there, back in town and all grown up.

Dead animal, Dylan knew that was what he was thinking. But a dead animal didn't make a path like that through the woods.

Turning his head, he met the cool blue eyes of Sheriff Alex Denton. They nodded at each other. Dylan went back to studying the trail as he waited for the sheriff to close the distance between them.

CRCRCRCR

The body had just been deposited there sometime in the middle of the night. She'd been dead about two days and was starting to smell something awful. Dylan was waiting out of the way when Denton called for him. He walked around the trail, placing his feet on rocks and tree branches, leaving no sign of his passing, more than most of the sheriff's men could say as they had trampled in and out.

"How did you know she was here?" Denton asked, eying the man in front of him.

"I smelled her."

"You started up the hill and smelled her?" he asked, pulling out a pad, not taking notes, but doodling, as he watched the hazel-eyed, rangy man in front of him.

"No. I never left the trail. I was out taking pictures, just walking around. I saw some broken branches, and smelled something off. The wind changed, for just a second, and I caught it."

"It's still cool out. And she's not ripe enough yet. I had to be practically on top of her to smell her," Denton said, narrowing his eyes thoughtfully.

Dylan lifted one brow. "You have too much civilization bred into you still. I was a Ranger in the Army, Sheriff. Your sense of smell can be unbelievably acute, if you let it."

The sheriff's mouth firmed out. "I can't believe you smelled her body from the trail a hundred yards away."

Dylan's nostrils flared and his eyes closed briefly as he sought to block out all else. "You held somebody this morning, not long ago, who wears perfume from Victoria's Secret...*Amber Romance.* My sister loves it."

The sheriff's eyes widened. Standing five feet away, the smell of death thick in the air, the man across from him had smelled the lotion he had rubbed into Shara's body after she had climbed naked from the shower. After he had pushed her against the wall and covered her mouth, kissing her deeply and cursing the demons that wouldn't let him tell her he loved her.

"It was that body cream."

Dylan flashed a grin. "Probably why it's still so strong. That stuff is thicker, has a better kick and clings to your clothes longer, it seems. I smelled the death, saw a body trail and called nine-one-one. Then I waited right here until you showed up. I have no desire to be wandering around a crime scene, Sheriff. None at all."

"Well, that's too bad. Because you're going to. Come on."

ႸᏟᏰᏟႸᏟᏰᏟ

The woman's name was Ann Archer. She hadn't been reported missing. That in itself was odd. From the looks of her body, she had also not died pleasantly. Somebody hadn't liked her very much.

In fact, they had downright hated her.

Dylan's mouth spasmed once in sympathy as he knelt beside the body alongside the sheriff. "I'm not sure what you want me to look for, Denton. I'm not a cop, never been trained in forensics."

"You've got eyes and a nose like I've never seen," Alex said easily as the coroner's people waited to bag up the body. "I've made my take. I'd like to get an idea of yours, GI Joe."

Dylan slid the Sheriff a bland look before he studied her body. "She didn't die easy."

"Is death ever easy?"

"I'd take a quiet easy death in my sleep, or a bullet to my head over this. Hell, almost anything would be better than what she suffered. Whoever it was beat the life out of her. Slowly."

"What makes you say that?"

"Healing bruises, new bruises. Old cuts, some already almost healed over. Then brand new ones with blood still drying around them. She was tied up, several times, different ways, and I'd say with different things, rope, a chain, I think." Dylan's mouth compressed to a flat, grim line. Lowering his head,, he studied her hands. "She was put someplace dirty, tried to get out. Her nails are broken down to the quick and her nail beds are bloody and infected, filthy. She was trapped, penned up like an animal. Poor thing," he mused, shaking his head.

"Ann wasn't an easy woman to get along with, liked to run her mouth about herself, her company, everything. She'd tell you in a flat second how incredible everything about them was, and how you sucked...but then if you called her on it, she'd be telling you that wasn't what she meant. But I don't see anybody she knew professionally doing this. This was personal," Alex decided, eyeing the numerous insults to her body.

Dylan had to agree. "Very personal. Nobody deserves to die like that." He pointed to the ugly marks on her back, the long, dark contusions. "These here? I've been hit with a pipe before, that's what those look like. I imagine some of her bones have been broken." Rising, Dylan slid a hand through his hair and closed his eyes. The image of her face, turned to the side, staring into forever, would haunt him. It was one thing, dealing with terrorists, and fighting somebody you knew was an enemy, seeing death that way, seeing the death you knew they could bring.

It felt different, somehow, seeing it like this.

"I don't know why they'd dump her here. Easy to find her," Dylan mused, eyeing the hill. It was a little steep, but not much. And the trail was popular on weekends. "I smell rain on the air, but that only washes away physical evidence. It won't hide the body."

Alex glanced up at the sky. Clouds were already rolling in. "I know why. That rain is gonna be a downpour." Jutting his chin the direction of the creek, he said, "We get that downpour in a few hours as the forecast predicts, this body would have been gone come morning. Water comes through there, fills up in here, and rushes to the creek and the creeks all through here flood and rush to the river. It could have been weeks or months before body her was found."

"You think the one who did it was planning on her not being found yet? Planning on reporting her missing later?" Dylan asked.

ଓଓଓଓ

"Mom's gone to New York for a lingerie show." The sulky face and oily complexion of the teen in front of Alex had him gritting his teeth. "She made me take her to airport myself on Sunday."

"You watched her get on the plane?" Alex said. He had to ask, he knew that, but he already knew the answer. This boy had killed his mom. Alex knew it as sure as he was standing there. Another killer, trapped in the body of a child. Jeremy Archer was a bright, sharp kid who hated authority figures, hated his mother, hated just about everybody.

Not a nice kid, all in all. He'd been in trouble before. Somerset wasn't as small as it had once been, but it was still small enough. He knew many of the people that lived here, and all of the troublemakers. Jeremy was one of the worst.

"Yeah. Stupid, why in the hell I had to go and kiss her bye, I dunno," he groused, shrugging his thickly muscled shoulders. "Dumb bitch. Hate her."

Normally Alex could overlook that as regular teenaged angst. But something in this boy's speech was, well, more real genuine hatred. Lowering his brows over his eyes, he asked, "Mind if I get your mother's hotel number? I really would like to have a word with her."

"Lost it."

"Well, then, you'll just have to come with me to the station. You're only sixteen. Seventeen is the age you need to be to stay alone," Alex said easily, stepping aside and waiting for him to step out. "We'll have somebody from juvenile services stay with you until we can contact your nearest relative."

The boy sneered, and Alex could see he looked ready to bolt. Arching a brow, he laid one hand on his gun and said softly, "Think long and hard before you do that, kid. Real long and hard. I'll run ya down, kid. You'll still end up in the same place, down at the jail while we wait for your *mother* to come home. Come with me, nice like, and we can get ahold of an aunt or uncle, whoever your relatives are and you can home with them."

He saw the flicker in the boy's eyes. Knew there were all sorts of uncles and aunts around, even though the dad had hightailed it years ago. Watched as the boy made the decision not to bolt. Alex fought not to laugh. *Like taking candy from a baby.*

CRCRCRCR

Dylan eyed the boy from behind the one-way glass. Jeremy's eyes were cold, angry and merciless. He sat at the table staring up at the sheriff, looking bored. He wasn't the least bit sorry for what he had done.

In fact, as Alex laid out the pictures before him, Dylan watched a flicker light through his eyes. The flicker of pride. He wasn't upset. He wasn't horrified. He was pleased.

Oh, he hadn't been happy about being caught. It finally dawned on him that Alex wasn't taking him to juvenile services, but instead, he was taking him to the station to question him about his mother's body. He had fought bloody hell, and when the child's advocate was brought in, he'd told them to go fuck themselves.

The advocate still sat there, but he was silent, cold-faced and still. This child wasn't a child and the advocate knew it. Right now, as Jeremy studied the bloodied, battered body of his mother, he was smiling a grim, pleased smile.

Whether he admitted it or not was moot, but the boy had done it. There was no soul in those eyes. None.

"You say you saw your mother get on a plane two days ago, Jeremy. She's been dead for two and a half. Can you explain that to me?"

In a bored voice, the advocate said, "I'd advise you not to answer that."

"Go fuck yourself," Jeremy said with a sneer. Then he turned his muddy brown eyes to Alex and laughed. "She was supposed to go to New York more than a week ago. She's been in the basement, in a hole I dug for her a year ago. She screamed herself hoarse, and when I started beating her, she had hardly any voice to cry with. I wished I'd gagged her so she had been able to scream at the end."

His voice had gotten rather dreamy there at the end. Dylan's mouth twisted in a snarl. *Sick little bastard.*

The advocate closed his eyes. "Jeremy, I would advise, again, that you not speak."

"Shut up, you fucking maggot. Stupid whore, she deserved it." Jeremy's eyes gleamed manically. "Always telling me how and what not to do. When to do it. Parading around the house in that fucking lingerie she buys, like I couldn't see her. I hated it, and she always did it. Never stopped it. Chased Dad away. Always yammering about her business, the website, the store, her books. Gonna be a bestseller, and she couldn't write tripe.

"I finally shut her up," he whispered, his eyes narrowed down to slits. "Finally."

The advocate, Mike Farrell, slid his eyes over to Alex and shook his head.

Dylan saw the message in those eyes. *Crazy.* Maybe, a little. But it was just plain evil in those eyes. Too many people thought mental problems could be fixed in a few years. This boy's problems went straight through. Through and through to the core, and a few years away wasn't going to solve them. Not at all.

"Jeremy, how long have you wanted her dead?" Alex asked, leaning back in his chair.

Dylan imagined he wanted away from that evil. Dylan certainly did.

Jeremy lifted his eyes to the glass, and Dylan had the odd feeling he could see him. Moving closer, he stared at the angry boy through the glass with narrowed, disgusted eyes. *All your life, boy, haven't you?*

"All my life," Jeremy whispered as he started to rock. "All my life."

CRICBCRICB

Kris listened with horror as Dylan repeated what he could. She heard the exhaustion and the fury in his voice and she wished she could hold him. Kacie was watching her closely, and Kris folded her hand around her friend's thankfully. "Dylan, that was evil you were looking at."

"Yeah."

His voice was tight and strained. Her heart ached a little. "I wish I was there. Are you okay?"

"Hearing your voice helps," he said.

"Where is he now?"

"Isolation in the county jail. They won't put him into juvenile. This isn't a child's crime."

She heard his sigh through the phone, and there was a world of weariness in the sound. He never sounded that tired. "No. Definitely not. I knew Ann, vaguely. I've run into her before when I visited Nikki. She's asked a million times about getting her some inside help, as she called it with B&M. I told her I wasn't an employee there, and if she wanted to get pubbed there, she needed get an agent. It's awful, thinking her own son would kill her. Nobody deserves to die like that."

"Except maybe those who kill like that," Dylan said darkly.

"Not even them," Kris said softly. "Because whoever had to kill them, their madness would infect you. Don't let his madness infect you, baby, not even in thought."

Kacie said loudly, "Dunno what you are talking about, *yet*, but that is good advice, Dylan."

Dylan's laughter drifted through the phone. "Tell that weird boss of yours to hush so I can talk to my girlfriend. I was

131

planning on phone sex. How can I have phone sex with your boss in the room?"

"Oh, that is easy," Kris replied. "We can go ahead and have phone sex. I don't mind her witnessing my moans. She could probably give me some really good suggestions. You wouldn't believe what a freak Kacie is. She's a sex fiend."

Kacie giggled and Dylan said, "Oh, really... Why don't you give me some details? You're not involved in any of this fiendishness, are you? Are there pictures? Can I have copies?"

"You're just as weird as she is," Kris said, smiling as some of the tension dissolved from his voice.

"I didn't hear a no," he said. "And you haven't kicked her out. I guess you don't mind me getting started on the phone sex, mind if I go ahead and tell you how much I wish I was there with you, stripping your clothes off, kissing your pretty breasts before I go down on you? I love your taste..."

Kris's eyes fluttered closed, her breath caught in her chest, and her cheeks flushed. "Oh, man."

"Oh, please," Kacie snorted as she rose from the couch, fluttering her lashes at Kris and giggling when Kris glared at her.

Dylan laughed. "We'll wait. When I get my hands on you in a few days, I will just do it, instead of talking about it." Then his voice dropped huskily and Kris's body quivered as he whispered, "But you'll dream sweet dreams of me tonight, won't you?"

CRCBCRCB

Kris woke with a smile on her face. Dylan lifted his head and looked at her with slitted eyes and she pressed a kiss to his mouth. "Go back to sleep, hot shot," she murmured. "I can't sleep any more."

He grunted and buried his face in the pillow after passing his hand down the front of her body, setting every last nerve ending to sizzling. Her eyes widened and she was tempted to climb atop him and take him for another test drive.

But—

Kris had an antsy, nervy itch in the pit of her belly that had nothing to do with lust. So she rolled out of bed and grabbed the T-shirt he had discarded the night before and tugged it on over her head, smiling with an odd satisfaction as his scent settled around her.

Padding out of the bedroom, she slid a hand through her tangled hair.

Coffee.

She needed coffee.

Within five minutes, the smell of it was drifting through the cozy little house and she was starting to feel much more human.

But something was calling her.

It was like she had forgotten to do something.

But she hadn't yet discovered what it was she was *supposed* to be doing, so how could she have forgotten it?

Coffee in hand, she opened the door and shivered as the cold morning air struck her flesh. November in Kentucky was much better than November in New York, but damn, the wind coming off the Kentucky River was cold. She waved absently to Raintree who was already in place, drinking from a Styrofoam cup, which he tipped at her before returning to just...watching.

How long would he watch?

Dylan had said until Max was either dead or they caught him.

She knelt to pick up the paper Dylan had bribed the delivery guy into actually bringing up to the house. It cost him an extra ten bucks a month, but it saved him from having to walk or drive a half a mile to get his paper. Of course, he did that more for her on the weekends than for himself.

He'd just as soon walk or not bother reading the paper.

No sooner had she touched the paper than it happened—a child, shaking in the cold, flashed before her eyes.

Kris froze. Her lashes lowered and she whispered, "Not again."

She didn't want to be haunted by faces of a child she couldn't help.

But this one was familiar.

She had seen her before. Months ago. The dreams. A tiny little girl with wispy blonde hair and big, frightened eyes. With a scowl, she grabbed the paper and stood up, closing the door. Leaning back against it, she mumbled, "I'm losing my mind. Drugs. Lots of drugs and a trip to a shrink will help this problem."

But ten minutes later, she stared at the paper spread out before her and it was only worse. Because there, on the front page of the small hometown paper, was a wide-eyed, grinning child, blonde, young and innocent. She smiled up at Kris from the grainy paper, her expression as carefree and loving as could be. She was angelic-looking and lovable, and her face made Kris's heart stop.

She was also missing.

Dylan lifted his head groggily.

Kris stood beside his bed, her eyes wide, the pupils so dilated, just a thin rim of green showed around them. In her hand she held the morning paper, and her entire body was trembling.

Slowly, he sat up, his voice gentle and soothing. "What's wrong, rich girl?" He reached out and caught her other hand, bringing her into his lap. "What's got you so spooked?"

She licked her lips. "It's happening again," she whispered, her voice fragile.

Dylan frowned. Reaching over, he took the paper from her, lifting it so he could see the picture. A pretty little faerie of a child stared out at him. Another kidnapped kid, he thought, sighing. He could see why it bothered her so badly, after what happened to her. He didn't exactly know how to approach it, because he'd never told her that Nikki had told him about it.

But she couldn't take every missing child like this. It would tear her apart. "Kris, sweet, you can't—"

He heard her swallow, felt the shudders wracking her body. "I dreamed about her. Months ago. For weeks. And I searched the web, every day, and never saw her. Until now. She was kidnapped two days ago," Kris said, her voice breaking.

Dylan felt his blood run cold as he studied her face. "Are you sure about that?"

Tears streamed down her face as she said, "I've never been so sure about anything in my life. And I hate it."

Dylan blew out a rough breath. "Okay. Okay. Just give me a minute." He eased her off his lap and grabbed a blanket. He tucked it around her and then stood. He snagged his discarded jeans from the night before and pulled them up over his hips. Knotted muscles in his back protested but Dylan ignored the discomfort while he zipped his jeans.

Facing Kris naked wasn't a good idea, especially not when she was upset. "You okay?" he asked gently.

She just looked at him with miserable eyes. Dylan rubbed a hand over his neck and then took the paper from Kris's hands. He noticed they were shaking and a fist closed around his heart. By the time he'd finished reading the article, that fist had closed so damn tight, it felt like it was choking him.

No wonder she was so damned upset, he thought as he turned to look at her.

Shit.

This was a little more than he was used to handling. Dally had been prone to odd little feelings, like when an op was going to go badly or if they should pull out. Sometimes a contact they had trusted for ages had suddenly just changed, and Dally was the only way they had known that.

But this...this was a hell of lot more than that.

This had crossed the realm of unusual and gone straight into the extraordinary. *If* it was for real.

"Tell me about the dream, Kris," Dylan said quietly, rubbing the back of his neck, watching her as she rocked back and forth on the bed.

She lifted her eyes to his and blinked, just staring at him. He swore as a fine shudder started to wrack her body. Her eyes were glassy and wide and when he moved over to the bed, lifted her on his lap, her skin was cold. "Damn it," he muttered, holding her up against him. "Kris, are you okay?" he asked gruffly, rubbing his cheek back and forth against hers.

"She's four, and blonde...and there's a scar on her back from when she fell while visiting her dad's. He was an alcoholic, and had been drinking. Went to take a nap, and left the back door open. She fell down the steps, a nail gouged her back," Kris murmured.

136

Dylan frowned. That wasn't in the paper. "How do you know that?" he asked.

"She remembers," Kris said. She whimpered, pressing her face against her knee. "It just happened last year. She remembers the smell of his breath when he came running outside when she screamed, and how he yelled at her. She hasn't seen him since then."

Dylan felt his skin crawl. This was just a little too eerie. "Can you tell me anything else about the girl? Who she is?"

"Her name is Codi Marie," Kris said.

"I read that in the paper," Dylan said gently. "But something more. Why are you having dreams about her?"

Kris licked her lips. Softly, she said, "I...I uh, I think I'm supposed to make you find her."

ॐॐॐ

Dylan repeated the story in a low voice to Ethan Raintree before he brought the ex-Ranger inside. The Native American studied Kris through the window and shook his head. "Well, it would explain how in the hell she saved your sorry ass," Raintree decided. "What you are going to do about it?"

Dylan blew out a pent up breath of air and admitted, "I'm going out to talk to the kid's mom. I don't see what choice I have."

Ethan closed his eyes.

"You realize they may think you did it."

"Yes. I thought of that," Dylan said, shaking his head. "What kind of dumb ass do you think I am? But what choice have I got? She's just a kid."

Ethan pinched the bridge of his nose between his fingers as he followed Dylan inside the house. Kids were also a weak spot, for almost anybody. Somebody who couldn't be bothered to help a child just wasn't worth bothering with, he reckoned. "Just be careful how you walk, buddy, okay?"

Kris caught sight of Raintree over Dylan's shoulder and she scowled. "What in the hell is he doing in here?" she asked, lifting her eyes skyward.

"He's here because I'd rather you not be alone when you look so spooked," Dylan said. "He's harmless."

Ethan stood there, trying to look harmless. Kris's laugh was weak, but at least it was better than that pale, shocky emptiness. He was about as successful at looking harmless as Kris was at looking plain, Dylan decided. But at least Ethan wasn't as imposing as Luciano was.

Dylan leaned down over her, nuzzling the soft skin behind her ear and whispering, "Get some more sleep. I'll be back when I can."

ᘓᘔᘓᘔ

When Dylan knocked on the door, he was surprised when a cop didn't answer. Cautiously, he said, "I may know something about your daughter. But I'm not exactly sure yet. Can I talk to you for a few minutes?"

The mom's face was lined, worried and pale from exhaustion. Her voice was hoarse, from crying, most likely. "We already know who has her. We just need to know where they are. But you can come in."

Her mom's name was Alyssa Morgan. She was a young state trooper, divorced for a little over two years, and the child's dad had relinquished custody of Codi after the little girl had gotten hurt at his house one day last year.

"Her name is Codi. Codi Marie. She's four. She was best friends with our next-door neighbor's daughters, Bethany Hart. I didn't care for the parents much, they were too...intense. Focused too much on being *the* perfect family. Never let the poor kid have so much as a candy bar, wouldn't let her watch cartoons, she was always dressed so damn perfectly..." Alyssa Martin's eyes filled with tears as she spoke, though her voice never wavered.

"Our daughters looked amazingly alike. We even had pictures of them in similar outfits, her idea, not mine, though they looked so sweet. People even asked from time to time if they were twins."

Taking a deep breath, Alyssa said, "About four months ago, Bethany took sick. Very suddenly. Fever, sore throat, coughing. She caught pneumonia and the doctors treated her with antibiotics but it didn't help. She took nearly a month to start feeling better.

"About a month after that it started all over again and her fever skyrocketed. She started having seizures and they had to hospitalize her. They couldn't break the fever and they couldn't stop the seizures. Nearly a week of them, and then they just stopped, like it had never happened. Bethany was smiling and acting like she had never been sick. The doctor wanted to keep her a few more days to monitor her, but her parents insisted on taking her home and took her out against doctor's orders.

"They found her the next morning, dead. She died in her sleep the day they took her home," Alyssa said, staring off into the distance.

"Codi was heartbroken. She'd go play there and act as though Bethany was still there... I didn't say anything at first.

The doctor said she had to grieve in her own way. But then, Vanda starting calling Codi Bethany, and dressing her in her daughter's clothes.

"I had to tell Codi she couldn't go over there anymore, and watch her start to cry. Codi didn't like wearing Bethany's clothes, but she knew wearing them made Vanda stop crying for just a while. Codi's just got such a soft heart." Her voice fell into a monotone and Dylan suspected she wasn't really seeing him right then. She started to rock back and forth, staring at a picture of her daughter that she held in her hands.

"Vanda was furious. Started saying things like I had stolen her daughter away. Her husband took her into the house, but you could see an almost desperate look in his eyes as he looked at Codi."

Lifting her eyes, she stared at Dylan, and he felt the punch of that look in his gut. "They took my baby. My heart is broken that they lost their daughter, but they *stole* mine."

"You think they have her," Dylan said quietly.

"We know she does," Alyssa said softly, her pretty blue eyes confident. "She was in her room, napping. Vanda came by, and I let her in. We were in the kitchen, talking. I thought it was a little weird, at the time, but...Bethany had died and I felt so bad for her, so sorry. We were in the kitchen. I thought I heard the door open, but then Vanda spilled her drink and while I was cleaning it up—"

Dylan felt his heart squeeze in his chest as tears filled her eyes.

"We think her husband just walked in and took her," Alyssa whispered brokenly. "He just *took* my baby. Vanda left a few minutes later and I heard their car drive off. I went to check on Codi about ten minutes later but they were gone."

"You called the cops right away?" Dylan asked.

Alyssa gave him a dirty look. "No. I sat and twiddled my thumbs and moaned and screamed for an hour. Yes, I called it in right away. But either Morris knows too much from watching TV or from living next to me. He had changed the license plate on his car. *With mine.*"

She started to reach into her pocket and then she stopped, a half a grin forming at her mouth. "I stopped smoking when I first got pregnant, but sometimes I still forget," she said.

Dylan smiled back. "I stopped when I joined the Army, otherwise I'd offer you one," he said, shrugging. "Have your contacts in the field found anything?"

Leaning forward, Alyssa said quietly, "No. They've disappeared into the wind. But now I want to know what you are doing here."

Dylan was now wishing he had a cigarette tucked away somewhere. He had the choice here—he had enough information, he could make up some bullshit story that would lead her nowhere. Or he could tell her what Kris knew.

Hell, he already knew what his choice was going to be.

Had there ever really been any doubt?

"I'm retired Army, you know that?' Dylan said conversationally. "Little over a year ago, I got a call from a friend of my sister's. She had this dream..."

It took nearly an hour to explain it all, and when he was done, Alyssa hadn't done much more than nod and stare at him.

"You realize that sounds absolutely crazy," she said softly.

Rising, she walked out of the room.

He listened, ears pricked, as she opened the refrigerator, and was still waiting patiently when she returned, a beer in hand. Popping the top, she drained half the can and continued to study him.

"I don't drink much. After my ex-husband, I sort of lost my taste for it," she said, licking her upper lip. "You know, about four people know how my daughter got the ugly little scar on her back. He knows, my lawyer knows. His lawyer, the pediatrician. That's about it. Both my parents and his parents are dead. We mentioned a birthmark in the paper. Not that scar."

She settled back on the chair and stared at him with unsettling eyes. "Okay, so...can you find my daughter?" she asked.

Can you find my daughter?

രുരുരുരു

He pushed his palm against his forehead, trying to silence the voice in his head. Ever since Kris had wakened him, shoving that paper into his hand, he had known it would come to this.

Did I ever really have much choice?

No, not really, Dylan thought as he studied the water line. He bypassed the rickety old dock and headed for the shore of the hidden cove. The moment he had seen that picture, he had been lost. Those innocent blue eyes, that sweet smile. *Bring me home...* He had felt those words being whispered, deep in his gut. *Bring me home...*

Once he had the light little craft on shallow ground, he leaped nimbly onto the dock, holding the rope loosely. Glancing over his shoulder, he checked the lake, made sure nobody had seen him. None of the early morning fishermen came in this area and hunting was off limits in this heavily wooded part of Rough River.

He had the boat shored and ready for his return, tied in a complicated knot nobody but him could hope to undo. Tossing a light pack over his back, he drew one last item from the boat. Hoping like hell he didn't need it, he holstered the sleek semi automatic easily. In his boot, he had a knife sheathed, as well as another one at his hip. There were a pair of handcuffs he'd borrowed from Raintree, rope and a first aid kit in the pack. Hopefully, he wouldn't need anything else.

Bring me home...

If worse came to worst, and that little girl was being held there, he could always take up a position in a tree and radio his position to the police. But if she was being hurt, or if they were getting ready to bolt, he couldn't take that chance. So Dylan was prepared to do what he had to do to get that little girl home.

Bring me home...

"Hell, she probably isn't anywhere around here," he muttered to himself as he started moving on silent feet through the dense undergrowth.

But his gut told him otherwise. Kris had told him about her dreams, and in most of them, there was a cabin, near the river. Place like this had plenty of cabins. But all the other little details led him to believe it was in this area. The gas station she described. A certain landmark. Yeah, she was here all right.

Somewhere.

He walked for hours, slowly, checking for any sign of somebody other than fishermen. Several cabins were scattered all throughout here but none revealed anything more than fishermen, the occasional odd poacher or honeymooners.

Dylan crossed the gravel road nearly five hours after he had sped across the lake in his small craft, tired, hungry, frustrated. His back hurt like hell and his head wasn't much better. Worry had burned a hole in his gut and he was about ready to give up.

Then an image of Codi's little face flashed through his mind and he muttered, "Little while longer." He moved off the road and took a path directly into the woods this time, instead of the marked path. He moved soundlessly, his booted feet moving from rock to leaves to ground without disturbing anything.

.He walked and walked. He wondered what in the hell he was doing here and he cursed the bum back that kept him from moving the way he wanted. Just when he knew it was time to call it quits, he caught sight of something.

Bring me home...

Kneeling down, he eyed the small, torn scrap of silky pink. Grim, he looked all around, searching the ground until he found what he was looking for. The broken trail of people moving through the woods, people who didn't know how to do it.

Finally, something to track. Something to follow. Taking the tiny bit of pink, he rubbed between finger and thumb before pushing it into his pocket. He focused his eyes on the trail. They'd been moving in from the reservoir, the way he had come, heading west.

Hunger, pain and frustration forgotten, he continued to move, now following the broken trail.

It took him roughly an hour.

At some point they stopped letting her walk. He could see her footsteps from time to time, over the rocks, muddied little impressions from her sneakers. But she had tripped, and then the woman had knelt down in the leaves and picked her up, probably held her and loved on her, convinced herself it was her child.

"Some people are going to feel sorry for them," he muttered to himself, shaking his head. They would see a grieving woman who had lost a baby and latched onto something to comfort herself.

But he was having a hard time doing it. Nik had lost a child herself, to a terrible tragedy, after living through a life of them. Had it driven her to steal another person's baby? No. Moving on, he knew he was getting closer. The smell of smoke was getting thicker in the air. And food, then finally, voices. Raised ones.

"We can't stay here! Her face is all over the news!" Morris yelled.

Sliding behind a tree, watching in shadow, Dylan eyed the cabin, looking for the best way to get closer. A red Blazer was now parked in front of it. Dylan checked the license plate and shook his head. The guy was smart. He had changed the plates, again. But the red Blazer was way too noticeable.

"Not her face...Codi's face. Poor Codi died, and they are convinced it was my Bethany. I won't let them take her away again," a woman hissed.

The voice was full of passionate fury that made Dylan re-evaluate all he had ever known about sanity. That woman, without even looking at her, Dylan knew she was crazy.

"I know, I know," Morris crooned. "But, baby, if we stay here, they will take her. Her mother is a cop. They'll believe her before they believe us. Damn cops, always so fucking crooked."

Dylan edged around the tree, dropping to the ground and creeping along it as he moved closer. He had to see Codi, see if she was awake, able to move, able to scream.

Their voices carried on over his head and Dylan had to focus on them as well as being quiet. *Shoulda brought a recorder. I'll do that next time...*

Next time?

"What about going to Arizona?" Morris asked. "We can cut her hair, dye it red. That will change how she looks..."

"But I love her hair," Vanda sobbed.

"Honey, if they see her—"

A soft, tired voice broke into their conversation. "When is my mama coming to get me?"

Vanda started to sob. "Why doesn't she remember me? Damn it, you ungrateful brat, I *am* your mother! You call me Mommy! Now! Do it! Do it!"

Dylan's lips peeled back from his teeth and he started to rise from the ground into a crouch, but Morris said, "Vanda, that's enough. She's been sleeping. Had a nightmare, that's all. We'll give her some of the nice medicine and..."

Dylan reached the window and rose, watching from the side. Drugging her. He watched Morris feed a spoonful of clear liquid to the child and within minutes, her lashes were fluttering, and her eyes, already cloudy, went glassy and opaque.

"Vanda, you can't yell at her like that. She doesn't remember yet. But once we get her safe, we'll take her to a special doctor, like the one who gave me the medicine and he'll make her remember what we want her to remember," Morris said, turning and focusing grim eyes on his wife. "But no more yelling at her. It's cruel."

"And her not calling me mama, or not remembering who I am isn't cruel?" Vanda shouted, throwing a glass against the wall, her long red hair flying around her shoulders.

Dylan saw the knowledge there, the refusal to accept. Oh, she knew she was wrong. She was deluding herself and she knew it. Crazy or not, part of her knew that wasn't her child.

"She lost her best friend. Give her time."

"That boring, plain little Codi. Little brat," Vanda muttered as she started to pace back and forth, her legs scissoring angrily as she stared feverishly into nothing. "We're better off away from them, from them both."

'Honey, I need to go out, get supplies for the trip. While she's sleeping, I want you to cut her hair, get it dyed. The color kit is in the bathroom. We bought it so we'd be prepared. Color and cut yours as well. We need to look as different as we can, so if we're stopped we look nothing like who we are," Morris murmured, catching his wife around the waist and stroking her back.

"Yes, baby. I know. I understand that, I'm just so upset with Bethany right now. She should be coming out of this... It's those drugs we have to keep giving her," Vanda said, her face folding into a perfect little pout.

Melting back into the forest, Dylan hid away from sight and waited for Morris to leave. He'd wait until the man was gone.

Then he'd take care of the woman and get the child back to her mama.

QRCBQRCB

"Women are the damnedest creatures," Dylan swore under his breath.

She ended up bolting out of the house, with the kid, although how she'd figured out he was there, Dylan didn't know.

He knew he hadn't made noise when he hauled himself into a tree to watch and wait. He'd hidden there and watched as Morris came out and climbed into the red Blazer. The guy's face was pale and nervous, his eyes darting all around. His hair stuck up like he'd run his hands through it, repeatedly.

Settled there in the tree, Dylan had waited until the truck was gone, eyeing it until no sign of red was filtering through the trees, until the faintest sounds of motor had died away. When he had slithered down from his post, he'd made a few soft sounds that could have betrayed his position, although he seriously doubted Vanda had heard those slight noises. Still, he didn't like it—just a year or so out, and look...

Of course, the stiffness of his back could account for it. He no longer trained for field operations.

All had been well and good as he'd moved toward the house, keeping out of the line of sight. Listening, just listening. He hadn't wanted to do anything until he could decide if the woman would hurt the little girl. She'd been crying again, in soft, broken little sobs as she slept. The pitiful, heartbreaking mewls tore at Dylan's heart like daggers.

Vanda had been pacing the room, swearing under her breath. "When, damn it? When is she going to remember?"

A woman's instinct would undo a man's most careful plan. Every damn time. Dylan had made the fatal error of backing away for a few minutes, not trusting her erratic mood. But something—not a sound, not a sight of him—but something alerted her to him.

As he stood in the woods, wishing for the cigarettes he had stopped smoking years before, she bolted, seizing the girl and running out the back door. Dylan heard the door slamming and his head whipped around with a snarl on his lips. He took off after her, running lightly through the undergrowth.

The poor baby was crying loudly now, screaming, "I wanna go home! I want my mommy!"

"Shut up! I am your mommy!" the woman shrieked.

The strained, harsh sounds of her voice, followed by a wail from the little girl, brought every instinctive urge Dylan had to the surface and he sped up. He hurtled through the woods after them, running all out, his eyes locked on the red of her sweater, his nostrils flaring as he scented her perfume, her fear. And the poor baby...

Codi bucked and threw herself out of the woman's arms suddenly and took off running away. She ran down the path, away from Vanda, at a ninety degree angle, up the hill, and away from the lake.

Thank You, God, Dylan thought as he lunged for Vanda and took her down before she could leap after the tiny little faerie in her little blanket pajamas.

Vanda swung out, trying to scratch his eyes out. Dylan grabbed her hands and pinned them down.

"Mrs. Hart, I presume?" he mocked lightly. Then he forced himself to straighten and wipe the cruelty from his face. She had, regardless of her crimes, lost a child. Bitch, she was, she had lost a baby. Maybe it had driven her a little crazy.

She had known what she was doing, though. He could see it in her eyes.

"Get the hell off of me. Who do you think you are?" she hissed. "Get the hell off of me."

"Can't," Dylan said easily. She struggled again and he grunted as she tried to ram him in the balls.

"Who in the hell are you?" she demanded again. She bucked and struggled and finally, Dylan flipped her over and pinned her wrists at the small of her back. Onehanded, he dug

149

through his pack and found the handcuffs. She started to screech.

"Listen, I'm a friend of the little girl's mama. I'm going to call the police and I'll take those cuffs off once they get here. I'm not going to keep dodging those nails of yours."

"You can't just—you aren't a cop?" she stuttered.

"Nope," Dylan said as he rose, scanning the hill. Cocking his head, he studied the tiny little bit of gold crouching at the top. Kids were such amazing things. He had heard her stop running, almost as soon as Vanda's pursuit had stopped. And now, like a little kitten, she was watching the show. "Miss Codi? Your mama sent me to bring you back to her."

"Go away." The little girl's voice floated down to him like a faerie's whisper. "You're a stranger and I don't talk to strangers."

"Well, hell." The kid sounded just like Mandy.

Sliding the woman at his feet a look, he said, "This is a bitch. I don't want to let you out of my sight, but it's too damned cold to leave her up there. I'm taking her to her mother."

"*I'm* her mother," Vanda snarled, kicking at him.

"No, you're not," Dylan said firmly as he shrugged out of his backpack, reaching for the slim, strong rope he had brought with him. With an arched brow, he said, "Move over to the tree."

She didn't.

Kicking and screaming, she fought him the entire time until Dylan jerked her upright and said coldly, "I can knock you unconscious and tie you that way. Or you can sit nice like while I bring that pretty little girl down here so she doesn't catch cold before her mama can get here. Your choice."

The sullen silence that ensued had him smirking inside. Stupid bitch. While the knocked unconscious held its appeal, he couldn't really say it was very likely to happen. As pissed off as he was, he was glad she shut up and settled down. He hated to hit a woman, but he'd do it if he had to. It had happened before when he was still in the Army. The world was changing and he didn't always fight up against just men anymore.

He was pretty sure hitting Nikki when he was a kid didn't count. At least he hoped not.

Stepping over her legs, he glanced down at her. "If you're good, I might untie you and take you to the house before I take her home. Otherwise you can freeze your ass off while you wait for the cops."

"You're going to get your ass thrown in jail, treating me like this," she hissed.

Quirking an eyebrow at her, he asked, "Why? For getting a little girl home where she belongs?"

Then he headed up the hill to play tag with a cute little blonde as he reached for his cell phone.

Chapter Seven

Six Months Later

"Hell, Kris. I don't know about this." Dylan studied the website with a scowl on his face. Then he looked around the office and shook his head. "I really don't know if this is a good idea." With his hands jammed in his back pockets, he walked around the office.

He looked like he was still trying to figure out what he was doing there. It had taken Kris six months to convince him to give this a shot. He wasn't going to back out now. Kris wasn't going to let him. She knew he was still rather reluctant. Kris eyed him and wished that he could see himself the way others saw him, the way she was seeing him now.

Well, besides unbelievably sexy that is.

There had been a look in his eyes, a glow of satisfaction, as he turned that little girl safely over to her tearful mama that Kris would never forget. Since that misty, late evening, she had been thinking about this.

Alyssa Morgan had apparently been thinking something similar, planting little seeds along the way. She had made the three-hour drive from Somerset to Wagner a few weeks after he'd returned Codi to her mother. On her face had been a casual, easy smile and in her hands she'd held a stack of papers and a picture.

A cute, towheaded boy with sparkling green eyes that made Dylan's mouth tighten and his eyes darken.

Kris had thought she would have to talk him into that one—looking at that little boy hurt him. The little guy reminded him of somebody, she suspected. She could feel that in her gut. But Dylan had taken the papers and politely asked about Codi. Then he rudely slammed the door in the state trooper's face.

Beacon Investigations had been born as an online site four months ago, and since then, Dylan had returned two Kentucky children to their parents, one from Tennessee, and had helped a federal marshal break up a drug ring. The federal marshal had come to him via the sheriff, Alex Denton. He had turned down far more jobs than he had accepted and was working a half dozen right now.

Four kids returned home, a drug ring broken, and he still didn't know if it was the right thing. Kris had come to the conclusion he wouldn't know the right thing if it bit him on the ass.

"Dylan, you were born to do something like this." Kris moved to stand in front of him and caught his face in her hands. She stared into his eyes as she pressed her lips to his mouth.

Deepening the kiss, Dylan searched out her tongue. Warm, strong arms wrapped around her waist as he backed her up against the desk. He rocked forward and Kris whimpered a little at the feel of his thick, hot sex cuddled against her belly. His scent, strong, clean, male, flooded her senses, overpowering the smell of pine cleaner and new paint. He stroked one hand down to palm her ass, gripping her firmly, steadily as he slowly withdrew, kissing his way along her jawline to her neck, scraping the pulse there with his teeth before nudging her shirt out of the way with his chin.

"Now this," he purred roughly. "This is right."

"This...doesn't keep you occupied twenty-four seven."

"It could," he responded with a wicked grin. He stared at her from under a thick fringe of lashes. "You've never let me try." He rocked against her as he spoke and Kris gasped as a hot wave of need flooded her belly. Her nipples tightened and her blood sang.

"This doesn't pay you, boy. Although, damn, it could..." Kris groaned as he slid his hands up her thighs, pushing her skirt up. "You're distracting me."

"Damn straight."

The telephone rang and Dylan sighed, letting her skirt fall as he rested his forehead against hers. "I love you," he murmured softly. "I don't think I've told you that before."

Her eyes flooded with tears. "Umm. No. No, you haven't." When he started to turn away to reach for the phone, she threw herself at him and wrapped her arms around his neck. "Not so fast, hot shot. I love you, too."

The answering machine came on and Dylan's slow, confident easy voice rolled out, "You've reached Beacon Investigations. Leave your name and a number."

Nikki's voice, light and easy, filled the room, "Hey, guys, just wondering how you were settling in. Just wondering how tricks are going in Lexington. Hope the new office is as good as you two were planning. Gimme a call."

Kris tuned her out. "That's how I know this is right, Dylan. I saw it in your eyes, each time you closed a case, each time you took a child home. When you helped that federal marshal break the drug ring and close his case. I saw the satisfaction in your eyes. You haven't been that pleased with yourself since you left the Rangers. I know it."

Catching his face in her hands, Kris rested her brow against his and whispered, "This is right, Dylan. It's right."

"Not just me, though, is it?" he said quietly, stroking his fingers through her hair. "You do know you're an editor, right? You aren't supposed to be trailing any of my people, asking questions, nosing around...or acting as a tag. Although I do have to admit, you've gotten pretty good at it."

She fluttered her lashes at him. "It must be my very own tag," she said. "Speaking of which, do I ever get to lose mine?"

Dylan grinned. "Sure. When we find Blessett," he said, slapping her butt lightly. "And I'll be sure to let Luciano and Ethan know how much they *shouldn't* have been teaching you. But this means a lot to you. I know that. That last kid, she threw herself at you and I didn't think you'd ever be able to let her go. Although I could have paddled your ass for sneaking along. You are not supposed to *tag...*"

Shrugging, she fought the blush that crept up her neck. "Well, hey...grooming the next Stephen King has merits, but every now and then you have to take a break and do something different, you know?"

"Hmmm, something different."

Kris shuddered as he knelt in front of her, pushing her skirt up, pressing his mouth against her through the fragile lace of her panties. "Let's see what all we haven't tried," he whispered gruffly.

"Is there something we haven't tried?" she teased. Then her lids fluttered and closed as he licked her through the lace.

"We'll just have to see." He slid his hands under the lace and stripped her panties down her thighs. His palms were hot and rough as he boosted her up onto the edge of the desk. He pushed her thighs apart. Automatically, Kris leaned back against the desk's surface and used her hands for balance. The

155

strength drained out of her body as he pushed his tongue inside, caressing her with slow and devastating thoroughness.

"I love your taste," he muttered. His voice vibrated against her, echoed inside her and turned her to mush. In, out, slow and steady, until she was rocking against him and pleading with him. She squirmed and tightened her knees, trying to hold him closer. He shifted away and Kris cried out, but he didn't leave her. Instead, he pushed two fingers into her and rotated his thumb around her clit.

She climaxed with a wail.

The world spun. She felt him pull her off the desk. Then she was facing it. Cool air caressed her bare flesh as he bent her over the desk and pushed her skirt to her waist. "I won't ever be able to sit at this desk without thinking about this." Dylan lowered his head and kissed her neck, biting down lightly. He wedged a knee between her thighs and pushed them apart. "Open for me," he muttered.

Mindless, Kris spread her legs wider. Her palms pressed flat against the desk and then tightened into fists as he pushed inside her. Her breath hissed out of her lungs and her heart slammed against her ribcage in a fast, furious rhythm. He pulled out and then pushed back in. He slid a hand around her hip, his fingers seeking out the hard bud of her clit.

His other hand held her hip, holding her steady as he shafted. Long, deep strokes, slow and thorough. Kris's world dwindled down to just that, his thick cock moving inside her, his fingers caressing her, his lips at her ear, muttering her name, telling her he loved her. Heat, hunger, need, love, they tangled inside her, pulsated through her, wrapped around her heart and tightened, tighter and tighter until she exploded with it.

As she screamed out his name, he stiffened behind her. A guttural moan left his lips and she felt him climax inside her. Kris was still gasping his name sometime later but whether or not they had discovered anything new, she wasn't sure. Her mind had long since stopped functioning.

ᘯᘓᘯᘓ

Dylan held her against him on the couch, resting his chin on her hair, breathing in the scent of her body, the smell of her lotion, her perfume, the scent of his sweat mingling with hers. Damn it, he still couldn't believe he was with her—Kirsten Everett.

She pushed him.

If she hadn't told him to do this—yeah, outright *told* him— he wouldn't have done it. Oh, Nikki might have nagged him into it sooner or later. It wasn't that Dylan hadn't considered it. But he more than likely would have gone and hired on with somebody else. Taking on shit cases, skip tracing, divorce cases, spying on people cheating on each other, instead of what he really *needed* to be doing.

Kris pushed him into this place, the place he really wanted to be, making the choices he wanted to make, but usually would have put off.

She didn't understand the fear of failure. Kris didn't understand how to not succeed. Hell, she had never done anything outside the world of editing, but that hadn't stopped her from going out and asking a million questions with this last case. Or the one before that, the one about a little boy kidnapped by a friend of the mother's.

He suspected eventually she was going to nose her way in further and further.

157

She was getting good at it, too. She nosed around. She asked the questions. She'd looked, she'd listened to those gut feelings and she'd figured it out. One of the neighbor's other neighbor, an old woman, one everybody thought was senile, had taken Kris inside, talking slow and loud, and *forever*... Kris had sat there for two hours. Listening. Actually, she had been having fun—the little old lady reminded her of her grandmother. Then she mentioned the other neighbor, the one who had moved about three weeks before the boy had disappeared. The lady had returned the day before the boy had been kidnapped while walking home from school, just visiting with the old lady, or so she claimed.

The police had questioned the lady but she'd had an alibi and they didn't pursue it. Kris did.

Kris had strolled into the small, cramped office that Dylan had set up with a cat's smile and an address three states away, dropped it on his desk and walked away, tossing him a smile as she said, "You might want to check that out."

Brat. Nikki was rubbing off on her.

"You're thinking so loud, you woke me up," she muttered.

Dylan laughed softly, glancing down at her. "Mind reading now?"

"No. You just aren't sleeping," she mumbled, cuddling against him. "If you aren't gonna sleep, I can't."

"Why did you talk to the old woman so long?" he asked out of the blue. "You homed in on her like a pigeon. And stayed for too long."

"She's a sweet old lady," Kris said, rolling her eyes.

"And you don't even need to ask which lady," he murmured, frowning. "What about the dad? Hannah's dad? How did you know he didn't take her? How did you know it was his ex-girlfriend?"

158

"Lucky guess," Kris said, arching a brow.

"Ahhh." Dylan closed his eyes. Thinking of a blue chemise she had worn last night, he asked, "What color am I thinking of?"

Kris snorted. "Are we playing twenty questions?" she asked before yawning into her hand.

"Humor me."

She snickered. "Royal blue."

Dylan opened his eyes. "What color would a woman call that thing you had on last night?" he asked casually.

"Royal...blue," Kris replied, her eyes meeting his. "What are you getting at, Dylan?"

"I'm curious how a woman who has never had any kind of security training *at all* knows what questions to ask...and what people to talk to. All the time." Threading his fingers through her hair, he shifted her until her weight was on top of him and he met her gaze. "I think a part of you just automatically knows. But I think there's a little more than that. Dallas Conroy, one of my friends from the unit, he...he didn't want to go on that last assignment. Told Jerry something wasn't right. Said something was just plain *wrong* with the whole damn thing."

"And the entire time, I remember he was staring at Max. Part of Dally knew. If he had pulled out, he'd be alive now. You've got something inside of you that knows things. Just like Dally had a part that knew things."

Kris started to snicker, but Dylan laid a finger across her lips. "Don't laugh. It's a part you oughta listen to. If we had listened to Dally... Well, we should have listened."

"Like I'm wondering now why I didn't listen to you when you told me to take the back door in when I went to get that little girl the last time," he drawled. "You remember. The time you tagged along. In a separate car. Twenty minutes later. When you know damned good and well you aren't supposed to. If you hadn't, the little girl would have died. But the back door was a security risk... Of course, we weren't expecting the guy to lose his marbles..."

"I...I've kinda blocked that out, babe," Kris said, a bright false smile on her face. "Something about seeing a gun swinging in my direction makes me queasy."

"How did you know, Kris?"

Dylan watched as her pretty green eyes darkened to near black in the dim room, as she swallowed, ran her tongue over dry lips. "I don't know. I just did."

CROSCROS

The ad in the phone book read:

Beacon Investigations

Missing Persons, Specialty Cases.

No Divorces Handled.

Jackie had called the number, even started to leave a message, but she was afraid when she told him that she didn't have any money he'd laugh and hang up on her.

But something about that simple ad... *Beacon Investigations.* Well, it had been a beacon out of all of the others in the phone book. Tearing it out, she had slipped out of her parents' house, against her dad's express orders.

He didn't care that Melissa hadn't been seen in months. Didn't care that she was missing. "Came to a bad end, I told her she would. Not listening to her father, not following the Good

Lord's word," he had ranted, pacing up and down the aisle at church.

The Good Lord wanted Melissa home and safe. Jackie knew that much. She closed her hand around the cross her mother had given her. It was the last thing Mom had ever given her. She'd died a few weeks later.

It usually comforted her. Today? Not so much. Still nervous and scared, she studied the wooden door and took a deep breath. Slowly, she reached for the doorknob.

Dylan sat in his chair, eyeing the girl through the security camera link on his computer. She had been pacing in the lot for about twenty minutes, slowly circling closer, slowly, slowly, until she was finally at the door. Grinning, he shook his head as her hand slowly lifted for the third time before falling away. But before it reached her side, she gritted her teeth and reached up and closed it around the handle and turned the doorknob.

Dylan blanked his face so that when she got past his newly hired secretary, he'd be able to listen to what she had to say with a straight face. He had to wonder what on earth the kid wanted with a private investigator.

What was she? All of fourteen? Hell, she maybe thought her boyfriend was cheating on her.

Then again. Maybe not. The look on Pat Halie's face was rather grim when she led the girl into his office. Her normally laughing brown eyes were not laughing at all. As she escorted the kid into the office, she had an odd look on her face and Dylan grimaced.

Hell.

He wasn't going to be sending this kid home, was he?

At least not right away.

Shiloh Walker

"The young lady has a problem, Mr. Kline. One her father has not reported to the police. Miss Duncan did, but they have not done much to pursue it," Miss Halie said quietly as she led the kid to a seat. As quiet as her voice was, it didn't hide the underlying fury there.

"My sister is missing," the girl said, her voice shy and hesitant. Her eyes moved all over the room, cataloguing everything, filing it away.

There was a sharp mind behind those eyes, one that didn't miss a damn thing, Dylan mused.

"She...she ran kinda wild this past year. Our mom died a few years ago. We both miss her but Melissa... I don't know. It messed her up a lot. She was settling down some, though. Met a new guy, was going to school, stopped doing drugs. Then one night she didn't come home. But Dad wouldn't tell the police. He said she'd come to a bad end. I've talked to everybody—nobody has seen her. Jake is going nuts—he doesn't know where she is—"

"Jake?" Dylan asked, interrupting for the first time.

"Her boyfriend. The police talked to him, but he was out of town at a basketball game the night she was missing. He's a senior on the team, a good guy. Missy couldn't believe it when he started acting really interested in her, said all he wanted was to bang her, that was all guys ever wanted from girls like her.

"But Jake was different," she said softly. "He liked her, a lot. Called her a lot, stopped by to see her. Then one time he came by the house, argued with her, told her she deserved better than she gave herself. I was upstairs and heard them. She...um, I think she tried to get him to sleep with her and he wouldn't. He told her he wanted her, but he wanted it to be special and he didn't want her strung out when it happened."

162

Jackie looked up, tears in her eyes. "Missy wasn't used to guys wanting something special with her..."

Dylan glanced at Pat before looking back to the girl. All right. The kid wasn't going anywhere.

"Can you tell me how long she's been missing?"

ℭℜℭℬℭℜℭℬ

Dylan flipped his wallet shut after holding the ID up to the peephole and waited for the door to open. He hadn't exactly been expecting this. Jacob T. Warner was pretty much at the top of the social ladder.

In the few short months since he and Kris had set up the office here, he had only taken one case from anybody who had lived in this income range.

The missing child had been kidnapped by her mother and lover just before the custody hearing. Dylan had found the kid, all of seven, alone in a hotel in Tijuana, Mexico, while the mother and her twenty-year-old boyfriend were getting it on in another hotel. Needless to say, her custody rights were terminated.

The door opened slowly and the boy, a tall, sandy-haired kid, eyed Dylan with narrow, distrustful eyes. "I already told the police. I didn't do a damn thing to Missy—I love her, damn it. I wish you all would get that through your heads and actually start *looking* for her, instead of hassling me," he said through gritted teeth.

"Well, I guess it's safe to assume you're Jake," Dylan drawled as he tucked his wallet away. "Relax. I'm not a cop. I'm a private investigator. Jackie came and talked to me today. And face the facts, kid. First suspect with teenaged girls is usually

Shiloh Walker

the boyfriend. So let's get you out of the way so I *can* go looking for her."

Dylan suspected his matter-of-fact speech was something the boy hadn't heard before. Snapping his mouth closed, the kid settled back and studied Dylan again before turning over his shoulder and hollering, "Hey, Dad!"

Then he glanced at Dylan. "Dad's a lawyer. I'm not talking to anybody without him around. Not after the hell they gave me at the station. They just wanted to pin something on me and sweep it away. But then, after they couldn't, they just stopped looking."

Dylan saw the impotent anger and decided on the spot Jake was innocent. He knew it in his gut. But that didn't mean he was walking away. He still had questions to ask.

The man approaching down the hall saw Dylan and instantly tensed, though you wouldn't know unless you knew how to look. His face stayed easy, his smile polite. There was just a flicker in his eyes, a grim tightness in his shoulders for the quickest of seconds before he reached out, offering his hand. "Hello, can I help you?"

"This is a private investigator. Dylan Kline. He's here about Missy. Jackie hired him."

"I'm surprised that bastard father of hers is willing to do anything."

"He isn't," Dylan replied, shaking the offered hand. "Jackie is my client, Mr...?"

"Beau. Beau Warner. You say Jackie hired you?" he said. Silver eyes crinkled at the corners and he smiled, brilliant white teeth flashing. "Oh, man. That's...very Jackie-like."

Jake laughed. "He wants to talk to me about Missy."

164

Beau's face sobered. "Jake doesn't know anything, Mr. Kline. She's been missing for three weeks and Jake's been through the wringer. I'm afraid—"

"Doesn't she deserve every chance to be found?" Dylan asked, meeting Beau's eyes. "If it was your kid, wouldn't you want every question asked a thousand times? Poor kid's dad doesn't give a damn, but she does have a sister who's got a heart of pure gold. Let me do what she's asking. Work with me."

"It's just a few questions, Dad," Jake said softly. "I want her home. I *need* her home."

Beau sighed and shook his head. "She's a sweet girl. Had such a rough time, with that dad of hers. Crazy son of a bitch. All right, come on in."

CЯCБCЯCБ

Dylan studied the boy in front of him, then his notepad. Precious little to go on, the clothes she was wearing, hell, he described those down to a tee, save for undergarments. But no new job, no new friends save for the ones she had started hanging out with she started dating him the past summer. Nobody particularly angry with her for leaving the crowd she'd left behind, no dumped boyfriend.

"What did you see in her, Jake?"

"Don't talk about her like she's dead, Mr. Kline." Jake's face paled a little and his mouth firmed out. "Don't. She's not."

Dylan rubbed a hand over his face. It didn't exactly look good. "Sorry, Jake. I was talking about when you first started seeing her. She wasn't exactly your type. What do you see in her?"

"She had sad eyes," Jake said distantly. "I dunno. I ran into her at the mall one day. I'd seen her around before. She was sitting in the food court. I don't know why but I sat down with her. She told me to leave her the hell alone." A ghost of a smile appeared on his face and he said, "I almost did."

"How long have y'all been sleeping together?" Dylan asked casually, sliding it real easy like, glancing at Beau, who just closed his eyes and shook his head.

Jake's eyes flew to Dylan and his mouth twisted in a sneer. "We haven't. Not once. I told her it would be special, and I meant it. And I'm gonna tell ya what, I don't think she's ever had sex. I think it scares her. We can only go so far when we...ah..."

"I bet the term you're looking for is making out," Beau supplied. "Unless it's called something different now."

Jake's face flushed. "Yeah, well. Anyway, then she gets tensed up and nervous. I don't want to push her. She's special to me. I meant it when I said I love her. And I don't plan on messing it up for anything."

Dylan studied the kid in front of him with appraising eyes. Hell, did they still come that...*pure*? With a small smile, he tucked his notepad away and wondered if he had ever been like that.

No. Never.

He had been out for everything he could get.

And more.

CRCBCRCB

Kris settled into the sunken bathtub with a deep sigh of satisfaction. The jets had bubbles dancing around her, working the stiffness from her muscles with a steady, soothing motion that would no doubt put her to sleep if she wasn't careful.

The past year had been the most exhausting one of her life.

And the best.

Wiggling her toes, she fought the urge not to grin like a loon.

Then she gave up and let the smile take over.

"He loves me," she murmured in the quiet room.

Music played from the radio in the other room, the strains floating just barely to her ears as she leaned her head back against the pillow. Staring up at the ceiling, she said softly, "He loves me."

"Yeah, he does."

Shrieking, she sat up, water splashing over the side as her eyes flew to the door. "Damn it, Dylan! Are you trying to scare me to death?" she asked, her heart pounding like a drum in her chest, her entire body shaking. "I'm going to put a bell on you or something. Rig the floor so it makes a noise when you walk on it."

He grinned at her, his mouth curving up in a hot, slow smile as he studied her in the tub. "Sorry," he said easily. Moving across the bathroom, he knelt by the tub and eased her back into the water. Then he rolled up his sleeves up and settled his hands on her shoulders. "You're strung as tight a bowstring, you know that?"

"Worn out," she murmured. "Busy couple of months."

"Hmmm." His thumbs dug into the muscles at her neck and Kris moaned, her head falling forward.

"I've got a new case. Not going to get much money though. Guess it's a good thing that last guy was so happy about getting his daughter back as quick as he did."

Kris rolled her eyes. Happy was an understatement. He'd given Dylan a bonus in the neighborhood of fifty thousand dollars. Dylan had been in the middle of declining when Kris had breezed in, smiling and thanking him in one sentence.

"What exactly is the case, and how much is not much?"

"Not much is none. A girl came in about her sister. She's been missing for almost a month and her dad didn't go to the cops, the sister had to. But the cops aren't doing much," Dylan said.

"None." Kris took a deep breath. "No money?"

"It's a missing kid, Kris. I can't tell the girl no," Dylan said flatly. His hands moved back to her shoulders without breaking pace, but she knew there wasn't any argument.

"Hell, I know that. But that means when somebody offers you a bonus, you don't even think of saying no," she said in a voice just as flat, leaning her head back and glaring up into his eyes. "Got it? You'll do this, too often. You have a living to make."

He slid his hand down in the water as he stared into her eyes, cupped a breast. "You mean I can't be your love slave and you take care of me?"

The spit in her mouth dried up and Kris swore the bones in her body melted. "Ahhh..."

A smile curved his mouth as he arched his head around and covered her mouth with his. "No? Okay. I guess I'll have to do it your way then." Pushing his tongue in her mouth, he drank in her taste and massaged her breasts as the water pummeled her body.

Kris turned and reached up, twining her arms around his neck, plastering her wet torso as close to him as she could. *Damn it, you drive me nuts.*

He moved his lips away and she opened her mouth to tell him that but then he slid a hand down her front, into the water, down over her belly. He cupped her and then pushed a finger inside her sheath. Kris tightened around him with a moan. Water splashed around her as she moved against his hand. She wrapped her arms around his shoulders and tried to move closer.

Dylan chuckled against her neck. "You're going to drown us both."

"I don't care." But instead of trying to pull him closer, she rolled to her knees and leaned up against him. His arms came around her and Kris gasped as he stood in one fluid, easy motion, lifting her wet body out of the tub.

Cool air danced on her flesh and she shivered a little. Blistering heat replaced the chill as Dylan turned and pressed her up against the wall. The tile was icy but she didn't notice. Dylan leaned into her and all she could feel was the heat of his mouth on her neck, the strength in his hands as he skimmed them down her sides and the throbbing of his cock against her belly.

His jeans felt rough against her thighs. Then they were gone and all she could feel was the heat of his skin against hers. She tangled her hands in the cotton of his shirt and tugged upward. He obliged and lifted his arms, letting her pull the shirt off. When his arms came back around her, Kris sighed at the pleasure of it.

"I want to be inside you," Dylan murmured against her neck. He traced his tongue up her neck and then bit her ear gently.

"Hmmmm…" Kris lifted one leg, hooking it over his hips. "Then what are you waiting for?"

Dylan laughed. "You're so impatient," he teased. But he cupped her hips in his hands and lifted her. Kris wrapped her legs around his waist and stared at him as he rubbed his cock back and forth over her slick, wet folds.

"Quit teasing me." Kris fisted her hands in his hair and arched.

"Bossy, bossy." His mouth covered her and he shifted the angle of his hips. He entered her and they groaned into each other's mouths. "Fuck, you're so tight," Dylan muttered against her lips. "You feel so good."

Kris whimpered and rocked against him, taking him deeper. His hands squeezed her ass as he moved her. He held her steady as he pumped in and out. Under her lashes, she could see him staring at her, his eyes dark, glittering and intent. He looked so hungry. So focused. That raw, blatant hunger on his face was as erotic as the feel of his hands on her body. It went deeper than sex, though. She could see it, could feel it in the way he touched her, like nobody else would do it for him.

Like she was the only one who mattered to him. For always.

Tears stung her eyes as he pressed a gentle kiss to her lips. So gentle. So at odds with the hungry demands of his hands and his body. His cock throbbed inside. Kris clenched around him. She moaned out his name. He stroked one hand up her back, over her neck, fisted it in her hair. Using that hold, he angled her head and made her look at him.

"Say my name," he whispered.

"Dylan." Her lips curved as she said it.

"Tell me you love me."

The rhythm of his hips slowed as he waited. Kris cupped her hand over the back of his neck. "I love you. I adore you. I need you."

170

His lids drooped. Then he kissed her. As their mouths met, he started to pump inside her again, fast and hard. Low in her belly, she could feel it, her muscles tightening as climax approached. Her ears buzzed, blood roared in her head and her heart raced away inside her chest like she was running an Olympic marathon.

The hand on her ass tightened. His fingers dug into her flesh and he pressed deep, his thrusts going from deep and hard to short, desperate little thrusts. The hand in her hair clenched. She felt a sweet, erotic pain from it and then she exploded.

He called out her name as she screamed.

Her last conscious thought was that this was a hell of a lot more relaxing than any bath.

CRCSCRCS

Dylan was slowly going insane a week later. Pounding his head against the wall.

Melissa had simply vanished from the face of the earth.

After a week of searching, there was nothing. Her old friends hadn't seen her. Her new friends hadn't seen her.

Her father... Well, he hadn't seen her, and his words had Dylan burning at the core. "She is paying for all her wicked ways, I will tell you that," he had intoned in a deep, sorrowful voice, with eyes that gleamed maniacally.

Dylan had offered him a pitiless smile. "No, sir. God doesn't punish kids. He punishes the bastards who abandon those kids to wolves. Have a good night." Walking away at that point had been necessary. Otherwise he would have killed the miserable fuck.

A girl just doesn't disappear into thin air.

Then there was the phone call he had just gotten, totally unrelated to the case, but very related to him. Raintree had just gotten pulled from Kris. He'd no longer be watching her, and neither would Luciano.

Dylan swore softly. He didn't know what to think of that. Max had been in hiding for close to two years now. He could be dead for all they knew. Damn it all. You can't expect Uncle Sam to do it forever, but he didn't like it either.

Too soon.

It just felt too soon.

The door swung open and Kris sailed in, a sunny smile on her lovely face, that wine red mouth curved up in satisfaction, her green eyes glowing with smug pleasure. She strolled over to the chair and settled down, curling her legs up in a graceful, feline movement. The position had her skirt riding high up her thighs. The smile on her face, so female, so sexy, made his blood pump a little hotter.

"Hmmm...I've got some interesting news."

"What are you doing in this neck of Kentucky, darling?" he asked, swallowing tightly. He hadn't expected to see her for a day or two. This long distance thing really, *really* sucked. Especially now that he knew Ethan and Luciano weren't there anymore to watch that fine ass of hers.

She smiled again, a hot little smile that seemed to whisper *secret...* Dylan licked his lips.

"Hmmm, well, that's more news. For later."

He was rather enticed by the bare length of leg her position was revealing and the words coming from her mouth took a minute to penetrate his head, especially since he still had the problem with his IQ dropping those fifty points any time he

Always Yours

looked at her. Finally, he blinked and made himself meet those sparkling green eyes. "Ahhh...ummm, more news?"

"Yes, more news. But the interesting news, first," she said, grinning at him.

Swallowing, he shifted again as his cock pressed uncomfortably against the fly of his jeans. "We wouldn't want it to be uninteresting news, I guess," he said dryly. He managed a half smile while he tried to make himself think. He had been doing a decent job of that. Until she strolled in. Damn it.

All he had to do was think of her and he lost all thought.

He hated this—her living half her time in Louisville, the other half in Lexington. He wanted her with him, all the time.

That smile, hot and female, widened and her eyes dipped lower, as though she knew damned well exactly what he was thinking. Like a caress, that gaze moved over him, but she never moved that lazy cat's pose in the chair. Cocking a brow, she said, "I met an unusual woman today. She seemed to know everything about everybody. But nobody's name. She has newspapers from thirty ago. A memory like nothing I've ever seen. Damned near photographic. She quoted damned near half the original Constitution to me...and that was before tea."

Dylan tensed. "You've been out asking questions again," he said softly. "Darlin', don't you have an editing job? A boss who might get upset with you if you aren't working?"

"Well, that's part of the news," she said, grinning.

Damn. He didn't like the sound of that. She was sliding too seamlessly into this part of his life and he didn't know half the time if he wanted her in this with him or not.

It didn't help that she had fit so smoothly. So perfectly. That she seemed to follow everything so damned well. Damn it, he was doing this by the seat of his pants.

173

So was she.

And look how far it had taken them.

"So this old lady is what has you smiling like a loon?" Dylan mused, scratching his chin. He wouldn't ever understand women.

"No. What has me smiling is what she saw a few weeks ago. '...that pretty girl, used to act so trashy, just acting out, that was all. You could tell. She had a good heart...'" Kris voice had deepened as she spoke, raspy, like an old smoker's. Studying the ceiling, she sighed in satisfaction. "She watered her plants every day at three-twenty p.m. Do you know who she always saw?"

"Missy," Dylan murmured, shaking his head. "I'll be damned. You did it again."

"Missy," Kris repeated with a smug smile. "That day, she recalls seeing a van in the area, one she had seen before. An old, nondescript blue Chevy. One that seemed to have been in the area before, why...around the same time as Missy, come to think of it. She was looking down, remembered seeing Missy on the corner as the van was slowing down. When she looked up, the van was driving away and Missy was gone."

Dylan's eyes narrowed with the hot, urgent need to hit the trail and go *hunt*, go find his quarry. "A blue nondescript Chevy van. That's more than we had before."

Not as much as he'd like...but still. A license plate would have been nice.

"Oh ye of little faith..."

Glancing up, he saw Kris studying his face from under her lashes with an amused smile on her lips. Then she said in a singsong voice, "Ten-E-four-two-zero-one. Kentucky plates. Jefferson County."

Shaking his head in admiration, he said, "You did it again it, girl. Damn it all."

"Why, thank you," she said, fluttering her lashes. "I'm telling you, that old woman has a mind like a steel trap. She's scary. I bet she knows what color underwear she wore on May 26, 1972. Hell, I bet she knows what color underwear I'm wearing right now. The FBI needs to hire that woman. She's a gold mine."

Striding over to the computer, he said, "Give me that license plate again." In under five minutes, he had a name and an address. Jotting it down, he handed it to her and said, "While I'm gone, see if you can find anything interesting out about this guy. And later, I'll find out what color underwear you're wearing."

"While I'm riding *with* you, I'll be more than happy to." Kris tossed her legs over the arm of the chair and stood, meeting him in the center of the room, toe to toe. "I'm getting a little tired of being left behind while you go and have fun."

"Fun." Dylan ran his tongue over his teeth and studied her porcelain face, the green fire that was suddenly blazing in her eyes. "You consider talking to scum fun?"

"Why not? You do. You're dying to get up to Louisville and see if you can pound some information out of that guy about that pretty girl. And leave me here. *Again.* Doing all the legwork. Which I don't mind, except it means leaving me out of the action all time. Damn it, this is about the fifth time I've gotten something good for you and you want to just leave me out of it."

"That's what you're good at."

"Yeah, well of course I'm good at being left behind. You're making sure I'm getting plenty of practice." Frustrated, she shoved a hand through her hair. Storming away, she strode to her desk. She hit the power button to her computer with more force than necessary and when Dylan moved closer, she ignored him.

"I want you safe."

Kris snorted. "I spent most of my life in New York, pal. Safety is a fool's paradise. After 9/11, you ought to know that. After what Max pulled that night in New York, you ought to know that. I can take care of myself against anybody who isn't an Army Ranger or armed lunatic. I'm a brown belt in karate, Dylan, and you haven't been taking me to the firing range so I can file my nails and work on my social skills. *And* I've got two yahoos who like to... What? What is that look for?"

Dylan felt his face freezing over as he studied her. "I got a call earlier. They are pulling them off. Max hasn't shown his face and it's been too long. They need the men for other things. Raintree tried to argue, but he...well, he's under orders," Dylan said quietly.

"So I'm alone again," Kris said quietly.

"I'm not going to let anything happen to you, Kris," he said softly.

Her eyes met his for a brief second and she nodded. "I can accept that. And I believe you. I didn't expect them to keep it up this long. But I want to be alone right now. Go away."

"Kris—"

Lifting glacial green eyes his way, Kris said through clenched teeth, "Go fuck yourself, Dylan. I'm too pissed off to talk to you right now."

Dylan opened his mouth to say something, but Kris shut him out. From the corner of her eye, she saw him leave the room. Then she focused her eyes on the computer as the familiar pages of the web came up and she started her search. Oh, yes. She was very good at this. It was second nature now.

But was this all he ever planned on letting her do?

Hell, maybe she should rethink what she planned on telling him.

CR&CR&CR&

Dylan slid on his sunglasses as he climbed into the black jeep. Brooding, he sat there for a few minutes and stared up at the second floor window, half-waiting to see if Kris would come and look out.

She didn't.

Damn it. Nothing wrong with wanting to keep her safe.

Except if he knew a damned thing about Kris, she just might go and find trouble all on her own.

That was a very disturbing thought. Especially since Luciano and Raintree weren't going to be around to help watch her butt anymore.

Dylan didn't like it. Blessett wasn't dead. Rats like him just had the damnedest luck and tended to turn up in the most unlikely places. Dylan spun out of the parking lot and wondered if maybe it wouldn't be a better idea to keep her with him. The better to watch her with, my dear.

Of course, the point of having a partner was to split the work. Not worry about her pretty, sweet little ass all the time.

Partner.

Sweet hell. How had she ended up in *that* position? Of course, she was supposed to be a *silent* partner, providing him with a little more money than he had ready, once he had bought his house. Although taking money from her, even as a loan, had grated on him, and he had only done it because she had stared at him with injured green eyes when he had just said he'd go to the bank.

"So you'd rather pay interest than borrow money from me?" she asked, her lower lip protruding just slightly.

Hell. He should have just done that and told her about it after the fact. He didn't want her involved in this part of his life. He didn't want to risk anything happening to her. But doing that was proving damn hard, he mused as he sped down the highway. Bad enough she had kept having dreams off and on. Then she was taking a few names and researching, finding out little bits and pieces of information while he was out talking to people, handing him a rather useful sheet of details that would have taken him several days or weeks of phone calls to try to get. If he had known where to look and who to call.

It wasn't until she actually took some of that information though and started talking to people that he discovered just how damned *good* she was at this. She had a knack for handling people. He suspected it wasn't exactly...a normal skill, either.

She had known with a non-custodial parent abduction case that the grandmother knew where the mom was. But she hadn't told him a damn thing. Not the boyfriend's name, who had bought the tickets, nothing.

Kris had waltzed in, while Dylan was out trying to get the information from somebody else, and had basically tricked the information out of the old cat in under twenty minutes. The lady was still convinced that Kris was a high school friend who had fallen out of touch with her daughter. And while Dylan was en route to Tijuana to pick them up, Kris had settled back down in her office in Louisville, like she had done nothing more than taken a long lunch break.

Oh, she definitely had a talent for this. Working people, solving puzzles, like she'd been doing it all her life. But he couldn't see risking her.

CRCBCRCB

Kris rubbed the bridge of her nose. Jadus Monroe had a few petty convictions, marijuana, resisting arrest, soliciting sex from a minor. That one...maybe. Didn't feel right, though.

She'd spent the past few days gathering information. Where Missy liked to hang out. Who her friends were now, who her friends used to be. What she liked to eat, and where. How she liked to spend her free time.

Alana Chasteen said that Missy and Jake loved to chat online when they weren't able to go out. All of their gang did. One room in particular, *letnloose*. Going to the screen names, she picked a different one from her normal *KTE1973*, goofing off until she came up *kyteendreaming93*, making her seem that ripe old age of fourteen, just the youngest edge of those allowed into Missy's group.

Then she searched for the group and found about ten people there.

Right away, about four people said, *"Hey a newbie! Welcome!"* or variations thereof.

"Hi," she typed, a foolish smile on her face, wondering if she had lost her mind.

Someone with the moniker of *Silverwolfrising* asked, *"Welcome in, Dreaming. Isn't it school time in Kentucky?"*

"I'm homeschooled. Supposed to be researching,"

"*Homeschool sucks. I'm right there with ya,*" bright pink font came through. That was a female, she assumed, since the name was *Daizeegirl2.*

"*That is why lots of us get to be in here during the day. Homeschooling,*" *dumedumegood* said. Kris rolled her eyes. *Oh, please. Kids.*

"*So what do you like to do, Dreaming? Tell us 'bout yourself,*" *Daizee* said.

Kris's mind whirled. "*Movies, shopping. I like reading, but don't tell Mom. 'Please', don't tell Mom, lol. I dunno. Just the normal.*"

"*Kewl. I like reading, too. I love LOTR. Tolkein rocks. Have you read Nicole Kline's stuff?*"

A grin a mile wide split Kris's face. And she lied. "*Never heard of her.*"

And the chat room lit up with all sorts of different colors as about seven of the ten people decided to tell her about how awesome her best friend's books were. Oh, Nikki would be pleased.

She left after about ten minutes. Didn't ask anything. But something felt *interesting* here.

There was a tugging in her belly as she left the room and scanned over the names. Yeah, she'd come back.

Logging onto the database of missing Kentucky children, Kris propped her chin in her hand and studied the faces. Too many. Some young, some teens who most likely had run away. And a few who were listed as being returned safely back to their families, though not enough. She wanted to see Missy's name there.

One face caught her eye. An extraordinarily lovely face. Andrea Silver, sun-streaked, tousled blonde hair, an innocent smile, big dark eyes. Fourteen, missing for about five months. Her eyes were happy, sparkling with the joy of life. Clicking on the link, Kris read the little bit of information that was available.

Walking home from work on a Saturday afternoon in Louisville. Never made it home. Her parents had a bad fight with her the day before. It was assumed, though, from what she was reading, that the girl had run away. Shaking her head, Kris caught her lip between her teeth.

Nothing really, at all, to relate to Missy.

Except this odd little buzzing tingle in her head as she stared at the face.

No reason for that one to have captured her attention out of all of those many faces. *Loves to sing, very talented, amazing dancer...*

Kris shook her head as a deep voice, unfamiliar, but sounding so very real, echoed through her head. Ticking off talents of a child Kris had never met, or seen, before tonight. "You've lost your mind, Kris."

Young, young enough to be broken, a virgin...

Now Kris was starting to feel ill. Hot, sour licks of nausea rolling in her belly as she stared at the innocent, lovely face. A shadow passed over that face and Kris felt her mouth tremble. That pretty girl...*dead.* She refused to let the thought enter her mind, but in her gut, she felt it. In her soul, she felt it.

Slvrnghtgale.

She didn't realize she had been touching the keyboard until the word was already typed out. Jerking her hands away from the keyboard, she hissed. *Damn it.* Kris leaned away from the desk, closing her eyes. All her life, she had experienced *odd* things. Not just the dreams, more than that. She had never questioned them, but she had never pushed too hard to learn

181

more about them either. She had ignored what she could push away and what seemed of little use to her. Used what seemed to be of benefit, and some things, she had little choice as some other part of her kicked in and took over.

It had been that part of her dictating when she had come down to find Nikki that first time. Why she hadn't just let it go when the girl ignored her letters. It had been more than just a feeling that the author behind those roughly written, but amazing stories. And it hadn't been about the stories.

It had been about the woman.

It had been about Nik. Nik had needed her.

Kris had been following that urging each time she had given Dylan information which had led to one of his cases being solved.

But this—this was stronger. This was unlike anything she'd ever felt before. A compulsion stronger than anything she'd ever known. And that voice, it was foul. The voice... It rubbed inside her head, like raw silk, *poisoned* raw silk that would touch her skin and let something evil seep inside and fester, and kill.

"Damn it. What in the hell is going on with me?"

But she knew. Dylan, damn him, had gone and made her acknowledge something she had been pushing aside all of her life. She was different, at least a little. Subconsciously, Kris had known that for a while. The less she pushed it aside, the more it came out.

CRCACRCA

When he got home, Dylan came through the door expecting to find pretty much anything from the War on Terrorism to the Cold War. He got... Kris on the computer, her eyes with that glassy look of somebody who had been chatting a while and didn't intend to stop any time soon. She mumbled something in his direction and drew her feet up under her as she shifted position on the couch. She had her laptop open on her lap, an uneaten sandwich on the table in front of her and a half empty bottle of water beside it.

"Ah, what are you doing?"

"Working."

"On what?" he asked, cautiously. The terse tone of her voice didn't exactly sound angry, but she sure didn't sound welcoming either.

"Projects."

Projects. Hell, with her that could be something for Nikki, editing something for Escapade, or something for the investigation.

"You going to be any more detailed than that?" he asked. Dylan decided this caution was for wimps and slid closer, stroking his hand up and down the smooth naked skin of her back. There was certainly a wealth of flesh bared by the low-lying back of her chemise.

"Haven't decided yet."

"Aren't you being talkative," he muttered, rolling his eyes.

She snorted and flipped her laptop closed after pass protecting it when he craned his neck around to better see what was on it. Dylan could always snoop, but she was kind of funny about that. And a damn good computer person. The last time he had tried, her files had sort of shut down on him, and she had known. She had also been pissed. The ice in her green eyes had been cold enough to freeze a man's balls, and that haughty demeanor had returned. In spades. Of course after a day or two having to crawl, he finally figured out that was exactly what she wanted. Him crawling.

She was just waiting to see how long he would crawl... She hadn't been all that pissed off *then*.

Pass protecting her laptop was just habit. Dylan suspected at the time she hadn't really cared that much. That time. But this time? She left the room in silence with her laptop against her chest and he knew that if he so much as tried to touch that laptop, she would have his hide. Stretched, cured and hung on the wall. Oh, he could get past whatever fail-safes she had on the laptop. No way whatever setup she had would hold against him if he really wanted to get into the computer. But he didn't have any reason to break her trust like that. And right now she was mad about this morning.

Damn it, could he blame her?

Not really. Leaning his head back, he stared at the ceiling and wondered if there was anything he could have done differently. Likely not. Kris was too damn smart, too damn brave, too damn natural at this. Sooner or later, he should have known she would be itching to do more than just give him a little bit here and there, give him the start. Sooner or later, she'd want to see a case through.

But how in the hell could he risk her? Dylan honestly didn't know if he could.

If I don't, I'm going to lose her.

Chapter Eight

Dylan headed down the hall, his mind still heavy with thought when the shower came on. A groan rumbled out of his chest. A wet, naked Kris. How in the hell could he resist a wet, naked Kris?

Dylan padded on silent feet into the dimmed bedroom. His eyes tracked over the little pile of clothing she had had left by the bathroom door. Her tiny lacy panties on top, a black silk bra lying just to the side. The steam drifting out of the bathroom was redolent with the scents of vanilla and peaches, the soaps and lotions she loved.

Placing the flat of his hand against the bathroom door, he pushed it open and felt the blood drain to his groin as the outlined form of his lover appeared in the foggy glass of the shower door. Damn it, she was *his*. After all this time. His.

As he watched, she lifted her face to the spray of the shower and slicked her hands over her head, trailing them down her arms and wrapping them around her torso. Kris stood under the spray of water with her head down. Steam thickened in the room and billowed around him. As Dylan watched, she propped one shoulder against the wall and let the water pound around her body.

That dejected slump wasn't like her. Unable to take his eyes away, Dylan watched as a deep sigh wracked her body and she pushed her streaming hair away from her face, still unaware of him.

What is inside your head, darling, that's got you so down?

Shit, was it from this morning? Had he made her look so dejected? Reaching up, he flicked open the buttons on his shirt, one after the other, until he could shrug it off. It fell to the floor and he reached for the buckle of his belt, his cock jerking within the snug confines of his shorts. Then he freed the button from its hole and lowered the zipper.

Kicking his shoes aside, he shoved his jeans and socks off and moved across the bathroom. He moved loudly, purposely making enough noise that she lifted her head and stared at him. She blinked the water out of her eyes and stared at him. Her gaze was dark and intense as she watched him through the clear, treated glass.

He reached out and pushed open the shower door. Steam wrapped around him as he moved into the oversized shower stall. "You're too quiet," he murmured. He closed the door behind him, and crowded her against the wet tile at her back. He reached up and fisted a hand in her wet hair. The scent of her body flooded his senses, added to his already raw hunger. "I don't like it—can't stand it. Open your mouth."

Kris stared into his eyes, mute. Against his chest, he could feel the hot, hard little points of her breasts and lower, the quivering of her belly, the soft, wet curls of her mound against his cock as he rubbed against her.

"Open your mouth," he whispered again, dipping his head and licking her lips, cupping her face and using his thumbs to angle her jaw up to him. "I want to taste you. I want you to open for me."

"Dylan, don't..."

"Perfect," he muttered, ignoring her words and pushing his tongue inside her lips, past the barrier of her teeth. The wild honey and wine taste exploded on his tongue as he pushed inside her mouth. She didn't respond at first but slowly, she relaxed against him and moaned under his mouth. She tilted her head back, letting him take the kiss deeper.

When he had her moaning, he trailed one hand down her thigh and gripped her knee, pulling her leg up. The position spread her thighs, exposed the damp, wet heat between them. He groaned at the pleasure of it as he pressed the tip of his cock against that silky warmth. Anchoring her knee against his hip, he dragged his throbbing length against her. A growl worked its way out of his tight throat as the dewy heat caressed him, teasing him.

He nipped at her lip before kissing his way down her chin, her neck to capture one hard swollen nipple in his mouth. When she moaned and arched against him, he pushed inside her, slowly, withdrawing and then pushing back in. Slowly, each time barely breaching that hot, tight sheath. He watched her face as he fucked her. Her lids were low over her eyes, shielding her gaze. Her cheeks were flushed.

She moaned. Her heart beat madly within her chest. He could hear the ragged cadence of her breathing, the low, sexy moan rising out of her throat. Her hands came up and clenched on his shoulder, a delicious little pain from her nails as she raked him and demanded roughly, "Stop teasing."

"I love you," he said gutturally, anchoring one arm beneath her buttocks and bracing her more firmly against the wall as he pulled his cock out, feeling the sweat on his brow as he sank back inside, feeling each exquisite tightening of her muscles around him. "You know that, right?"

"Ummmm, stop talking," she urged, digging her heels insistently in his ass, arching her back and forcing her body to slide further down on his cock before he pinned her against the wall, leaning forward and nipping her lip. Her lids drooped closed, hiding her gaze away from him completely.

"Uh-uh, sweet.Look at me. Tell me you love me."

She wouldn't look at him and she didn't speak. Dylan felt a dangerous heat building in his gut. There was a senseless rage inside him. A need to break through the wall she had built between them. He slowed his thrusts and used his hands to hold her when she tried to take him deeper by rocking against him.

"Open your eyes and look at me," he rasped.

She did, but that barrier was there. She held herself apart from him. He raked his teeth down her neck. "Tell me," he cajoled.

"Make love to me," she countered. A hot, seductive smile curled her lips and her eyes warmed a little. It wasn't enough. She still wouldn't take him close like she always did—not his body. She was perfectly willing to accept that but she wouldn't let *him* in.

Dylan wanted to pull away. He was weak though. Her hands left his shoulders to slick down his chest before coming up to cup her own breasts, stroking her thumbs over her nipples lazily as she leaned up working herself up and down lazily on his shaft as best she could with his hands limiting her movement. He felt frozen inside even though his body was flaming and burning for her.

"This is no good, Kris." He went to set her down but her hands slid back around his shoulders, holding him tight.

"What do you want from me?" she whispered hoarsely. Her pupils were huge, nearly eclipsing the green of her irises. "You want me to tell you that I love you? You already know I do. That I need you—I need you. More than I need to breathe."

Dylan's control snapped with a near audible pop as he drove upward into her, pinning her against the wall and plowing upward into her channel, growling and driving deeper and harder. She tightened around him and the sound of her screaming out his name was almost as sweet as feeling her climax around him.

As she cuddled against him, he smiled. That was Kris. This hot, loving woman. Not that cool stranger he thought he had seen.

CRCBCRCB

But that cool, distant woman was there again the next morning.

Dylan eyed her narrowly as she slid from the bed, her eyes blank, a half-hearted good morning on her lips. She barely looked at him when he spoke to her.

"Fuck."

He was getting pissed.

Very pissed. And confused as hell. If she was pissed off, why in the hell didn't she start a fight? Or finish the one from yesterday? Sliding from bed, he snagged his jeans and drew them up his hips. He followed her into the kitchen where she was already pulling her cup of coffee from the automatic coffeemaker. He hated to admit how much he had come to love watching her wake up in the morning, how much he was coming to need it. Her eyes were heavy lidded, dim and would stay that way until after she had finished that single, crucial cup of coffee, followed by a cup of yogurt.

It was Wednesday. She spent most Wednesdays at the office with him, but at the end of the day, she'd head out the door and he wouldn't see her for a few days. He didn't want her to leave here angry.

"Do you have to go to Louisville later?" he asked levelly, keeping his temper under careful rein.

She blinked and frowned, looking up at him absently, like she had almost forgotten about him. "Oh, I forgot to tell you. Kacie is hiring in another editor. I'm going to telecommute for half the workweek. We've started taking email queries and synopses, and I'll bring home a set amount of work with me. It's a trial run for now, but it should work. I'll head home in a while, but—"

Dylan interrupted. "If you can telecommute, maybe you'd like to move in." Damn it, she *would* move in. "It's a long drive a couple times a week, but..." He shrugged, lamely. Maybe he should have thought that out a little better. But he wanted her here, where he could keep her safe, where he could have her with him all the time, not just two or three nights a week.

Kris arched a brow at him, looking for a minute like her slick, cool self. "Charming offer. I'll think about it."

He moved up behind her and hooked his arms over her waist, whispering in her ear, "What's to think about? In the name of conservation, you know. No reason to pay a mortgage payment on your house when I've got a perfectly good bed I'd love to share with you. And I want you here."

Kris shrugged. "I said I'd think about it."

"So you're still pouting."

Kris glanced at him over her shoulder, one slim, perfect brow winging up. Dylan had to fight the urge to grit his teeth. That royal, devil may care, queen to the serfs look enraged almost as much as it aroused.

"Pouting? Is that what I'm doing?"

Dylan snarled and stomped away. "You've been pouting for the past twenty-four hours."

Kris gave him a cool smile and sipped from her coffee cup. She stared at him over the rim of it. She shrugged and murmured, "I didn't realize I was pouting. I thought I was drinking my coffee. Hmm. Well, I'll be drinking my coffee for about another five or ten minutes. Then I will eat something and get dressed before I get back to tracking down some information about something that caught my interest last night. I'll do that for a few hours, then I'll work on Escapade for a little while. I've got to get back to Louisville tonight but I had planned on us getting dinner first. Of course, plans can change."

All interest in kissing that arch look off her face fled. Instead, he homed in on her words and moved across the kitchen, crowding her against the counter. He didn't like the look in her eyes. Or the gut feeling that she wouldn't share what had caught her interest. She was up to something, damn it. He felt it in his bones.

"What exactly caught your interest? And did you forget, you agreed to do some work for *me* today?"

Now both of those deep red brows rose before she smoothed them down and lowered her lashes over her emerald eyes and studied him through the heavy fringe. There was a small, cool smile playing over her lips. "Working? Is that what you call what I do? On occasion, I get an odd feeling and investigate it. Then I give you the details and you act on them. Leaving me out. I research information and turn the details over to you. You never officially hired me, never officially made me any kind of partner. Granted, I get a decent cut from the fees you bring in." Lifting one shoulder, Kris made a small moue as her eyes trailed over his face before locking on his mouth. "More often than not, I think you just like having me on hand so you can fuck me when you see fit."

Dylan battled the rage building inside him, knowing it was a lost cause, but hoping like hell he could find some reason for the fight she seemed determined to start.

She watched him, that mild, almost amused look on her face and when he said nothing, she continued, "If that's the case, you know where to find me. There's no research that needs to be done at this point. And if I get an odd little itch I need to go investigate, well, there's no reason for me to be in the office for it. You fucked me twice last night and once already this morning. You should be good to go for a few hours so I'm free to do what I need to do."

Cupping his hand over the back of her neck, Dylan leaned in and laid his finger over her mouth. The words he squeezed out felt like shards of broken glass as he growled, "Enough. Got it, babe? Enough. I'm not sure where all this anger is coming from, but that's enough."

Kris smiled against his finger, and the feel of that mouth, those silken lips moving against his work-roughened skin drove him nuts. But he was too fucking pissed. The chilled anger in her eyes only added fire to his rage.

"You don't know? You really don't know?" Blinking her lashes once, slowly, Kris shook her head and pulled back slightly, arching her head so that her mouth wasn't pressed against his finger. Then she slid her tongue out and stroked it against his finger. "You should. Haven't you been paying attention, *babe*? I'm tired of being left out. I'm not the brainless, helpless little airhead you seem to think I am. I'm capable, perfectly capable of taking care of myself."

With a suddenness that surprised him, she moved into him then slammed her elbow into his gut, sliding away from him.

Her hair was settling around her shoulders as she leaned against the opposite counter, arching her brow and lifting her chin in challenge as she stared at him. "No, I could never take you down. I'd never be fool enough to try. But how many people could even manage to move away from you like that?"

Very few. Dylan lifted a brow in acknowledgement. "It takes more than getting away. It takes taking down. It takes a willingness to hurt, to kill if necessary. It takes—"

Kris laughed. "I have everything it takes, Dylan. You're just too damned blind, or too damned protective to see it. That's fine. You try to keep me in this silk cage you've pushed me into." With a final, brittle smile, she whirled on her heel and left, the dark red banner of her hair streaming down her nearly naked back.

Kris shoved the anger aside. She couldn't do the work she had to do and be angry as well. A time would come when she could let all the anger she felt out, and she could let it rain down on the bastards who were really responsible.

It wasn't Dylan. Damn his fine ass for trying so hard to push her into a corner and keep her there. It wasn't him. But he needed to stop trying so hard to protect her. If he didn't want her in danger then he never should have let her near any of this, from the beginning. Damn it, she'd been living in near constant danger since meeting that bastard Blessett anyway— she sure as hell hoped that sorry son of a bitch was dead.

It was too late now to try to move her back into a world where she was ignorant of such things. She would always be watching over her shoulder from here on out. Damn it, she was *tired* of being the one who felt helpless.

She wanted to help somebody for a change.

Settling down in front of the computer, she listened to the breathing she could hear just behind her. Oh, she hadn't heard him come in the room. But he was in there all the same.

And furious.

Part of her was just the slightest bit sorry for that.

But she had to get this done.

There were pieces of a puzzle she could solve lying all over the place. She could all but see the outline of the puzzle, could almost imagine it. Just a little more time and she'd work the pieces into place. But she couldn't do it with him around. Besides, if he had *let* her do what she was capable of, instead of trying to confine her to a damn desk all the time, this sneaking around wouldn't have been necessary.

Kris had to get him out of here. She had to get this done.

For the girl.

This was for the girl.

But the faces were starting to blur in front of her eyes. Missy's, Andrea's, and others. How many others were there?

Many... I've taken many butterflies... Kris slammed a door in her mind shut against that dark, insidious voice. Then a shudder wracked her body as Dylan's long-fingered, warm hands came down on her shoulders, thumbs and forefingers nearly encircling her neck as he lowered his mouth to whisper, "This isn't over, sweetheart. You can bet your sweet little ass on that."

She couldn't stop the smug smile that curved her lips as he stomped out of the room, slamming the door behind him. "Hope not, handsome."

Then she focused her eyes back on the computer.

That bastard, that dark, perverted bastard, was here. Somewhere.

CRCRCR

Kris pursed her lips, studying the pictures her mom had emailed her. Sheesh. That one would work, easy enough. She had developed early, and her hair had been woven back in a French braid so it would hide the differences in style. Her complexion had always been clear, thank the Lord.

She looked innocent compared to some of the pictures she'd seen posted online. Except for her eyes.

Kris studied the eyes of her own picture, nearly twenty years old, and frowned. Her eyes looked...old. Far too old. She remembered when the picture had been taken, a few months after she'd been kidnapped. That would definitely force a kid to grow up fast, but Kris sometimes thought she'd been born old.

Sighing, Kris settled back and uploaded the picture. It would have to work. There were a few others that didn't show her eyes so completely, but they looked too *eighties*. This one could easily have been taken now. And it was a damn good picture, showing her well. If there was a man on there preying on lovely young teenaged girls, that picture was the best bait she had for herself.

With a smirk, Kris said, "We can only hope it will be this easy." Not that she was expecting easy, but a screen name, a first name, anything. Something pointing the way to Andrea or Missy—

When the phone rang, she lifted it up and said, "Stop growling at me. Your papers are exactly where you left them. If it's that damn bad, let Pat in there to do her job."

"Ummmm...ooookay," Nikki said, laughing.

Kris laughed, running a hand through her hair and settled back, drawing a leg up under her as she smiled, a real smile for the first time in days. "Sorry. I thought it was Dylan. He's pissed at me."

"Yeah...I got that. Just talked to him. He bit my head off when I mentioned your name earlier. He told me you were a crazy, insane female and he was madder than hell I let him let you talk him into this blasted fiasco. It took me a bit to untangle those words. Usually Dylan doesn't say more than five at a time. So that really confused me. I almost pity Shawn. He's heading your way as we speak. Going to drop in on Dylan... ah...unannounced."

"That will go over well," Kris said, a grin lighting her face. "Maybe they will get into a fight then go get drunk tonight. I can get some peace and quiet."

"You're that mad?"

"Yes...no—I don't know. He's frustrating the hell out of me. I don't think he realizes I can take care of myself. I'm not made of glass, Nik."

"I'd have to agree," Nik said succinctly. "I've seen you in class, remember. And I've seen you knock a man down when he didn't back off. I know you aren't made of glass. But Dylan, well, he's got this odd idea about protecting the women he loves. Even me. He's just rather, well, *wrong* in this situation."

"I can't keep working with him if all he wants me doing is crying on his shoulder when I have a bad dream, or researching somebody for him while I have a few minutes during my day. Hell, I don't even know if I want to keep editing. Sometimes..."

Turning in her chair, she stared out the window over the rolling hills that were the Lexington bluegrass area. It was so much *more* than New York City. There was life here and not just the hustle and bustle of big city. She was tired of big city. This was life. This was family, home, friends, country... It felt real.

She hadn't realized how hollow *her* life had been leaving her until she had come here and found this, found a life with Dylan. But it was still just a half of a life unless Dylan decided he could trust her to take care of herself.

"Sometimes what?" Nikki asked.

"Sometimes I feel like I'm not doing what I'm supposed to be doing," she said quietly. "Then I do something like what I've been doing when I'm helping him. And that feels right."

"Have you told him that?"

Kris sighed. "He doesn't want to hear it."

Nikki laughed. "I understand that. Men tend to want to...overprotect a lot. Sometimes to the extreme."

"Would he trust you?" Kris asked thoughtfully.

Nikki hesitated. The silence on the other end of the line echoed so loudly, Kris fought the urge to gnash her teeth. Finally, a long sigh passed over the line and Nikki said, "Yes, likely he would if I had gone into this with him from the beginning or if I knew something and insisted from the getgo I follow through. But Dylan knows me. Knows what I was like growing up. He looks at you and sees this lovely woman he fell in love with. He doesn't see somebody trained in karate or a woman I watched knock a guy's teeth down his throat. He doesn't see a woman who can be hard. He sees...well, soft skin, boobs, a big heart, a sharp mind. Nothing hard. He's in a business where you need to be hard." Nikki chuckled. "He obviously knows nothing about the world of publishing or he'd realize how cutthroat you can be."

"I guess it's time to show him I can be hard." A small tune played from her computer and Kris looked up. She smiled with satisfaction. "I think I was already on the right path... I think anyway. Listen, hon, I gotta go."

Focusing on the IM on her screen, she tapped out a "Hullo" to the other person on the box and waited. "Well, well, well, what have we here?" she mused. She hadn't been expecting this at all.

Not at all.

ॐ॰ॐ॰ॐ॰ॐ

The girl on the other end of the IM was nervous, very nervous, but not so nervous that she was going to pass up this chance to fix what she was responsible for. She had never meant for any of this to happen.

She should have tried harder to warn them away, *Slvrnghtgale* and *Exxiled*. There were others. She knew there were. But they were lost. Maybe forever. If she could stop it from happening *again*, that would be enough. It would have to be.

When the new name had appeared in their chat room, *Kyteendreaming90*, an itching had settled in her belly, in the back of her head, followed by a fierce, violent joy. *Finally.* Somebody who would help her drown out the evil voice in her head, the suffering screams she heard at night when she laid her head down.

There was another one, a man. When she closed her eyes, she could picture him, just his eyes, grim, hazel eyes. Those eyes would almost be as scary as the other man, but she knew this one would never look at a child with greed or lust. They'd flash with violence and fury as he came down on those who had taken two of the voices that had helped fill the girl's lonely life with laughter.

"My fault," Pamela Jo Atwood whispered quietly. "I've got to fix it."

CRCЗCRCЗ

The girl was a bleeding genius.

Kris had no idea how old this child was, and for a few minutes, she had questioned whether or not it was a child. Though the girl's fear was obvious, as was her naiveté. She had tried to go to the police, and couldn't understand why they hadn't done anything, just based on her feelings.

A cop couldn't do anything based on the feelings of a kid. Even one as extraordinary as this one seemed. The girl was also the best damned hacker Kris had ever come across. She had known a few, not many but a few. And they were damned good ones.

But this child blew them out of the water.

The oddest thing of all, though, was she was like Kris. She IM'ed Kris with the disconcerting message, *"You're not a teenager. You made an itch start in my belly and in my head the moment your name appeared in the chat room. You know what kind of itch I'm talking about. You get them too. You've listened to them, or ignored them, just like I do, depending on whether or not they help you. This time we can help somebody else. Are you going to listen?"*

"Bet your tail I'll listen. Exactly what do you know and how long has this been going on?"

For a long moment, there was nothing. Kris wondered if she had left. But then the letters assured her partner was typing away.

"*Slvrnghtgale was the first one that I know about. But it started long before her. Then they took Exxiled. She's the one you came looking for.*"

Kris's breath locked in her throat. Damn. The kid really did know. She hadn't asked about *Slvrnghtgale*, hadn't done more than look for her.

And *Exxiled*... Was it Missy? "Shit."

Yeah. Shit. It totally freaked me out when you came into the chat room.

Kris jerked her hands away from the keyboard. She hadn't typed a damn thing, had only spoken the word aloud. Slowly, she tapped out, "*Kid, you're starting to freak me out.*"

LOL. ☺. I've been freaking myself out for a couple of years. You've been blocking this longer than I have. I'm a little more used to it. I was five when I started to realize I was different. And not just because I could read the Magna Carta in Latin as well as English.

Ahhh...Kris was dealing with a child protégé. Narrowing her eyes, she crossed her arms over her chest and asked aloud in a slow, purposeful voice, "How much do you know?"

A smiley appeared in the IM box, followed by the familiar acronym, *LOL*. The girl had heard her. Somehow. "*Enough to know that I'm being tested right now. And...enough to know that Exxiled...Missy...is running out of time. But you can help her. You and that guy. He has intense eyes.*"

What guy? Kris already knew the answer to that one, though. The girl was talking about Dylan.

"*Can you tell me what you know?*" Kris asked.

"*He bought her, ya know. For his master. He isn't from here. He's from Turkey and he was getting ready to take her back to his master, but Missy won't eat. She hardly sleeps. She just* sits.

And stares. *He's angry—he's going to bring her back. They don't want her now. She fought at first. That's the way they like it. His master wanted a young, pure American, one he could break. But Missy—"*

Quietly, Kris whispered, "Missy is already broken."

"Yes." The words, even though they only appeared on the screen, seemed forlorn and full of desolation.

Kris shook her head, clearing it. "What did you mean he's bringing her back?"

"His master doesn't want a girl that's broken. He wants a girl that is fighting and struggling. That's what he is going to bring back with him. Well, he is going to try. There's going to be another sale and he knows about it."

"A sale?" Kris demanded. She stood slowly. The blood drained out of her face. Her hands were sweating and she felt both hot and cold at the same time. *A sale...a sale...a sale...*surely, she had misunderstood. *Please, let me have misunderstood.*

"Yes. The buyer isn't the real bad guy. He's just a minor player. The real bad guy is the one online trolling for girls he thinks might work to pick up, girls who might look like runaways, who won't be missed. And he sells them. He took Slvrnghtgale and he took Exxiled. He's been taking more, for a very long time."

Kris felt her legs give out from underneath her. Her hands clutched at the arms of the chair and she shuddered while nausea, hot and rancid, roiled in her gut. *I will not be sick,* she told herself.

The IM box sounded.

Glancing up, she read the message and couldn't help but smile slightly at the words, *"Why not? I was."*

ଔଔଔଔ

Dylan slammed the door. He hurled his jacket at the couch and in a blind fit of fury, slammed his fist into the oak filing cabinet on his way to the desk. Stubborn, *stubborn* woman.

This place hadn't ever seemed this quiet before. Even on the days when he wasn't planning on her being here, it didn't seem to be this quiet. "What in the hell happened to her coming in here and running names for me?" he swore.

He still couldn't fucking believe what she had said. *More often than not, you like having me onhand so you can fuck me when you see fit.*

His temper had been simmering just below murderous all damn day. His smart ass sister's call hadn't helped. Damn it, Nikki sounded like she already knew how badly he had fucked up and she didn't even know what in the hell had happened. He had even lowered himself to asking if she'd talked to Kris.

She hadn't. And worse, now she knew. She knew he was having a fight with Kris. He didn't like it. At all. Then he launched into Nik, yelling at her for talking him into letting Kris help him so much. That was bullshit. Nikki hadn't talked him into anything.

"Shit."

Dropping his long, rangy body into his chair, Dylan muttered again, "Shit," as he stared up at the ceiling. How long was he going to have to crawl to get them back on an even keel? To get her to understand that he needed her to be *safe*? Damn it, she just didn't understand how dangerous this could be. Her life hadn't prepared her for any of this.

What was it going to take for him to come to grips with that fact that he couldn't leave her out of this part? He couldn't.

Dylan was trying to work himself into leaving and seeking her out when the door swung open and Shawn walked in, whistling tunelessly and cheerfully, his pale green eyes youthful, cheerful, direct as always. Scowling, Dylan settled back. "What the hell are you doing here? Don't you have some men to boss around, little brother?"

"Vacation. Wanted to check in on my big brother. See if you needed any help with your pretty girlfriend," Shawn teased, waggling his eyebrows. Skimming the office with a quick glance, he added, "I talked to Nikki a few minutes ago. She seems to think there is trouble in paradise. Last I heard, you were foaming at the mouth because Kris talked to a grandma and got some information that you didn't. The rebel. That old lady must have been real dangerous to get you into such a mood."

Dylan's brows dropped in a scowl. Fuck. Was it that noticeable? Shawn wasn't even *around* and he knew how damned bad it was. "She's at home sulking because I don't want her following me when I go talk to scumbags," Dylan said flatly.

"Surprised she didn't kick your ass. Especially if that's how you told her."

Dylan briefly recalled how she had thrown his hands off her, slamming that powerful elbow into his solar plexus, evading his hands and sliding away like smoke in the wind. Easy and quick, competent. Kick his ass? No. That wasn't likely. But the average guy? She damned well might have a chance at laying somebody out long enough to get away. Guys didn't expect a woman to know how to fight.

"I didn't say a damn thing to her," Dylan said, lifting one shoulder and dismissing his smart-assed brother.

Or trying to.

Shawn on the other hand... Dylan suppressed a groan as Shawn flung himself into a chair across from Dylan's desk, chuckling. "She faced you down on it, didn't she? And you weren't expecting it. Dylan, that is one lady I wouldn't worry about. Hell, she'd probably freeze a guy in his tracks and chop him down to size with that tongue for daring to look at her wrong. And if he laid hands on her, well, then she knows how to break them, too. Kris isn't helpless."

So I'm learning, Dylan thought sourly. But he'd be damned if he'd take advice from his baby brother. No fucking way. "Why don't you go jack off or something?"

Shawn smiled slowly. "Don't need to. Spent the night with a pretty little waitress. So feel free to unload all your lady troubles on me," he drawled, kicking his black boots up on top of the edge of the oak desk. He had a pleasant smile on his smug face. His hair, longer than Dylan's, tumbled into his eyes, dreamy pale green eyes that no longer looked so grim and dull. Dimples still lingered in his cheeks, though Dylan suspected in the next few years they would deepen to slashes like those Dylan now sported. It would take a while longer for Shawn's newness to wear off of him.

Hell, the kid lived in a dream world half the time.

Unless you did or said something that threatened his adored big sister, Shawn was entirely too affable.

Only two years Dylan's junior, Shawn still had a mantle of youth that Dylan had never had, and a dreamy air, combined with that quicksilver temper and his everpresent grin drew ladies like bees to honey. Shawn drank the honey down and moved on to the next, leaving them all sighing and smiling and wishing.

Clucking his tongue, he shot Shawn a narrow glance and said, "What's the point of that? Can't expect your help with a woman when all you have experience with is girls."

Shawn grinned. "Ouch. That hurt. Can't you do any better than that?"

Dylan grunted and plowed a hand through his hair, feeling the curls wind around his fingers. Needed another damn haircut. "Can't you go find somebody else to annoy? An old girlfriend? Maybe go pay some of the speeding tickets you collect?"

Shawn just smiled, folding his hands over his lean belly, looking like he could settle in and hang for a good month. "So what are you doing now? Another missing kid? They are calling ya a hero back home. Some kind of crusading angel."

A guffaw spilled from Dylan's mouth before he could stop it. Now that was a joke. "You are out of your mind. Where in the hell did you come up with that one? You take up smoking weed again? Nik will kick your ass."

Dylan snickered, leaning back in the chair, kicking one foot up on the edge of the desk and resting his elbow on his leg as he shifted slightly, taking some of the weight of his back and rolling it to his hip. The midday sunlight streamed in, spilling on his desk and Dylan squinted in the brightness. Kris always closed the damn drapes.

"Honest truth," Shawn said, smiling widely, starting to rock as he studied Dylan's face. "Rescuing the defenseless, the innocent, the poor. You almost sound like Robin Hood."

"You sound like a comedian," Dylan muttered, rolling his eyes. Moving his eyes back to files he had already read through, he said, "I've got to get to work. Go hassle Kris."

The smile on his brother's face almost worried him. "Oh, I'd love to..."

If he didn't trust Kris, it could worry him. If he didn't trust her...

CRICRICRI

Kris made notes for everything.

Neat, precise notes. By the time she was done detailing her conversation with—whoever it was, she had filled more than fifteen pages of notes, with the actual conversation, with her own speculations, and with the facts she had unearthed on her own.

Turned out *Slvrnghtgale* had a blog. Kris had meant to hit the search button for the message boards on her internet service provider to see if the girl had ever hit those, and hadn't been paying attention, hitting instead a world wide web search. But the search yielded anyway.

The blog had been dormant, with the occasional *Hey, Sil, where ya at...*or spammers hitting it for a good year now. Before that, *Slvrnghtgale* had posted religiously. She had talked about her singing, her dancing, her family, guys, mostly about her singing. Lots of people loitered on her little piece of cyberspace.

But most importantly—that blog wasn't one of those freebies. She'd purchased a domain for it and that meant it had to be registered. Which would yield a name, a phone number, address. In the right hands.

None of the people in the guestbook jumped out at her but Kris had merely glanced down, barely doing more than reading the dates before she signed off. Later. She'd look more closely there later, though she didn't think it was anything there. Whoever had taken her had come looking for her.

More than four hours had passed, and she hadn't gotten a damn bit of work done for Escapade. Kris groaned as she glanced at the clock. She didn't want to be here tonight when Dylan got home. She was too tired to argue with him. If she got out of here quick enough, she could hit the road before the traffic got bad. After she got back to her condo in Louisville, she'd put in an hour or two at home. And all day tomorrow, she'd do her real job.

Cussing, Kris hurriedly finished up the rest of her neat little concise notes in her notebook. As she crossed the last "t," a loud, boisterous knock sounded on the door.

"Damn it." Rising, she shut the computer down and closed her notebook, tucking the spiral-bound pad out of sight before she left the room.

She already knew who that was.

Her luck wasn't that good for him not to come calling. And the timing was just right, long enough for him to finish his bat out of hell drive up from Somerset, a detour by Dylan's office, long enough to have Dylan growling at him and snarling before he decided he had wreaked enough havoc.

Shawn's devil-may-care attitude and proverbial charm was endearing as hell.

He was also entirely too damn nosy.

Sauntering down the hall, she waited until the second knock rattled the door on its hinges before she opened it. "I need to hit the road, handsome, so if you need something, make it quick."

Shawn smiled. "Quick? How quick? And exactly how much are willing to give?"

Kris tsked. "Not enough. You need more than I have. Plus I like you too much. Dylan would kill you."

Shawn grinned, shoving his hair out of his face with a wide-palmed hand, his clever fingers catching her eyes. Damn, those Kline boys sure had grown up nice.

"Lady, I can handle my brother. Don't worry about that. I was kicking his ass back when Nikki was still daydreaming about being a writer."

Kris hummed under her breath and stepped aside, letting him come in. Being a carpenter could sure as hell do fine things for the bod, she decided. He filled out the well-worn T-shirt in a way she was pretty sure he hadn't done even two years ago. And those lean hips, long legs...day-yum.

Entirely too much like Dylan.

But he didn't have the shadows in his eyes that Dylan had.

Did that say something about her taste in men that she preferred her brooder over the charmer?

Rolling her eyes, she followed him on down the hall and into the living room, curling into a chair opposite him as he flopped onto the couch. "I hear you're on vacation," she said, cocking a brow, drawling out the last word the way Nikki would. "Letting somebody else run things for once."

Shawn closed his eyes. "Don't remind me. He fu..." His words trailed off as one eye flew open and his lean cheeks flushed. "If he messes it up, I'm gonna kill him. But I wanted a couple of days off in between jobs. All he is gonna do is answer the phone, give estimates. He should be able to do that without me babysitting him."

Kris grinned. "You sound so protective. You're awful young to be running your own construction business."

"I took it over and fixed it after Buddy Matthews nearly ran it into the ground. It's mine, all right," Shawn said, smiling a crooked, self-conscious smile. "Not exactly the exciting, hellraising career I imagined ten years ago, but it pays the bills and then some. Plus, I enjoy it. And it's mine. I did it. Just me. I didn't..."

"You didn't need Nikki helping you out," Kris finished. "I guess that would have bothered you. But she wanted to do it."

Flatly, Shawn said, "Doesn't matter. She kept me off the streets and out of trouble for the most part. Kept my sorry, stupid ass in school and made sure I passed, even though I barely have a lick of sense. I didn't want to keep taking from her."

"You're not stupid." Kris sat up straighter, scowling.

"Not far from it," Shawn said. He shrugged dismissively as though it didn't even matter to him. "I had to have her help me through elementary school. Couldn't figure out how to write my name. Reading killed me. Damn it, I couldn't even write a book report unless she helped me get through the damn book, and she had to help me write the report, too. I may not be stupid, but I wouldn't have passed school without her. I wasn't going to keep on taking from her. Not anymore."

"It's not taking if they freely want to give," Kris said simply.

"Maybe not. But she had been giving all her life to us. And not taking a damn thing in return." Shawn forced a tight smile. "I'm good with my hands. I've got more common sense than Nik and Dylan combined. I'll have to be happy with that."

Kris leaned forward, propping her chin on her hands, waiting until he was looking at her. "Nikki and Dylan both have heads as hard as rocks. They could use a hell of a lot more sense than they have. A man who is good with his hands isn't to be taken lightly." Rising, she held out her own and said, "Come on. I'll fix you some lunch."

Shawn wasn't stupid, not by any means. He just had a problem with words on paper. He and his secretary had an

209

understanding. She could watch her soaps during the day, get great raises, a great Christmas bonus, provided she help him with this problem of words and paper.

She also kept it to herself.

No. Words, paper and Shawn, they all hated the other. Numbers weren't really an issue. He had done great in math, geometry. Even chemistry hadn't been such a problem because that had seemed like more math. But words...hell, he was embarrassed even to admit how bad it was. It took him nearly a month just to read each of Nikki's books. He adored his sister, was so damned proud of her so he read each and every one faithfully. So what if reading twenty pages from one of her books could take him two hours?

Up until he'd hired his secretary, he'd had to labor his way through way too many words. Thank God for Christi Sue Markam, called Boo by everybody. Hell, even he had started calling her Boo. She went everywhere with him. All the OSHA crap he had to put up with, all the training, she would help him through the written part and then he was fine. His memory was phenomenal. He could hear it once and then it was saved, like on one of Nikki's damned computers.

He just had the little problem of getting it inside his head.

Wandering the house, Shawn slapped his work-roughened palms against his thighs and glanced toward the kitchen. Whatever in the hell she was cooking sure smelled good.

Better than the golden arches or a cold sandwich for lunch, that was for sure. When his cell phone started to ring, Shawn saw the number and swore half-heartedly. The damned fool hadn't even made it a day without needing some help. Swearing, he flipped the phone open and headed into the small office just off to the right, looking for some paper as Max started with, "Well, I'm not too sure how to figure out the estimate for this one. She's wanting something kinda different..."

"And if they asked for a doghouse, could you figure that out?" Shawn grumbled, grabbing a pen but not seeing any paper on hand. Reaching into the drawer, he cocked an eyebrow at the desk. Nice. Doesn't squeak, doesn't shift...nice... Smoothing his hand down the wood, he admired it a minute before spying a notebook. He flipped it open to the back, scrawling down the measurements and the figures.

"Well, I dunno. Is it gonna be a round one with a balcony, a bathroom and a terrace?"

"Don't matter. It's still just a job," Shawn snapped, tearing the sheet out. He started to flip the notebook closed but something on the notepad jumped out at him. Words didn't do that very often. Frowning, he cocked his head. Sharp ears caught the sound of a female sigh and he closed the notepad, sliding it out of sight.

Leaning back in the chair, he said, "I can't ramble off an estimate without sitting down and writing down some numbers, having a calculator...but we're prolly looking at..." He rambled off some fairly accurate numbers as he watched Kris's shadow coming down the hall. Tucking the paper lower, he added, "I can give a better estimate when I actually have something in front of me to *write* on. But seeing as how I'm supposed to be on a vacation, I didn't bring notepads and pencils and a calculator with me."

Kris came to the door and stood there, an amused look on that pretty face and Shawn gave her a frustrated look, rolling his eyes.

"Okay. Well, Luella is still just thinking, anyway, she says. She can wait until you're here, she thinks."

Shawn listened to female chatter on the other end and wanted to groan. Luella Markham Shit. If he had known that, he would have added another thirty percent. Simply for the pain in the ass of having to put up with her. Overblown, overdone, pain in the ass.

Kris cocked a brow at the look on his face. Keeping the piece of paper hidden in the palm of his closed hand, he made a stabbing motion to his belly and mouthed, *Kill me now...please...*

She laughed.

"Okay, boss. Luella's gone. Between you and me, I think she just wanted to see you," Max said. The older man laughed as he hung up the phone and Shawn one-handedly flipped the phone closed and returned it to the loop on his hip before running his hand down his face.

"I think I'd rather work for ZsaZsa Gabore. Tammy Faye. Anybody else. Build pink palaces and cover them with gilt and flowers and lace."

"Isn't Luella only like nineteen?" Kris asked, her brow puckering.

"Good memory," Shawn said with a wide smile. "Nineteen and a nympho from hell. She had a coming out, for crying out loud. Invited the entire county. The entire thing was done in pink lace and her dress looked like a wedding cake. And she tried to tell everybody there we were getting engaged." A muscle started to tick in his jaw as he remembered. He hadn't even planned on going to the damn thing until one of his buddies called him with *that* piece of information. The little twit was going around handing people cards to their *engagement* party. So then he had been forced to go and correct that misinformation. "I'm not doing anything for her. I don't care if her daddy does own half the county."

"You said she was a nympho—does that mean you have...?"

Shawn jumped out of the chair, his brows drawn low over his eyes. "*Hell* no. She's a kid. And the last one on earth I'd ever touch. I can't stand that obnoxious, stuck up creature," he said honestly, shoving his hands into his pockets and conveniently getting rid of the paper he hadn't been able to find.

"Good," Kris said, laughing. "I'd hoped you had better taste. But then how do you know she's a nympho?"

"Because she seems to think she can jump on me at every chance she gets me alone? Or because she thinks stripping nekkid is going to turn me into a slobbering fool?" Shawn jibed, moving out from behind the desk. "I've seen her nekkid more times than I've seen...well...I don't know. I usually don't see a woman nekkid more than a handful of times. I've seen her at least five times. And she still can't get it through her head I'm not interested."

"That doesn't make her a nympho. A nympho needs sex all the time," Kris said, laughing. "Maybe she's ahhh...umm. Maybe she's a starving virgin. But she shouldn't be trying to rape you."

Shawn shot her a disgruntled look. "She's getting annoying. But she stopped it after the last time, at least with the planting her nekkid ass around me. I warned her to stop it or she'd be sorry."

Kris's brows rose. "Uh-oh. What did you do with her?"

Shawn smiled slowly, moving closer. "She kept swearing how she would do anything, everything I wanted. Well, she hops into my truck with me even though I told her to get lost. And she strips herself nekkid *again*. This time I'd decided I'd had enough. I let her think I was actually going to let her have what she wanted. And she was cuddled up against me, nibbling at my neck, trying to kiss me. Didn't let her though. She tastes like cigarettes and I hate it when a woman tastes like an ashtray. I reached around her and started playing with her hair while I was driving, her back, distracting her. She wasn't paying attention at all. I was about to die laughing. Told her we were going some place special. Where she could get the attention she had been asking for."

Shawn propped his shoulder against the doorjamb, watching as Kris's eyes started to sparkle. "I'm almost afraid to hear the rest of this."

He grinned. "I did have to kiss her while I was getting her out; didn't want her opening her eyes. And I timed it just right, too. Right as the bell was ringing to let out church. She opened her eyes and pushed me away and I started laughing, and hopped back in the truck, tossed her clothes at her. Told her that was it. She did it again, well, she didn't want to know what kind of trick I'd pull. And there was her entire congregation there to see her in all her glory as I pulled away, laughing my ass off while she screamed bloody murder at me. It was even worth having that taste in my mouth."

"You are *bad*." Kris was giggling, one hand pressed to her belly as she leaned forward. "Oh, that's priceless."

Shawn cocked a grin at her and shrugged. "She asked for it, little twit. Besides, she actually left me alone for over a month for that." A sigh left his mouth and he shook his head mournfully, his dark blond hair spilling into his eyes. "I had hoped she had finally left me the hell alone. But I am not so lucky."

"She's convinced she's your one true love."

Shawn's eyes darkened. "Not likely." That selfish, self-centered immature thing? No. He'd know. When he saw his own true love, he'd know. And it *was not* Luella.

ᏟᎧᏌᏟᎧᏌ

Human trafficking.

That's what had leaped out at him.

While he couldn't exactly go and surf the web the way Nikki could, he could do a few things.

Like call Renee. A state cop who had just transferred to Illinois. Now he had liked Renee. She definitely wasn't going to be the love of his life. But she had been...special. Yeah, Renee was exactly what he needed. And wasn't he just the lucky one, he had her number stored in his cell.

Strolling out the back door, he ambled along a path that led down to the creek as he called, hoping she'd be home and not out. Renee was a night owl. Terminally. It was late enough for her to be up for the day, though, so she might be out running around—

"Hullo!" that cheerful husky voice called into the phone.

"Hey, sweet, remember me?"

ᏟᎧᏌᏟᎧᏌ

Dylan saw his brother's Blazer and wanted to bang his head on the steering wheel. So what if he had told his brother to come here? Shawn didn't have to take him seriously, now did he?

He sat in the driveway for a few minutes, beating out a rhythm with his fingers on the steering wheel. Dylan was not in the mood for Shawn. His kid brother was annoying even under the best circumstances. This sure as hell wasn't the best circumstances. He'd called Kris three times today. She'd ignored each call. He had a feeling that her mood hadn't improved throughout the day. His certainly hadn't.

Dylan wanted to kick Shawn out and finish what he'd started this morning with Kris. He wanted to clear the air. That was what he wanted.

But that wasn't what he was going to do. Because Kris wasn't going to back down and Dylan wasn't so certain he was ready to make any kind of compromise. Fuck it all. Shawn wanted to get caught in the middle of a cold war, fine. Maybe the company would have Kris acting a little less...chilly. He needed her help with this—needed an extra pair of eyes and an extra pair of hands running things.

There was still a lot of work that had to be done here and Dylan wasn't going to be here to do it. Either tomorrow or the day after, he was going to have to head down to Slade, Kentucky, and follow up a lead. There was a guy living there who just might have a clue about where Missy had ended up.

There was a chance it could get ugly and Dylan was just fine with that. He was in the mood for a fight anyway. The redneck had been riding shotgun in the van when Missy had been kidnapped. And according to Jadus Monroe, he had gone on with Missy for the second leg in her trip. Jadus had been the pick up guy. But he said, after Dylan *convinced* him to talk a little, that the other guy knew more.

There was a good ole boy tight knit community in Kentucky and they weren't about to let a kid like Jadus inside. But Jadus had listened, and watched. Apparently Jadus had sensed there was a lot going on and he wanted in on it. Or at least more money. Mick Langley had taken the girl on down to Slade, Kentucky, without realizing Jadus was tailing him. Thank God for greedy bastards like Monroe, Dylan thought.

"Quit stalling," Dylan told himself, shaking his head. He grabbed the handle and shoved open the door. As he did, he glared at Shawn's truck and wished it was about a thousand miles from here.

"Don't look so happy there, bro," Shawn said from the left.

Dylan continued to stare at the Blazer without batting an eyelash. "I'm rethinking. You'd be more comfortable in a hotel. My treat."

Shawn laughed, but it was a humorless sound. Almost forced. But when Dylan looked at him, his brother just shrugged. "Your welcoming committee has already invited me to stay," he said. "She's cooking supper. Steaks on the grill. Potatoes. Salad. I think I wanna marry her."

Dylan snarled at him. Shawn's mouth quirked up in a halfhearted smile that had Dylan's eyes narrowing. "She's too good for you. Besides, you have to finish growing up, kid," Dylan said in an offhand manner, waiting to see the fire burn in Shawn's eye. His brother couldn't ever resist the chance to fight.

But Shawn only shrugged. "Way she's been snarling when she hears your name, I'm thinking she's probably too good for your sorry ass, too," the youngest Kline said, lifting one broad shoulder as he stared sightlessly into the woods just beyond Dylan's house. His eyes, usually so easy and carefree, looked troubled. "I'd suggest you start working on that, Dylan."

Then he turned and ambled up the walk, his booted feet falling silently on the brick way as Dylan stared after him.

Shawn had just walked away from an argument with his brother.

Something was definitely not right.

Chapter Nine

Kris flexed her hands nervously, letting them hover above the keyboard as Shawn and Dylan hollered at a baseball game on the TV downstairs. *Thank* God, she thought fervently as they had finally settled down to something. Besides hanging at her elbows, that is. After Shawn had gotten back from his walk, he had been watching her with dark, intense eyes that were far too unsettling.

And Dylan, well, he just *watched.* And everything about him had always unsettled. And aroused....

Aggravated? she suggested to herself pithily.

Smothering a laugh, she thought, *Yeah. That too.*

Loitering in a chat room full of teenagers could be so annoying, and so...enlightening, it was almost disturbing. Most of them were just frustrated kids. But others, others concerned her, bothered her. Every time *Silverwolf* came on, her instincts screamed at her.

Not to run and hide, but to run and find.

He was the link to Missy. There was something there.

Something...

A familiar little beep sounded. *"You're quiet tonight,"* the message in the IM box read. It was *Silverwolf.* Greedy bastard. Smiling, she typed out, *"Stuff on my mind. Sorry."*

"Need 2 talk?"

Kris replied in the negative and waited, holding her breath.

"Mom has 2 take me into Lex tomorow. We don't go there much. But I can prolly ditch her for a coupla hours if ya wanna go to the Greene Mall. We can talk, U can blow steam."

Kris's mouth curved into a hot, pleased smile. *"Maybe. When do you want to meet, Silverwolf?"*

CRCBCRCB

Shawn waited until Kris pulled out before he called Renee. The cop couldn't have been any more than five minutes from the house, he figured, because by the time he had pulled on a shirt and washed his face, she was banging on the front door, her pretty brown eyes hot and glowing with excitement, a lust he hadn't ever seen.

A need. Like what he saw in Dylan's eyes, he mused as he stood aside. "Damn, girl. You never looked that excited to see me," he teased gently as he led her down to Kris's office. "She might have moved stuff. I doubt she's worried about me snooping. But Dylan—different story."

"Anything. Find me something. Anything," Renee said. "That bastard Moorehead chased me off the force because I wouldn't let some cases go. Called me a hysterical female, theatrical, overimaginative... None of that would matter, except it turned the cases over to some jackass who couldn't find his dick with a roadmap."

The hungry light in her eyes, the tensed and ready set of her body made Shawn pause. "If this is nothing..."

Renee smiled, some of the tension easing out of her body as she lifted a hand to caress his cheek. "I got to see you, babe.

Regardless, it won't be...*nothing*." Her blonde curls danced merrily around her face as she tossed her head and smiled saucily at him. "I'd travel a day for that chance any time."

Shawn covered her hand with his and pressed it gently before kissing it and moving away. "Come on. Kris left in an all-fire hurry this morning. Something's not right. I can feel it."

It wasn't nothing.

Renee read the papers aloud to him after he simply barred her way when she tried to leave, her eyes dark and angry. "That's my brother's woman," he said quietly. "My sister's best friend—her other half. If you think you can waltz out of here and leave me behind, well, you had better remember exactly who it is you are dealing with."

Renee sized him up. She was pretty sure she could take him—hell, no she couldn't. The gun at her back wasn't even an option. Grimly, she said, "Your brother's woman is either a damned lunatic or a genius. How in the hell did she piece this together?"

Succinctly, she condensed it down as far she could, pacing the room as she read, knowing that watching him would only make him uncomfortable. Hell, so he had a problem with letters.

Renee couldn't understand algebra. Her tongue tripped as she came to the neatly printed entry about the girl who had IM'ed her out of the blue. The cop in her was tensed and ready, on full alert, even as part of her snickered... *phony!*

The talks about the other girls. Several of them.

There was a name that was far too familiar. *Slvrnghtgale...* A name Renee knew hadn't been online in months. Andrea Silver, the sweet-faced teen with the voice of an angel who had gone missing from Fayette County a year ago. This was the case that had pushed her into overdrive, into overtime, into near insanity.

Up and missing without a trace.

Loved to dance, loved to sing, most likely had a career in it. Overly protective parents who never let her out of their sight, and the girl was itching to try her wings. She had, slipping out of the house one night a year ago, last seen talking to two men, apparently, with very minimal descriptions available and then she continued on to her destination.

She was never seen again.

Renee had worked the task force that had been formed to locate the local celebrity with her bell-like voice and her innocent charm. She had fallen in love with the innocence that smile held and her heart had broken a little more every day as nothing had been unearthed.

"These are the people who took one of my kids," Renee said quietly, her fingers clutching the papers spasmodically, a muscle twitching right beside her eye. "I don't understand it. How does she know this? We couldn't find a *damn* thing. *Nothing.*"

Clearing her throat, she settled her hips against the desk and stared at the papers, not at Shawn, not out the window, but at the papers. "There is another girl, closer. Missy. Geez, this woman details everything. They took her, but she wasn't the fighter they wanted her to be. She's being returned..."

"Returned to where?" Shawn asked softly, a full-throttle rage just boiling behind his teeth.

"The slave house where they took her. She didn't meet satisfaction," Renee said "And he wants a replacement."

The rage shining in Shawn's eyes damned near eclipsed her own. Fortunately, she decided that having him ride with her was a good thing. Because driving around with him would be easier than moving him.

"Slave house?" he repeated carefully.

"White slavery. They take women, kids or young women off the streets and sell them into sexual slavery. It's not white slavery—it's sexual slavery, and the problem is growing like you wouldn't believe."

"And Kris is right in the middle of it," Shawn said softly, moving over and gently tugging the papers from her hands, staring at them as if they were written in Greek before taking them away and laying them face down.

"I'll go and catch up with her. We can follow her, keep up—"

Shawn laughed. "No. Darlin', that is my brother's woman. You will not be doing a damn thing without him knowing. If you want to go and find him while I go and tag Kris, feel free. But, babe, you are not leaving without one of us," Shawn said, his voice lowering, a soft, humorless smile creasing his face as he dipped his head. His mouth was just a breath away from hers. There was a warning in his eyes making her heart skitter in her chest even as she cursed herself.

"Shawn, babe," she said, mockingly, as she tried to remind herself not to be intimidated by the man standing in front of her. "I'm a cop. All I would have to do is make a few phone calls—"

He laughed. "Don't kid either one of us. They didn't believe you last time and you don't want to chance it this time or risk the bastards sliding any further away." Silky blond curls tumbled into his green eyes, keen and sharp, no longer soft and dreamy and he smiled a cold, knife-edged smile. "Now are we going to go and get my brother? I don't think he wants to let his woman get any closer to these guys than she already is."

That dark dangerous look on his face had Renee swallow and rub her hands down her jean-covered thighs. "Is she his woman or yours?" she asked, frowning.

Shawn laughed, shaking his head as he stepped back, skimming the back of his hand down her cheek. "Oh, Kris is all his. Pretty as she is, well... She's definitely not what I'm looking for."

"Hmmm, I remember. You'll know that when you see it, won't you, lover?" Renee asked, feeling an old burn of jealousy rip through her. Then she swallowed and pulled back. "C'mon, let's go get him."

ℭℛℭℛℭℛℭℛ

Kris sat on the high stool, sipping her cappuccino, waiting.

She was out of her mind.

So totally out of her mind. Waiting here for a man who would likely try to kidnap her. Well, the *her* he thought she was. But she couldn't exactly change her mind either. If she up and left, she was scared to death the bastard might show up and try to...

Kris sat up slowly, feeling a cold chill slide up her spine. All around her was the low buzz of a normal Wednesday in a busy mall, chattering parents, sedate music, nothing new that she could see. Nothing out of the ordinary. Not even a man. Very few teenagers, even. A few preteens, lots of toddlers, preschoolers, and parents...

A dark-haired, brooding girl entered her line of sight as Kris continued to stare and wait, breathing shallowly. He was coming closer. Kris's eyes flew to the girl. A red alert started flashing in her head. *Leave. Damn it. Leave.*

The girl glanced up, a frown on her pale, pretty face. And she was pretty, even though her dyed black hair made her look far too pale. Her spiky black brows gave her an almost elfin appearance and her mouth was rosy red even without lipstick. Her eyes danced over Kris without connecting and locked on somebody behind Kris. She looked almost hypnotized and Kris felt a fear slide through her belly as somebody entered her peripheral vision, moving past her and glancing at her, sizing her up and dismissing her.

It was him.

And he wasn't alone.

Kris couldn't see anybody, but she knew as well as she knew her own name that he wasn't alone. Shit. Lifting her eyes, she stood slowly, moving up to the girl who was still staring at the man who slid in and out of the mall customers, an idle, friendly smile on his face.

But his eyes kept going back to the girl who was watching him avidly, almost hungrily.

"He's too old for you," Kris said, keeping her voice light and friendly as she kicked her leg over the bench the girl was sitting on, straddling it and studying the girl's face. "And he's up to no good."

The girl gave her a snide look and asked, "He your boyfriend? Nah. Can't be. Doesn't look like he knows who you are." Pushing her hair back, she slid him a flirtatious glance as he circled back around and headed back her way.

Kris cocked a brow at her. "No, kid. He isn't my boyfriend. He's trouble." Taking a deep breath, she decided what the hell. "He's what they would have called a slaver a couple of hundred years ago. He is here looking for a girl to kidnap so he can sell her to the highest bidder, somebody who will turn that girl into a body slave. Preferably a kid, a young one who is young enough to be clean, healthy, hopefully a virgin, and sassy and feisty enough to fight, and keep fighting."

The girl's eyes widened, her brows disappearing under that spiky fringe of hair. She looked as though she didn't know whether she wanted to laugh or just get up and go call for the men in the white coats. Kris smiled and offered her own cell phone. "Go ahead and call the loony hospital. But stay here. Don't go with him. Don't leave here for a long, long time and have somebody you know come and pick you up," Kris said.

The girl's eyes dropped to the phone.

Kris could feel eyes on her. Angry eyes, *knowing* eyes.

Busted.

The girl frowned at her and asked, "Why? Are you nuts?"

"Could be..." Lifting her chin, she met the eyes of the man standing across the corridor. He was staring at her. No longer at the girl, but at Kris. Kris let a cool, cocky smile cross her face even as the fear that had been snaking through her came to full bloom inside her belly. Lifting her chin, she said in a level voice that carried, "I think you're looking for me."

And then she looked back at the girl. "I'm not crazy. And I'm not wrong. But even if I am, what have you got to lose by humoring me?"

The girl glanced over her shoulder as Kris spoke, catching a glance of the man's eyes.

Something she saw there froze her. "Holy fuck, did you have to do that?" she hissed, her head whipping around as she stared at Kris.

The sound of solid male boot heels on the ground echoed far too loudly in the crowded mall. Kris swallowed her fear and said quietly, "Go to the music store and hang out there. Take the cell phone, kid, and call whoever you know for a ride. Wait there—"

"Look, lady, if he's that much bad news..."

"So do I get two in exchange for one, I wonder?" a soft voice said, filled with humor. It was a warm, sexy voice, filled with humor, heat.

Lifting her eyes, Kris shoved the phone into the girl's hand and pushed her away. "I said, *go*."

"No. The girl stays. I don't know who you are, but you played a bad game with me. I'll take you both."

Kris smiled. "No. You see, I will start screaming. The worst you can do is shoot me with the gun I know you have." Her eyes flashed. "I know what you have planned, and to me, death sounds much more pleasant. You don't really want that attention, do you? So she is going to walk away, and I will watch her walk into the music store."

His eyes narrowed. "Guns... What is this talk of guns? I am a lover of flesh, which you somehow know. Why would I bruise such lovely flesh with a gun?" he said silkily, reaching out and trailing his hand down her cheek.

Kris lifted her head, far enough back that he wasn't touching her. "Because you do not like being surprised or outwitted by a damned bloody bitch of a woman," she sneered, curling her lip. "And don't lie. You have a gun. I know it. It's at the small of your back. You have one gun, and two knives, and your hands, the thing you prefer the most to use on women."

The girl was still sitting, almost afraid to move as though she feared drawing attention to herself. In her small, pale hands, she held Kris's cell phone and she started to shake, her entire body quivering.

"All right. She can go."

"And the men you brought are going to be in front of us when you head out. I saw them come in. If they even try to touch to her, I'll know. And my cooperation ends."

The cool, complacent look in his eyes faltered, replaced by one of pure fury. "Who the fuck are you? You are no cop—I know the smell of cop." A chilly smile graced his face. "I don't think that's what I smell here."

Kris fought the heated flush that raced up her cheeks at his offhand degrading comment. An icy glint slid through her eyes. "No. I'm not a cop. Not a private investigator, not anything. But I do know more than you'd like." Licking her lips, she leaned forward and whispered, "I know about the pretty little song bird... Her singing stopped, didn't it? And Missy, I know about Missy. So do plenty of ot—"

Kris's breath left her in a rush as he whirled her and pressed her against him in a bizarre lover's embrace, leaning down to croon in her ear, "Enough, bitch. Before I cut you open here and now and damn the consequences. I've run before, I'm good at it. And you'll be dead before you even hit the floor...know what a stiletto in your heart will do to it? And you'll still look so lovely too."

He flashed it long enough for her to see the skinny, deadly point before sliding it back inside the sleeve of his coat.

Fast... Her heart skittered in and out of her chest and she licked her lips, forcing the words out, "You can run, maybe from the cops who don't know that many personal details...*yet.* But can you run from the people you work with? A lot of them will be feeling their asses fry. And they will be coming after you, too." Stiffening her hands, she slowly pushed them away from her chest as much as she could. Her gaze jumped around and she knew to almost anybody who looked, they'd just see a man hovering over a woman in a tight embrace, his arms enfolding her from behind.

As his skin touched hers, her eyes clouded over, the feel of his skin on hers forcing a cold wind through her body as his mind merged ever so briefly with hers. "There's one man, in particular, that you don't want to have chasing you. He scares you."

"Shut up," he rasped in her ear.

Kris laughed shakily before she lapsed into silence, debating her options. She could scream...but if she did that, he might slide that stiletto into her heart, between her ribs, piercing the sac that held the heart, the tissue, the muscle... Kris swallowed, feeling a cold sweat breaking out on her body, a nauseating fear. But even more, if she screamed, she would never have the chance to get to the girls and *maybe* try to save them.

Dylan would come.

He would find her, the girls, and this man would be *stopped*.

Her breathing steadied and her voice firmed. "Slide that stiletto in me. Go ahead. And see how much trouble that doesn't save you. I'm not afraid of dying. I'm more worried about *you* not dying."

She felt the tension race through him and his hands tightened to the point of pain on her wrists. "Let's go."

Kris slid the dark-haired pixie a sidelong look out from under her lashes, hoping the girl would be *smart*. Or at least paranoid enough to not take the chance.

"Bitch, if you want to live, telling me you want me dead isn't a good way to get started," he said as he forced her out into the bright sunlight. She kept track of the men around them as they each exited differently, through different doors, one reading a paper, one munching on a sandwich, another just ambling out, staring at Kris with cold, soulless eyes. And he had one hand wrapped around the pixie's arm, who was staring at Kris with pleading eyes.

Kris could *feel* words in her head. *I'm sorry... They want to hurt you... I just wanted to help...*

Kris tsked under her breath and stopped, slamming her elbow back into the man's gut before aiming her chilly green eyes at a cruiser that was crossing the back of the mall parking lot. "And bringing her out right in front of my face was a very bad move," Kris said harshly, evading the hands that came from behind. "Let the girl go or the show is up. *Now.*"

"I decide when the show is up, bitch," he growled, trying to crowd her towards his car, but unwilling to make too much of a scene. *Yet.*

Kris could sense his reluctance to draw attention to them. He hadn't been prepared for this, for anything like this. And his eyes were gleaming with a half mad desire to get away right now. Without drawing attention, and *with* a girl. He was used to scared girls, ones who thought that if they did what he said, they just might be okay. Not a woman who knew she was likely good as dead anyway.

"Not this time. Not with me. I know the worst you can do. And I know what you have planned for any girl you grab off the streets is worse than anything you can do to me."

Kris had learned the art of bluffing very well. Tossing her hair back, she evaded yet another set of hands, not hearing them or seeing them, just somehow feeling the man behind her, rotating so that the parking lot was now at her back. The cruiser was moving closer. But he hadn't noticed her. Not yet. One man, though, the one who held the girl, was leaving the sidewalk, taking her with him.

"Don't take one more step," she called out, tossing caution aside. A couple of disinterested shoppers tossed her a look before moving on.

Kris turned and moved over to the man who had just tossed her a smirk. She smirked back and opened her mouth to scream.

"Steve. Look at her face," one of the guys said, shifting from one foot to another. "C'mon."

Smiling, Kris closed her mouth, swallowing the scream and said, "Yes. Look at my face, Steve. I'll scream."

His big, cruel hand fell away and the girl pulled away, gasping. Kris shoved her in the direction of the police cruiser. "Go to them. Fast."

The men had barely even time to blink before they swore heatedly, one automatically reaching for a gun only to have the ringleader grab his hand and hiss, "Are you nuts? Get the fuck to your car. *Move.*"

He shot Kris a lethal glance. "They die. Tonight. You could have saved them."

Kris smiled. "I already have."

He took off, sliding away from her like oil on water. Kris tossed the girl a glance, seeing her stumble to a stop right as the police cruiser noticed her, gunning the car in her direction, the lights flashing, a grim-faced, middle-aged lady riding shotgun with a younger man.

Kris smiled and retreated back into the mall.

She didn't need to be with that bastard to follow him. She wasn't exactly certain how she knew.

But he couldn't possibly hope to lose her now.

They always liked the same place, that luxurious cabin in Slade, perched over a lake, hanging onto the mountain, private, away from the city, where they could hear everybody who came and went. She had seen it, seen more than she wanted, the second he touched her.

With a little luck, she *might* get there before the others. Missy was there, right now, suffering and running out of time.

In her hurry through the mall, she didn't notice the slim blonde who came out of the crowd, a dark frown on her face as she started to tail the tall redhead.

Crazy, Renee thought, shaking her head in sheer shock. The girl had just totally broken every rule of trying to protect a kidnapping victim. *And totally inspired.*

That man wasn't *too* likely to kill somebody who could still bring him money, especially since Kris had made it clear that she'd rather die than fail.

When the phone rang, she didn't even glance at the number. "I'm babysitting. I'll call you when I have something worth sharing. Now go away."

Chapter Ten

Shawn barged through the door to Dylan's office just as Dylan was on his way out, ready to pound his fist through the wall from sheer frustration. Dead ends. Fucking dead ends. Everything had stalled. Damn it, he had left something unturned, something crucial and it was going to keep him from finding Missy that much longer. Damn it, Kris. Her and her selfish—

Selfish. Hell, he couldn't exactly say that, but what the fuck? Didn't she want to find the girl? What happened to that need he had seen burning inside her eyes?

"Shawn, I don't have time for your crap right now," Dylan snapped, shoving his arms into the sleeves of his jacket, adjusting the tail of it to make sure his gun was covered. "I've got a lost girl I need to find, no leads, no clues, because the one person in this world who seems to able to connect with people and track people down seems to have lost interest in doing that. Kris doesn't give a damn any more and I have *no* clues. I've no time—"

"Shove it up your ass and come on already," Shawn barked, jerking his head to the door without so much as another word as Dylan moved aside just in time to avoid them crashing face to face. "Your darling lady who has lost interest has just gotten ass deep in trouble."

Dylan paused, only long enough to take a breath, and asked, "What?"

A cool, feral smile curved at Shawn's mouth. "If she doesn't give a damn then maybe you need to go enroll in that clown college they got down in Florida. She's been investigating it all along, big brother. And she's ass deep in alligators...as Renee would like to say," Shawn said, heading down the hall, not even bothering to wait and see if Dylan was coming.

He bypassed Shawn in five seconds, a dark, dangerous look on his face, his brows low over his eyes and his hands clenching into fists. Fury and fear grappled for an even hold inside him as he silently kicked his own ass. Should have damned well known she was up to something. Kris didn't give up on anything and she had just let this go...in exchange for IM chats and surf the web?

"You're gonna tell me how you know this before I get rid of your useless ass, little brother," Dylan said, shoving the door open, feeling the rage course through him.

Shawn smirked. "Yeah. Sure. Keep telling yourself that, Dylan. You ready for a ride? She's en route to Slade, Kentucky, small town a little outside of—"

"I know where the hell Slade is. I've got a guy down there I've been needing to contact. If you tell me that Kris has gone to question him...I'll beat her ass," Dylan muttered, fury racing through him, mingling with fear. "What in the hell is she doing, spying on me?"

Shawn snickered, shaking his head and he shoved open the door to Dylan's Blazer and leaped in. "It's not one you have to worry about, Dylan. It's the whole party apparently."

Dylan growled as he gunned the engine and threw it into reverse. "How exactly do you know about it?"

"Ask Kris when you see her. Renee was reading some notes, very long, detailed notes." A wry laugh filled the air. "I figured out something wasn't right, but if I was reading them, I'd still be there working my way through them."

Long moments of silence passed as Dylan thought of her and that damned laptop, that damned office door she kept closing in his face every time he walked by, every time he tried to talk to her. He had assumed she was working on stuff for Escapade.

Pushing him back—that's what she had been doing, she'd been pushing him back, keeping him from seeing what she had been up to.

Because she had known he would stop her? Damn it, *stop*... That fucking word would have pissed her off. Fuck. He had known she'd want to be involved with this, from the time of that first amazing dream. But she could have found a little less *dangerous* way to show him how damn wrong he was.

Dylan said quietly, "I am going to kill her."

"You don't sound very surprised," Shawn said as they sped down the Mountain Parkway to Slade.

"Surprised. Maybe I should be a little. I should have figured she was up to something, should have known," Dylan whispered, shaking his head. He hadn't, though. If anything happened to her, it was his fucking fault. *His*. "How far are they ahead of us?"

Shawn shrugged. "Dunno. We may get there around the same time. And I reckon I ought to let you know about Renee."

CRCRCR

Kris knew the truck was on her ass.

Glancing in the rearview mirror again, she wove in and out of the light midweek traffic. The problem with rural Kentucky? Not enough traffic, no place to turn, no place to lose somebody tailing her.

She hadn't really had the opportunity to try in New York, but she imagined it would have been a hell of a lot easier to lose somebody on a road that didn't stretch out into the clear blue sky. Of course, there was also much less smog here...and Dylan.

Damn his stubborn ass.

"You ought to be sitting here with me, slick," she muttered, shaking her head as she punched the gas and shot through a narrow opening between a semi and a tow truck. The sporty little BMW handled it like a dream. She smiled as the distance between her and the truck grew.

She didn't feel anything *wrong* coming from whoever was there. And she was leaving herself wide open, more open than she had ever felt in her life. It was bizarre, like somebody had just taken the blinders off of her for the first time in her life. From the second she had stopped fighting it, everything seemed clearer, the colors, the scents, the sound of her own heart. She shot off the highway at the very last second and laughed as the truck missed it.

Once more alone on the road, she sped down the little two-lane highway, following that weird feeling deep in her gut.

Kris knew months before she would have shoved it away.

Now she clung to it, welcomed it.

If she was lucky, it would keep her alive long enough to lambaste Dylan for letting her feel like she couldn't take this to him.

But Kris was desperately afraid she wouldn't be able to save the kids and herself. "If I can keep you from doing it

235

again," she whispered softly. "That will be enough. I'll make it be enough."

In her head, she was starting to hear sobs and pitiful screams. They had to stop.

CRCICRCI

Kris was already out of sight by the time Renee was able to U-turn and catch the other exit, careening down the highway and slamming to a stop at the Shell station right at the base of the mountains. Renee climbed out, whirling and kicking her tire viciously, swearing in a long, heated litany, the words falling from her soft, rosy lips in a fashion that would have done Dylan and his Ranger buddies proud.

"How in the fuck?" she half shouted, slamming her fist on the hood. "She's an editor, for cripes sake. She plays with computers and reads books, and how the hell is she doing this?"

Taking a deep breath, Renee reached for her phone and hit the redial button. She was still trying to figure out how Kris had made her when Dylan answered the phone this time.

"Do yourself a very big favor, Chicago, and tell me that you have Kris standing there with you," he said.

Renee cocked a brow. Damn. Just like his brother, sexy growling voice and all. "Sorry, slick, and don't insult me by calling me a Yankee. That girl must have the instincts of a damned coyote or something. She's gone. Made me quicker than I don't know what, and she's long gone, flitting away to the mountains..." Her words trailed off as a familiar truck pulled into the Shell station.

The man from the mall. Grim-faced, furious, eyes full of death, he came out of the truck and headed into the station. Halfway there, he did a chameleon, as Renee watched. He went from a brutal man who looked totally soulless...to a sweet-eyed, simple-faced farm boy, tucking his hands into his pockets and nodding in that way only the men of the South can, making you feel as though you were sitting on a plantation porch, with a long lacy dress, sipping at mint julep.

Oh, his clothes were still the same, his hair hadn't changed, except for how he had run his hand through it, mussing it endearingly. But he looked...*other*... In a way that Renee simply couldn't describe. Hell, she was a damned cop and she would have been hard-pressed to make a connection between this sweet-looking old home boy and the bastard she had watched from the shadows as he loomed threateningly over Kris Everett.

Sliding back against the truck, she interrupted Dylan's rant of, "Where the fucking hell are you?" with a calm, "One of the ringleaders just appeared on the scene. Where are you?"

ᏣᏆᏣᏆ

This entire thing had gone to hell in a handbasket as far as Dylan was concerned. It was out of control, with a stray cop he didn't know out there watching a dickless son of a bitch, and his little brother riding shotgun.

Worst of all, his woman was out there.

Hell, all he needed was Nikki to complicate things. Nikki, *shit*. If anything fucking happened to Shawn—

"You're out of this, brother. We pull over at the gas station and I'm dumping you. Nik will have my ass for letting you—"

Shawn started to laugh, a deep amused chuckle rolling from his chest as he leaned his head back against the seat. "You still don't get it, Dylan. This isn't the Army anymore. You don't call the shots, you don't give orders, we don't take them. Now you wanna try kickin' my ass hard enough that I can't get up off the ground, well, you can do that." Then Shawn's voice went hard as steel. "But you don't get it. Kris is like family. She's Nikki's best friend. And she's your woman. People don't fuck with the family, Dylan. We stopped letting that happen a long time ago and I'm not about to change that now just because I didn't become a card-carrying, grenade-launching lunatic."

Dylan suppressed an amused laugh and said, "Damn it. These people…"

"I grew up in the same place you did, Dylan, I learned the same fucked up facts of life." He slid Dylan a narrow look out of flinty green eyes, all the humor and laughter gone as he warned, his voice low and hard, "Don't push me. I'm already pissed enough as it is."

As Dylan punched the gas and shot around the truck, his kid brother's words echoed in his mind. *She's your woman. People don't fuck with the family…*

My woman.

Mine.

Narrowing his eyes, he reached for his cell phone. "No. They don't fuck with the family." Casting the sun a glance, he wondered just how much time they had. How much he needed.

A low, gruff voice came on the line and said, "Unless the damn sky is falling, go the fuck away."

Laughing, Dylan said, "Come on, Chicken Little. I got bigger problems than the sky falling. I need hands and eyes."

CRCRCRCR

Flopping on his back, Jerry lay staring at the ceiling after Dylan had hung up. "Well, sure as hell beats just a Christmas card," he grumbled as he climbed from the bed and grabbed his pager before punching a number in and the last three digits, letting people know it wasn't an urgent *official* matter.

But it was something they'd want to know about anyway. Nearly a year. Nearly a damn year of silence and then this...hell. Well, it *did* beat a Christmas card.

And this could be...*fun.*

Within thirty minutes, he had gotten a hold of seven guys, seven Rangers, active or otherwise...and most of them could even be there by nightfall.

CRCRCRCR

"Sure she's a cop? I think she's got part bloodhound in her," Dylan said, shaking his head as Renee moved up on his bumper. He had exited the freeway and reached for his phone to call her, but there she was, right behind. The phone rang.

"Where is she?"

"So nice to talk to you, too, Dylan."

"Renee, where in the hell is Kris?" he demanded.

"Now that, I don't know. But there's somebody else you probably want to see. And I do know where he is. Well, where he will be."

Dylan snarled. "Damn it, I don't care about anybody or anything but Kris. Where in the hell is she?"

"You mean you don't want to know where to find the guy who tried to grab her earlier?"

Dylan fell silent. His hand squeezed the cell phone so tight, he was surprised the phone didn't shatter.

"That's what I thought. There's a campsite about two miles down. On the right. Pull in there." She hung up on him and in the rearview mirror, he watched as she stopped riding his bumper.

"Shawn, I'm going to kill your cop."

His brother laughed. "I've felt like that a time or two myself. You know, if you try to give her the same song and dance you read me, I hope you're ready to get her fist in your gut." He straightened as Dylan pulled off the road into a scenic, overnight campsite and he grunted. "Cops like her just might have kept you and me a little more on the straight, the narrow."

Shawn cocked his head, watching with interest as Renee climbed out of her truck a few heartbeats later. She didn't approach them—instead, she headed for the big map. The map was behind a clear piece of plastic, along with information about the local game, fish and camping.

Renee traced a hand over it and cast a smile at Dylan. She winked at him and headed back to her truck. He could hear another truck pull in. Renee didn't stop. She dropped something and Dylan looked down, watched the map flutter out of her hand. She climbed into her truck and drove away without looking back at them.

Truck doors slammed. From the corner of his eye, Dylan saw a couple of guys climbing out the truck. One disappeared behind the camper. The other headed in their direction.

Dylan kept his eyes on the camper as he deposited money in the self-depository. Shawn ambled over the map, studying it with narrow eyes as he slapped Renee's map against his hand, whistling under his breath. "I don't know why in the hell I let you drag me out here, Jackson," he said, reaching up and plowing a hand through his hair.

The "Jackson" elicited a sneer from Dylan. He had hated that name for as long as he could remember.

"Jackass," he said mildly as he came up to study the map. He looked at the place on the map where Renee had indicated. *Whispering Arches.* "Wish it was a little more detailed. The information about the park on the web sucked."

"You guys from out of town?"

Shawn's eyes widened. He hadn't heard him coming up behind them. Dylan had, but that silence, almost complete total silence as he moved, he didn't like that. "Yeah. Out of Somerset. Looking for a couple of places to maybe do some pictures later of my girlfriend."

"Pictures, huh?" Mick Langley asked, a hint of a smile on his mouth. He had a scraggly beard, dark blondish hair, powerful muscles under a worn blue T-shirt. He looked just like a hundred other guys in the rural Kentucky county looked. Except for those eyes, Dylan decided. He didn't like those eyes.

"I'm a nature photographer, freelance. But I do commissions from time to time," Dylan lied. "With fall coming up, I thought this might be a good place. The rocks, the untouched look of the place. The...privacy."

"Don't let him fool you with the professional talk." Shawn laughed. "He likes taking nekkid pictures of his girl."

Kris would either blush to the roots of her very red hair over that, or punch Shawn in the gut.

"Damn. Some guys have all the luck," Mick said, grinning, moving up to the map. "If you're looking for rock formations, privacy...then you need to steer clear of this part." He indicated a wide circle and said, "This loop here, all the rocks are too easily accessed and a bunch of new age hikers love to come out there anyway. What else you need?"

"Just good light. Good rock formation, I'd like some cliffs that don't have all the railing and modern touches added. We're hanging around for the night, pitching a couple of tents," he said smoothly. "I want to go ahead and scout out the areas I plan on using, maybe bring her up here this weekend and get a few done now, see what they look like. I want the colors of fall in it." Now that really wasn't a half bad idea...Kris naked on one of the rock formations, leaning against the arch with the sun spilling down on her face, that dark red hair spilling all over her shoulders.

A vicious smile curled his lips. Later. After he tore apart the bastards who had dared to threaten to her.

Something in Mick's demeanor changed, going from easygoing good ole boy to a watcher. Oh, he was still smiling, still laid back and easy as can be, but a subtle tension had filled him. They needed a better guy watching than this one. "Staying the night? Well, if you really have some hours to kill and don't mind a good long hike to get there, you need to try out this one," Mick suggested, pointing to an area far off the route, as far away from Whispering Arches as he could get.

"This area isn't really named, but it's full of younger arches and a ton of formations that just are out of this world. The younger arches aren't quite as pretty as Natural Bridge, but it's gorgeous. And it's in the national park, inside Daniel Boone. They kept a little more of the...nature there. Plus, not too many people hit that spot. So, there's your privacy."

Dylan studied the map and figured if the average Joe was going to hike that faintly dotted smaller loop, it would take the better part of a day. Or more. "How do I get there?"

CRCRCRCR

Mick felt the cold sweat dry off his body as the two men drove back out of the small parking lot, pausing to check the map, the younger of the two pointing down the road that would lead to Daniel Boone National. Shit. That little encounter had made him a little more nervous than normal, even though he had watched this area on these nights for the past three years. In that time, he had been forced to deal with yammering tourists, free-loving wannabe hippies, retired and vacationing cops.

Tons of photographers came through here. They loved the place. Mick couldn't care less. He couldn't hunt in the forest and he hated fishing. Well, he wasn't supposed to hunt in the forest. He had taken down a prize buck or two in here while killing time on sale nights.

Licking his lips, he wondered about the "return". It wasn't something that happened too often. But Courte hated lost revenue. And if no other buyer was interested, the good ole boys could buy her, combine enough money and have at her. Their own personal little slut.

He scowled, thinking of the last one. Little bitch had gotten away though—darting out into the woods, running like a demon possessed and screaming. Mick sneered. Stupid bitch. Her run had taken her headlong off one of the cliffs. She had still been breathing when they found her, some forty feet below, her breath rattling in and out of her lungs.

Mick had laughed at her. "Well, you ended up in a worse place, bitch, didn't you?" He had been *furious*. It had been more than a year since they had been able to keep a girl to themselves. All the merchandise had to be untouched, unsoiled. And if it came back, and it did, sometimes...of course, they never kept them for long. Around these parts, that was just foolishness.

But a month or so of having a piece of ass any time he wanted it, however he wanted? Nudging her with his foot, he had sneered and taunted, "Getting a coupla fucks looks pretty sweet now, don't it?"

But the girl...Mick shifted, wishing he hadn't started thinking of that.

The girl had looked at him, head on, as Courte came through the woods, his pale blue eyes icy with rage as they studied the dying girl.

She had looked at them and smiled, a peaceful, relieved smile before her eyes moved into the empty space just over Mick's head and she breathed her last. That smile had stayed with him, haunting him at night. Like a harbinger. Mick had decided maybe it was time to pull out. Not because he gave a damn about the fear he had scented on her. He loved that, but because when she had looked at him, *he* had felt a fear.

A sickening one.

Yeah. He was getting out. He'd collect his fee for tonight, get a piece of ass if it was there.

Then he'd clear out. Grab what gear from the trailer he needed and just be gone.

Courte could find another hardass for this job.

CROSCRO

Kris stood on the path at the foot of the small arch.

Something broken ran through her heart, twisting its way through her soul, until her throat ached with the sob that was inside, just begging for release.

The one called *Slvrnghtgale...* Kris had the oddest picture of a singing butterfly, captured in a cage, wings broken, battered. As Kris watched, something ephemeral rose from that dying butterfly with the sweet voice, and she watched as it rose upward.

Throat tight, Kris turned around and studied the small spot. She had to memorize, had to be able to find it again. She'd have to bring Dylan back here. Tears threatened to blind her before she blinked them away as she knelt as stroked her hand down the smooth piece of stone.

That girl had died here.

She studied the rather ornately placed steps that led up the rock wall. There was a security camera, well-hidden high in a tree. If Kris hadn't stopped exactly where she had, she never would have seen it.

She didn't know where to go from here. Her cell phone was gone so she couldn't call Dylan. Part of her knew she should turn back, get away from here and call Dylan. The other part of her wasn't willing to leave.

Her legs were aching, her body weary. Ditching her car in a parking lot more three miles away, she had followed something inside her gut to this spot.

But now that voice was silent. It wasn't going to provide her with a map to get up to whatever lay at the top of the carved and carefully set stone stairway. Not that it wouldn't be nice...because she was getting tired of standing under the camera, trying to figure out a way to move away without them realizing she was there.

That last, screaming warning, no words... just a sudden tension that tore through her when she stumbled onto the spot where a girl had died. It had been the last thing she had picked up on. Now, she was alone in her head. No voices, no crying, no evil whispers. Alone—and it terrified her. She wanted to leave. Wanted to go back.

But Kris wasn't going anywhere.

She had frozen as the camera started to swing back her way and with sheer desperation, she had dove for the spot under it, hoping for only *one* camera.

As the camera swung away again, Kris moved, refusing to look back. She had about fifteen seconds before it swung back to where she was...

Fourteen...

Ten. Rocks scrambled under her feet as she leaped over a stone and prayed there was no one around to hear her. Twenty more feet. She stumbled over a knobby, exposed tree root and hissed, mentally counting. *Five.* With a furious curse, she dashed behind the outcropping ahead right as she hit the mental count of *two.* And she hoped she hadn't messed the count up.

Of course, if she had... "I'll deal with that then," she answered, shaking her head. Right now, she had one hell of a steep hill to climb. It loomed up into the sky, and it looked more like a rock wall than she cared to admit. Plenty of handholds. Yeah, it was climbable. But that didn't mean she should climb it.

"Too late to go back." With a heavy sigh, she studied it for a long moment before picking her path. Then she set upon it, placing her feet carefully, reaching for every handhold and measuring every single step she took before making it.

If she fell, now wouldn't that just make a lovely surprise for these bastards to find? Maybe some of the men liked their kidnapped victims older, out of their teens... Kris's mouth twisted in a snarl. *Please, take me on.* Somebody out of the teenage years, somebody not so easily broken. Somebody who had learned how to fight.

They don't want them strong, not these men. They want them easy to break, and bend. The words, like so many things of late, whispered through her, not just in her mind, but *through* her, echoing inside her mind, her soul.

Others take strong ones, they love the breaking of them. These men want them—pliant. Accepting of their fate. They want them to fight at first...but that's just because they like breaking them.

Kris focused on the next set of rocks as she walked around the small, worn path. It was a rocky hike up, but she and Dylan had done harder climbs. *Dylan...*

Damn it.

He was coming.

She could feel it... *How* was that possible? Against the mossy green leaves that had wound their way up and covered the rocky walls of the mountain, she rested her brow. "This is...enough. I don't want or need anything else in my head," she whispered. "I've gotten this far, I don't *want* anything else intruding on my head."

Resolutely, she set her shoulders and shoved everything beyond getting to the cabin behind a stonewall she envisioned inside her head. After the cabin, she'd deal with these other chaotic, troublesome thoughts running loose in her head.

But for now... Reaching up, she grasped at an exposed root and hauled herself up grimly. For now, the cabin.

By the time she had cleared the mountain, her legs quivered with every step she took and sweat dripped off her body. Her stomach rumbled and growled demandingly and her breath was rasping in and out of her lungs. But she was standing on level ground. Through the trees, she caught the gleam of sun on glass.

"So. I'm here," she murmured. "Now what..."

Keeping behind the trees, studying the house, the ground, it wasn't easy crossing that distance. It should have taken no more than fifteen minutes. By the time she got done measuring every last footfall, and checking for signs of cameras, Kris had spent damn near forty-five minutes crossing the distance. And nearly three hours, just hiking to get here. Damn it, this was taking *too* long.

CRIESCRIES

If that woman's luck held out it was gonna be a damned miracle, he thought. His heart froze in his chest as she somehow managed to evade almost every single line, every laser that would have alerted the men of her arrival.

If he hadn't already deactivated them.

But damn if he wasn't impressed. Maybe Dylan had rubbed off on her, he thought. She was pretty damned good, not just for a civilian. Not settling for the fast route in order to get out of sight, but pacing herself, looking for the quietest way. He settled back against the rock and looked around. Idly, he wondered how much longer he was going to be waiting.

CRIESCRIES

They had windows all over the damn house. Even the part that butted up against the mountain at times had the ceiling angling in such a way so that whoever was in the room could stare up at the night sky through the opening in the trees, wide, open sun-roofs gracing many of the varying angles of the house.

It looked like a pile of wooden blocks gone mad, with the highest part built against the rock wall on all of one side, the angles of the house built into the sharp-angled wall before the mountain fell away into the open air.

Down there, through one of those windows, Kris saw a girl. And then another as she walked by the door, rubbing her bare arms, her head swiveling around madly. Looking for escape. And a third, sitting in a corner. Not cowering, Kris decided, more...accepting.

But she was a little too accepting. And her buyer hadn't wanted her that accepting. They wanted her to fight it a little. Just a little. Enough to make it fun.

Kris worked her way to the very edge of the flattened piece of rock she was sitting on, trying to figure out where to go from here.

Get the girls out. That was what mattered. Getting them out. But how...

Setting her jaw, Kris edged forward and started to swing a leg over. Might as well find out.

"Bad move, sweetie," a soft, low voice said.

Kris froze, fear skittering through her, freezing her blood, closing her throat. It took a minute, but then her heart started beating at a normal pace, and irritation bloomed. Then anger came.

She knew that voice.

Taking a deep, slow breath, she lifted her head and looked around. Damn it, where in the hell was he?

The wind came, bringing a different scent and Kris swallowed. *Is this what a rabbit feels like when the hawk is coming down?* She could smell him. Light sweat, and the scent of male. *All right, if I need to run, now is the time. I am* not *letting him take me away from here. Damn it I've got to finish this.*

But it felt as though as her senses had been totally and completely closed off.

Dampened.

He laughed, the sound a little closer. "Awful timid now, Miz Everett. And you were moving so fine through the trees. That would make some guys I know weep, how damn pretty and quick you moved through the trees. Then ya gotta go and get ready to ruin it."

Slowly, she turned around and stared at a wide chest. Lifting her eyes over that wide chest, up the deep olive skin tone of his neck, she recognized the shape of the face even under the paint that had been slathered on it.

"Is the face paint really needed for these guys, Raintree?" she asked dryly as she closed her eyes in sheer disbelief at her luck. "How in the hell did you end up here?"

"Your boyfriend," he said, a wide grin splitting his face. "And, lady, you pulled a bad move on Dylan. You'll be lucky if he doesn't spank you silly."

"Boyfriend?" she repeated, her brow winging up. It took every damn thing she had to keep her face cool. She was more worried about this guy than she had been facing that sonovabitch in Lexington.

"Yeah, your boyfriend," he said. "He's on your ass, you know."

"Then why don't you go meet up with him and leave me alone for a little while longer? I need to finish this," she said quietly.

He laughed, a low, deep chuckle as he reached up and ran a hand through black, silky straight locks that fell nearly to his shoulders. "Well, now why would I leave you be? He was damn nearly out of his mind thinking you'd get grabbed by one of the snakes he's hunting."

Kris narrowed her eyes. "*He's* hunting? It looks like I beat him here," she said.

"That's a fact. So why go and get your neck broken now?"

She angled her chin up at him. "Damn it, Ethan Raintree, I did a damned good job getting here just *fine* by myself, and I am not going to let you go hauling me out of here. They need me," she said, unaware of how haunted her eyes were looking.

Ethan sighed and reached up, brushing her hair out of her face. "I'm not hauling you anywhere. But I'm not letting you get yourself killed or hurt either. We're going to find someplace safe to wait, and to watch, until they get here," he said, blowing out a frustrated breath. "Something happens to that pretty butt of yours, Dylan would kill me. And I got rather attached to you, seeing how I was tagging you for more than a year. I'd rather you not get injured under my watch."

Kris flushed, shifting further away from him as subtly as she could. "I'm not under your watch anymore—the Army took you off," she reminded him.

He caught the little slide movement and grinned again. Moving back, he let her have a little more space, propping one shoulder against the rock wall. "Girl, you don't know a darn thing about us, still, do you? You are Dylan's. That makes you one of ours. Our watch doesn't end just because the Army says so. It doesn't end. Ever."

"I'm not nervous," she lied. "I'm—uh, I'm kinda tired. Long drive."

The surge of protection that gave her was unreal. He was telling her that because of her connection with Dylan, they would always watch out for her. Unsure what to think, confused, dazed, delighted...but now wasn't the time to think about any of that.

She licked her lips. "Ah, Dylan is coming. Correct? He knows what's going on?" she asked, trying to figure out exactly what had happened. How did Dylan know?

"Yup, he's coming. You don't seem very surprised by that, really. For somebody who was doing this under his nose, that is, wanting to be a cowboy. Cowgirl," he corrected, his eyes sliding back over her. "You sound kind of relieved."

Kris glanced around again, slowly lowering herself to the ground, her legs still weak and shaky from that steep climb. Just that climb, she insisted. Not scared. Not exactly. "I wasn't trying to be a cowboy. Or a cowgirl. I didn't have to do this on my own," she muttered, drawing her legs to her chest. "But I *know* things. He doesn't. I wasn't being left behind on this, letting him come out here blind. Those girls needed me."

Sliding his pale eyes to the cabin, he studied it. "Dylan didn't find them, did he? You did."

Lifting her chin, she simply met his eyes.

"Interesting lady," he murmured, cocking his head as he held her gaze. "Very interesting. But you could have just let Dylan know. He is used to going into things blind. He can handle this shit. He was trained for it. Were you?"

"Maybe not, but I'm the one who found them. They need me."

"So you say." Ethan said nothing else, just studied her for long moments before settling back against the tree, crossing his arms over his chest, his lids lowering over those very disturbing eyes.

The silence of the woods settled around her and Kris felt her lids getting heavy. But she forced herself to keep her gaze focused on the man in front of her. Friend of Dylan's he may way well be, but that didn't mean she could trust him.

Ethan Raintree had never in his life met a woman that stubborn, that resolved, that intense. Hell, she suited Dylan to a bloody T. Her eyes were heavy with exhaustion and fatigue was written in every line of her body. But she didn't sleep.

Didn't trust him enough to do it.

Good thing.

The bastards they were dealing with wouldn't hesitate to use her once they got their hands on her. Not that Ethan would let that happen. He waited, feigning sleep, knowing she wouldn't be able to fight it too much longer. She had expended far too much energy coming up the mountain out of sight the way she had, almost as silent as a whisper. The adrenaline that had been fueling her was seeping out at an amazing rate. She would lose the fight sooner or later and give into her body.

And what a fine one, Ethan mused. Dylan sure as hell had always been a lucky bastard.

CRCRCRCR

Dylan listened to the birdcall, a slow smile spreading across his face. "I'll be damned."

Shawn shot him a furious glance and muttered, "Yeah, you ought to be." Huddled up in a tree like a couple of squirrels, just waiting. "What are we waiting for again?" he whispered gruffly, staring at the house visible through the trees. "I ain't no fucking cat. I don't like sleeping in trees."

"Get over it. You insisted on tagging along. And I've spent the night in much worse places." Dylan sat in the tree like a fucking cat, his back against the trunk, one leg swinging loose, the other drawn up with him resting his elbow on it. But as the second call came whistling through the trees, Dylan cupped one hand next to his mouth and echoed it.

Shawn's eyes narrowed. "That isn't a bird in the trees making that noise," he said appraisingly, studying Dylan. "This some GI Joe crap?"

Dylan chuckled. "GI Joe crap would include a radio, com units, a surveillance team with me knowing where every damn member of the team was. This is...boy scouts," Dylan decided as he kicked one leg over the branch and started to slide soundlessly out of the tree.

Shawn tried to imitate it, but he was swearing and convinced half the mountain knew he was there by the time he had his feet planted on the ground.

"People aren't supposed to move that quick," he said flatly as he looked up at the tree. He had leaves in his hair and dirt all over his clothes from how many times he'd tripped while trying to tail after Dylan.

He was filthy. Dylan, on the other hand, looked like he was out for an easy, breezy walk. After the hike to get here, after climbing more than thirty feet up in a tree to make sure they were out of sight, and now back on solid ground again, and Dylan hadn't even broken a damn sweat. Damn it, hadn't he retired because he wasn't supposed to be able to keep up with the pace a Ranger would set?

"Ass," Shawn muttered, shaking his head.

"You know, it wouldn't do the world a lot of good if a Ranger moved through the woods sounding like a stampeding elephant," Dylan said, grinning. "But don't worry about it. I doubt they'd recognize the difference between you and a herd of deer. Even if we were close enough to the house."

Shawn shook his head and set after Dylan, endeavoring to be a little quieter. But he hadn't even moved three steps before he felt it, somebody else there with them. Instincts he hadn't had to use since his teen years suddenly sprang to life as he slid his eyes to the left, and then to the right, tension racing up his spine.

He was turning his gaze back to his brother when he felt him, the silent, looming presence of somebody behind him. He dropped to the ground, spinning out with his leg at the same time, catching somebody at the ankle, sweeping the bastard's feet out from under him. Then he tucked his shoulder and rolled away. He came to his feet with his hands raised.

"Mother fuck!" the man swore in a low furious whisper.

Shawn met a pair of cool blue eyes as the man slowly sat up, staring at Shawn, and then at Dylan with narrowed eyes. "This the way you say thanks, Dylan?" Jerry Sears asked.

"Not exactly," Dylan said as he moved back up to where his former commander was rising to his feet, staring at Shawn with icy eyes.

"If I wasn't so impressed, I'd be a little pissed off," Jerry said, waiting for Shawn to do something other than scowl at him. When he didn't, Jerry studied him more closely and finally decided, "Shit, Dylan. He's a fucking kid."

"He's louder than a damn buffalo, too," Dylan said agreeably. "But I really can't think of anybody I trust more than him. And for the record, he invited himself along. I wasn't wasting time trying to talk him out of it."

"If his head is anything like yours—"

Shawn made a rude sound finally, interrupting Jerry with a loud snort. "My head is nowhere near that thick, thanks." He

255

moved back off the path and out of the way as he folded his arms.

"Damn, he even has your attitude," Jerry said, moving around Shawn and studying the house through the trees. "Raintree is here already. He was already in Kentucky. Probably betting in Lexington at the track and making his wallet even fatter. Now he *was* supposed to vacate the Midwest more than a week ago, but...he doesn't always listen to his commanding officer very well. In this case, it might be a good thing he didn't. He got here within an hour of you calling and has been haunting the woods since then. He's not talking on his radio, though. Don't know if he's too close to the house or just ignoring me." He pushed a hand through his hair, the thick, straight locks sliding through his fingers, before he cupped a hand over the back of his neck.

Dylan smiled. "Knowing Ethan? Probably both," he summed up as he took point and started to work through the dense underbrush. Hot anticipation was filling him, the hunger for battle, something he had forgotten he missed. And the desire to throttle the stubborn redhead who was putting him through hell.

He'd find her.

Get to the house, check it out, put his brother in a tree where he couldn't do too much damage, and then he'd find her.

CRCBCRCB

Renee had left her truck behind a good two miles. She knew these woods. Granted, it had been years since she had done any hiking here, but she could get to Whispering Arch and take a spot.

Not that anybody had told her not to, but Renee was pretty sure that the men would scowl and try to placate her with something a little more—out of the way. So she had just placed herself out of the way and let them think that was what she was doing.

Not, she thought with a snort, following the faint trail through the trees. Not too many people took the steeper trails in this out of the area loop, which worked to her advantage. Of course, she wasn't too fond of how quiet it was. The wind moving through the trees and the calls of birds were the only noises she heard.

She jumped when a branch broke and froze, placing her back against a tree and leveling her gun, feeling like an idiot. "I'm drawing on Bambi, most likely."

"Nah. Bambi is more graceful. That was probably Thumper," a low, easygoing voice said from the side.

Renee swallowed the yelp that rose in her throat and closed her eyes.

"Now how smart is it for a woman to be hiking these trails alone?"

Opening her eyes, she leveled the gun in the direction of the voice and said, "I'm not out hiking for pleasure, sugar. Get on back to where you came from and be quick about it."

The cool breeze tickled her hair, her face, every bit of skin it touched as she waited. The voice laughed and trees just a few inches to the right of where she had the gun trained rustled only slightly before a man, roughly five-foot seven, with an olive complexion and chocolate brown eyes slid out to stand face to face with her.

"Miz Renee, I presume? Renee Whittaker who is supposed to be sitting on her fine ass in her truck, according to a kid by the name of Shawn Kline," he said, a slow smile spreading over his mouth.

Leveling the gun at him, she said, "I don't like when people know so much about me. Particularly when I know nothing of them."

Renee had barely registered the fact that he had moved and he already had her tucked against him, one hand wrapped securely around hers, aiming the gun safely at the ground. Then she started to swear in a low, heated voice, his amused chuckle only adding fuel to the fire.

"You're one of Dylan Kline's friends," she said, closing her eyes.

"Not exactly. I know him, know a lady friend of his. We did some training together, but we never went out for a beer together or anything," he said, still keeping his fingers wrapped firmly around her gun. "Don't think you could rightly say we're friends. But one of my best friends is a friend of his, so when he called, I figured I might as well come. Now why don't you let me have the gun? It's not a good idea to play with them anyway."

Renee kept the Glock firmly in her hand and ignored him.

"You know, that doesn't exactly look police issue to me," he said, his breath feathering through her hair, tickling her neck, her ears, as he arched his head around, resting his chin on her shoulder. The sounds of the forest seemed to fade away as he mused, "No. Not police issue at all. Makes a man wonder what exactly you're up to, pretty cop, walking around alone in the woods. You know there's all kinds of trouble here. I think you're looking for trouble, especially with that kind of firepower."

She didn't answer. The gun was registered and perfectly legal. So what if it wasn't police issue? Setting her jaw, Renee tried a little harder to pretend he wasn't there.

A soft chuckle drifted from him and he rubbed his chin back and forth over her shoulder. "Stubborn lady. Okay, I'll tell ya what. I'll let your hand go if you put that gun's safety on, and slide it back on out of sight. Then maybe we can talk. But if you try to pull a fast on me...I'll get testy."

"I'm not being set out of the way, or sent along home just because of a group of big tough Rangers showed up to help out a friend of theirs. I can damn well take care of myself," she said in a cold, stony voice. "But if putting it out of sight will get your hands off of me, you jackass, I'll do it."

"Hell, I'm almost tempted to say screw that. I think I like having my hands on you," he murmured, even as he released her other hand, sliding his hand up her arm, her neck, brushing a few stray strands of blonde hair aside.

Renee felt her heart stutter to a stop and she cursed the minute shaking in her hands at that soft comment, the light touch of his fingers on her. *Oh, no...*

Gritting her teeth, she slid the safety on and his arms slowly fell away, letting her tuck the Glock out of sight under her shirt as she slowly turned and stared at him. He winked, quick and friendly. "Good girl," he told her. "Now since I know I'd be wasting my time trying to talk you out of this, I'm not going to bother. Let's just get on moving. Sears is calling people to order and he and Kline are running the show around here."

Licking her lips, she settled on the path after him. "Isn't it kind of foolish of you to turn your back on somebody you don't know?" she asked.

One well-muscled shoulder lifted in a shrug. "No more foolish than you putting that gun away. Fair is fair."

ରେଓଃରେଓଃ

Dylan was standing in front of seven men, five of whom he had bled, sweated, and nearly died with. The seventh met his eyes and nodded, and said nothing, as the cop standing beside him fumed and crossed her arms in front of her, glaring at Dylan. Dylan could feel the stubbornness radiating off her and cocked a brow at Luciano, meeting his gaze and holding it for a long second.

"She's pretty insistent she be here, Dylan." Luc glanced at the cop and then at Dylan, a slight smile lurking at his mouth.

"I can see that," Dylan mused.

Dylan didn't miss this life. He missed the friends. He shouldn't cut himself so badly. He'd mourn Dom and Dally every day for the rest of his life, and Nick, he'd pray for some kind of miracle.

But he didn't miss the Army. He didn't miss being a Ranger. The life he had built here had come to mean more, and he had a bigger purpose in life than a Ranger. And his woman was somewhere in this huge forest, *alone*. And the kids...always the kids.

"So exactly what are we doing here?"

Dylan grinned. "Short and to the point, aren't you, Luc? Where's Raintree? I'd rather just explain this once, but I don't want to wait for the bastard to slide out of the leaves before we start looking."

"Boo."

Dylan had barely had time to step back out of the way before the tall, rangy Native American dropped out of the tree over them, with a wide grin on his face as he saw Renee jump and Shawn swear, one hand going behind his back. "I hope you didn't give the baby brother a gun, Dylan. He looks a little too jumpy," Ethan said.

Shawn pulled the knife from his back pocket, the six-inch switch butterfly fitting in his hand even better than it had when he had stolen it from a martial arts supply store when he was twelve. It flew open in his hand as Shawn met Ethan's eyes levelly, before he closed it and then it slid back out of sight.

Dylan smirked. "Baby brother doesn't likes guns, never has. But he has a fetish for sharp objects. And I wasn't about to try to take it from him. He gets testy about that sort of thing." He tossed Shawn a look that said *behave* before he said, "Well. We're here to find some ladies. A redhead is prowling around somewhere and if she gets hurt..."

"A redhead." Ethan laughed. "I have your redhead. She's...*napping.*" He paused before he said it, as though he was reflecting on that word. "Napping, dreaming hopefully sweet dreams, and not evil ones. But Kris is going to be mighty pissed at me once she wakes up."

Dylan couldn't stop the rush of relief that swept through him. "Napping...courtesy of you?" he asked carefully, trying to keep his emotions off his face, out of his eyes. *Safe...she was safe...*

"Well, partly. I thought I was going to have to do something drastic for a minute there. Stubborn lady." His storm cloud eyes met Dylan's and he said, "She was about ready to drop just from the adrenaline crash. She must have been riding it a while. She finally fell asleep. I—helped the process along. She won't be moving for a while."

"Kris is going to have your ass. How long did you spend around her? But I guess she wasn't nothing more than a fucking job to you," Shawn said flatly. "She has a fucking right to be here." Sliding his eyes to Dylan, he asked, "Was that your bright idea?"

"No." That, at least, was the truth. Not his idea, but he would be damned if he'd lie about being relieved she wasn't going to be in the line of fire. If this got bad... Clenching his jaw, he shoved it out of his head.

"She has a fucking right to see this through," Shawn muttered, turning around and moving outside the tight knit circle of men. His eyes met Renee's and she forced a tiny smile.

"If she's a smart lady, she'll see..." Ethan's words died out. Cocking his head, he said, "We've got company coming. We need to figure out how to do this, Dylan. Or are we going to worry about what I did?"

"She's gonna have his ass," Shawn reiterated. Glancing at Dylan, he said quietly, "You're breaking what you have here, buddy. She was just as lost as you were." Then before anybody could say another thing, he moved away and turned his back on them.

"Look, I spent more than a year watching that woman. I like her," Ethan said quietly, moving out of the circle and meeting Shawn's eyes. "But she is *not* prepared for this. She's too soft, too unprepared. Damn it, she grew up in a rich girl fantasy life. She got this far on luck alone and I'm not going to risk that luck running out."

"Enough," Dylan said flatly. Shawn's words spun around in his head. *She was just as lost as you were...* Dylan shoved the sick feeling those words caused him aside and wished to hell that his kid brother hadn't gone and gotten so damned perceptive. "Ethan, head back to where Kris is. That's what you have to do, just watch that area. Jerry, keep Renee with you. Luciano, hang with Jerry and Renee. She knows what's up, more than I do, I bet, since Shawn isn't telling me everything." His grim eyes moved to his brother's back and he shoved aside that niggling feeling.

He split the other four men up and sent them off, Davis and Collins heading down the ridge and Calhoun and Hobbes watching the trail up to the house.

"We're out of here," Hobbes said, a grin splitting his square face. His Queens accent grew softer as they melted into the trees. "Good seein' you again, man."

"Shawn, unless you plan on brooding all night, let's get moving," Dylan said, his voice clipped as he lifted his eyes to the faint sparkle of glass visible through the trees. Catching the set up that Jerry tossed him, he slid the radio gear on, feeling a little less blind now and then he tossed Shawn a questioning look.

Chapter Eleven

Kris could hardly think.

A thick, misty film enveloped everything and she could barely even recall her own name for the longest moments. When she finally left the darkness for the lighter sleep of dreams, she shrieked with rage.

She was stuck here.

Unable to move, lying there like a stone. The bastard had done something. The artificial blanket of sleep lay too heavy on her, and her thoughts were too cluttered. He had drugged her or something.

Wanting to scream, Kris resisted the pull of dreams and tried to focus. But it was so damn hard.

CRCRCRCR

Ethan knelt beside the sleeping lady and laid a finger alongside the pulse in her neck. "Good girl," he whispered. "Just keep resting. I know you're gonna kick my ass when you wake up. But at least you'll be alive and in one piece to do it. Something's not right with this set up. This is too slick. Too pat for some small-time op."

A soft sigh reached his ears and he settled down next to her, his weapon held loosely in his hand as he listened and waited.

CRCRCRCR

Dylan and Shawn waited.

Too fucking long.

Oh, Ethan had called it right. They were getting company. From their vantage point in the tree, they could see everything with too much clarity. So far seven men had come upon the place, four of them Dylan learned from Renee where the ones who had cornered Kris in the mall.

Three more men, then nothing for a good hour. More trickled in, at a steady pace, until more than thirty men were in the house. About a third of them left. The muscle. Going out to watch the grounds, patrol and guard, and Mick Langley was among them. Dylan had recognized one face and thought he'd tear something apart with his hands. Vance Ralston, a well-known sportscaster who had been tried a few years ago for child molestation.

The buyers, then.

People here to buy young girls for sport, to break them.

Shit. What in the hell is this going on here for? Dylan thought, the bark of the branch under his hand cutting into his flesh. *Here...* So close to his home, it infuriated him.

Hell, he knew realistically evil happened everywhere. It thrived on chaos, despair, need, things the young clamored to in droves. The bastard running this had locked into the teenager psyche and drew them out, compelling them.

But this was home.

265

Then there came a face that had him going blind with rage. Max Blessett came walking up those stone steps, side by side with an Arab man, their heads bent low, Max speaking to the gentleman in fluent Arabic. They passed close by where Hobbes and Calhoun were waiting and through the radio set up, Dylan heard the soft hum of them talking. Once they were out of hearing range, Dylan whispered, "What did you hear, Evan?"

Evan's flat voice said, "How in the fuck has he been hiding under our noses all this fucking time?"

"Forget that part. We deal with it, and we deal with him. What did he say?" Dylan asked quietly, speaking into the unit, keeping his voice flat and level. He wasn't going to think of that day, to see Dom's face, Dally's face. If he did, then he was likely to leap out of the tree and go after Blessett himself. Rip his head with his bare hands. The jagged scar at his back seemed to ache, viciously, for a moment.

Then he heard Evan's quiet sigh. "The Arab was making noises about how his boss wasn't going to be pleased if Max didn't provide a better girl this time. They had run out of patience. Max said he hadn't ever failed to provide on time before and he had the perfect girl this time. He was getting ready to start making some changes in his organization, some people had made a few too many mistakes and this girl would be the last. The Arab said he understands, it is getting very hard to find good people these days, but that wouldn't change the fact that the last butterfly had been sadly disappointing. That was why she was brought back."

"Butterfly," Dylan whispered, his voice thick, his throat feeling tight.

Unaware of what all was going on, Shawn murmured, "You don't really think we can take that fucking many people." His eyes were locked on the house, narrowed as yet another walked under the ceiling of leaves.

"Yeah. We can take that many. More, if we had to. But don't worry. You just have to look pretty, if you want the truth." Dylan clicked into the com and waited for Jerry and Ethan to come back. "We have...an interesting development."

Jerry asked softly, "How interesting?"

As Dylan watched Max and the Arab disappear into the house, he answered, "It's in the form of a rat."

The silence on the line was deafening. Collins was the first to ask, "I only know of one rat that would interest me. Nobody has seen him in over a year."

"I just saw him," Dylan said.

Jerry said, "That is a development. It ups the stakes. In a lot of ways. He sees your lady, Dylan, we got more problems. Plus, he knows how to play our games."

Dylan said, "I want to pin them in a room away from the girls. Up front?"

Ethan answered, "Yep. The girls are in the back western room, along the rock wall. Scared to death. There's a great room, down the hall from the girls, with windows facing every direction but the western. You're going to have to wait for nightfall for cover."

"Fuck that," Dylan muttered, shaking his head. "I'm ready as soon as we think everybody who is coming is here. I want them all to pay. Longer we wait, with the rat in the game, the more we risk him knowing something is up. You tampered with the cameras, but a good eye will see something is wrong. He's got a good eye."

The breeze came by, caressing his cheek, blowing his hair into his eyes as he kept his gaze on the house. *Soon.* A muscle jerked in his jaw as he thought of being able to get his hands on Max.

Kris would be safe. Finally, completely safe.

Dylan dropped from the tree sometime later, saying quietly, "Time to take care of the guards." He looked up at Shawn and said, "Wait here. Keep your eye out."

The sound of the guards' radios were ringing through the forest at a low level hum. That and their shuffling footsteps, their talking, the smell of cigarette smoke and body sweat filling the air.

Jerry grinned as he replied, "Guards? Is that what they call them? Radio silence, boys. We're playing with a rat now. New rules."

Dylan snorted in silence as he moved up behind two who were standing smoking and discussing a returned pet.

Like a fucking dog... Dylan came out of the shadows behind one and grabbed him, taking his neck and digging his fingers in roughly, one hand muffling the man's startled exclamation as he sent the bastard in dreamland even as the second guard was turning around to take a piss.

By the time he had finished, Dylan was lowering the unconscious man to the ground. He moved out of sight, circling around to come up behind the second one as he shoved his dick back inside his pants.

"Gus?"

"He's taking a nap," Dylan growled, reaching out, grabbing the second one and flinging him against the trunk of a tree, his hands fisted in the collar of his jean jacket. "Want to join him? Or die?"

Without waiting for an answer, he drove his knee into the shorter man's genitals and when he collapsed over, gasping, Dylan brought his hand down across the back of his neck.

He gagged and bound them both, one to a tree. That done, he moved on. He flashed Shawn a grin before he moved out of sight. He clicked into the radio as he moved on, signaling he had taken two down.

"No. Four," Luciano breathed into the radio. "This is too easy."

"Luc, silence," Jerry reminded.

When it had been quiet for nearly a half an hour, they all rose slowly and moved in.

"We're going in, Ethan," he whispered, almost soundless.

"All cool back here," Ethan said. "I've got this part."

So it was thirty something against the world. Shaking his head, Dylan hoped their luck held.

Drawing his gun, he moved behind a tree, keeping his eyes focused on the house, working slowly around the perimeter.

"Relax, Sergeant. She's sleeping now. But if she wakes up, I'll know," Ethan said when Dylan cast the ridge where they were hiding a glance.

"You got a good vantage point there, Raintree?" he quipped, not sure what to think of how easily they were reading him.

"Excellent. All the way around. And beautiful scenery," he smirked.

"Keep your eyes on the landscape, Ethan."

The Native American chuckled and said, "I am. Mostly. Chief just took down another. You got one getting worried. I can't see anybody else, but I've got their radios jammed."

"You're a handy bastard to have onhand," Dylan muttered, sliding through the trees as the one Ethan mentioned started to call out on his radio. "Mick? Gus?"

"They aren't around anymore," Dylan said.

From the other side of the trees, Luciano said, "I hope you don't mean permanently. We gonna have to do clean up?"

The man, his eyes a little more sharp, his hands a little quicker, lifted his gun. "Who the fuck are you?"

Dylan grinned. "Not the one you need to worry about," he said, lifting his hands, smiling easily at the gun three feet from his face.

"No. That would be me," Jerry whispered, only seconds before the gun went flying off into the distance. The man went down, with Jerry at his back, digging his face into the muck. "I want to know how many guns we're likely to find in there. Might be handy to know..."

The guards were left bound and gagged. With the exception of one. He had seen Luciano take down the ninth man and was lifting his gun, too slowly, too shakily, as though he couldn't believe they had been caught. But his finger tightened on the trigger. Luciano had drawn his own weapon, the man now had a neat little bullet hole between his eyes, his body off in the woods, away from anybody who might step out of the house.

Dylan moved ever slower, hoping.

Praying.

Missy, sweetheart, he thought. *Are you ready to go home?*

They burst into the house like wildfire. Dylan lifted his gun, aiming it at one of the sick fucks.

The smile on his face died away. In one hand, he held a fucking leash. And it was connected to a diamond collar that was wrapped around the neck of a tiny, sobbing creature who fought to keep from letting Ralston touch her.

The round, youthful face was that of a baby, and Dylan felt the rage tear through him.

He leveled the gun at Ralston's face. Coldly, he said, "Let. Her. Go."

CRCSCRCS

Ethan checked Kris one last time.

They were outnumbered. Too badly and he would be damned if he just sat there. Four men had already tried to flee and Ethan had dissuaded them via a hole through the leg. One had tripped, falling down and hitting his head with a sickening thud on a rock.

"Oops," Ethan murmured, sliding his eyes back to the house. Too many guns. Only seven good guys in there. Well, nine if he counted the cop and the kid with the butterfly knife.

CRCSCRCS

Shawn dropped out of the tree, swearing. "Bastards." They thought they were going to leave him behind? With Dylan in there? Kris? Renee?

Not to mention the kids...

He took the gun that had dropped when Dylan had taken the first out. "I can do that," he muttered. "I can make a man unconscious." Granted, he couldn't do it silently.

Then he moved towards the lit windows.

"They left us out," Renee said from the path. She tossed him a narrow look and said, "'Bout damn time you got here. Let's go."

"Ya know, if I wanted to be bossed around, I could have gone and joined the Army," Shawn said, shaking his head. But he fell in step behind her and listened to the roar coming from the house. He grabbed Renee and thrust her against a tree as one man came hurtling toward them, his eyes wild, a gun in his hand.

Odd, muffled popping sounds came through the air, and he prayed whoever in the hell was shooting had good nightsight. It was getting dark.

Then he lunged for the man who reached after Renee, wrapping his fingers around the man's wrist and slamming it into the ground. The gun fell and the man hissed, "Get off me, you bastard. Bunch of cop bastards, gonna kill you all—"

Shawn swore as a knife came slashing at him. He struggled to wrap his hand around the man's wrist with one hand.

In the other, he pulled his own blade, flipping the butterfly open, grunting as his hand slipped and the knife came closer to his face. "Stupid fuck," he whispered, using his weight to slam the knife down. "Stop it already. You want to fucking die?"

The fallen one swore and swung out and Shawn jerked back, and then he backpedaled as his opponent's hand closed around the gun again.

"That's it," he muttered as the gun swung around to face him. Diving low, he caught the weapon hand in his left as he struck out with the knife he held in his right. Bile tore through him, bubbled up his throat as he felt it slide through flesh, as he felt the hot wash of blood on his hand.

The man went limp, his eyes wide, a trickle of blood spilling from his mouth. His blade pulled from the chest with a wet, sucking sound and Shawn jerked away, still holding his knife as he watched the man crumple.

"I killed him," he said in a tight, rusty voice.

ରୁଓୠଓ

Dylan held the girl against his chest, crouched behind the bar. Yeah, there was some serious firepower in the room.

The girl was sobbing, crying, and scrambling to tear the collar away, pathetic mewling sobs coming from her mouth. "Get me out of here," she shrieked, clapping her hands over her ears and crying.

"Jerry?"

"Here, Sergeant." More muffled firepower in. Another body fell. "Luciano?"

"Gotcha, man. We're a little outnumbered, outpowered here."

"Everybody down," Ethan said calmly.

"Ethan, get back to—"

The house shook with the echo as Ethan came running through the door, his assault rifle aimed at everybody still showing their faces. "Stupid bastards."

The firepower shook the house and pain-filled swearing filled the room.

"Anybody else want to die?"

Dylan had to laugh. Ethan's calm, matter-of-fact question was answered by the sound of several guns falling to the ground. Only four more still stood.

But a few faces weren't accounted for.

The one who had originally been holding the girl on the leash. Renee and Shawn came running through the door and Renee swore. "The bastard from the mall, where is he?" she demanded.

Dylan said softly, "He's pocket change. There's a bigger rat here we need to find."

And soon. Before he got away. Again.

ᘓᘓᘓ

Kris fought the cloud of sleep and finally was able to open her eyes just as she watched the head of her guard disappear. "Bastard," she muttered thickly.

Come on... They don't have time...

Kris froze. "Not again."

This voice wasn't one she knew. Lifting her head, she said, "You know, for once it would be handy to have somebody around who can do more than talk to me inside my head."

A laugh caressed her skin, a sound that came more from inside her, than from without. *I helped you wake up, didn't I?*

Kris stood, stumbling into the wall, scrubbing at her eyes with her hands before she lifted her lids and looked around. She was alone.

"Where did you go?" she whispered, licking her lips. But there was no answer. Moving to the edge of the cliff, she watched as three men tore into the room, slamming the door shut behind them, staring at the girls with an evil smile.

Kris swallowed, feeling the spit in her mouth dry.

One was the bastard from the mall.

One was a dark-skinned man. Looking at him, she kept hearing the words, *I have taken many butterflies...*

But the third—

Max.

Her heart slammed against her chest and it was a wonder nobody else heard it. Max's lips moved but she couldn't hear him.

Leveling the gun at one of the girls, he smiled.

Kris screamed and jumped, landing on the window and feeling it break under her weight. Tumbling through, she landed on her ass on the bed and rolled away, keeping the bed between her and the gun.

Slowly, she stood, aware the girls had fled to the bathroom. The door slammed shut and Kris felt the band of fear around her chest loosen, just a little. Even though it was only the slightest bit of safety, it was something.

"You," Max whispered, shaking his head. "I couldn't figure out how in the fuck those bastards wound up here. This isn't anything that the Army gives a flying fuck about."

Kris smiled at the hatred he spat the word out with. "Nice seeing you, too." Then she added, "I'm what the Army gives a flying fuck about. Well, maybe not the entire Army. I've gotten...*involved*, I guess you could say, with somebody you used to know. And I was told not too long ago that they don't take it very kindly when somebody tries to go after their own."

"You think because you're fucking some soldier they'd do this shit, for you?" Max said, laughing. "No piece of ass is that good."

Kris smiled. "Well, you can ask Dylan that when he comes in here to kill you, because he's looking for you."

Shiloh Walker

"Dylan," Max hissed out. "Kline. You're fucking that bastard?"

She arched a brow at him. "In every way imaginable, and as often as possible. And I'm loving every second of it," she drawled, as the rage bloomed in his eyes.

"I should have shot him in the dick instead," Max snarled. "I will, this time. Stupid whore."

She laughed. "Even if you had, he'd still be more of a man than you could ever be."

"I'm going to shoot you in the belly. You die slow that way, bitch. And then I'll take my little sluts and start over."

Kris smiled. "You have to get past them first," she said as a furious bellow from outside the room filled the air. "I don't think they intend to make it easy."

"You die, either way," he hissed, aiming the gun at her face and squeezing the trigger.

"Max, we have to get out of here, *now*," the man at his elbow said, drawing a gun from his back and aiming it at Kris's face.

The third man, Middle Eastern looking, looked at Kris with appraising eyes. "Yes. Yes. Let us go. We shall take this...woman with us and—"

"My ass you will," she said.

Get ready, a soft voice whispered in her head. *They are here.*

Kris whispered quietly, "Who is here?"

"Who in the fuck are you talking to?" Max demanded.

Kris ignored him as she focused on the girl who had whispered to her so many times before. "Who is here?"

276

Us. We are. There was more than one voice now. There were dozens. *A ghost doesn't always haunt a place. Sometimes they haunt people.*

The sound of wind rushing past her ears filled the room, like the sound of wings. When the light went out, she dropped to the floor and huddled there as Max started to bellow in surprise.

Emotion clogged her throat, and she couldn't speak as her eyes moved over the room.

Sweet damnation, she thought, as lights swirled up out of nowhere, taking on faces, eyes, voices. The whisper of the young girls he had taken, too many silenced forever. He stared sightlessly at them, swearing and fumbling for the gun he had dropped.

The door came crashing open, light spilling in as he raised the gun, focusing on an insubstantial form and firing. Bullets went flying through the air, and one ricocheted, catching a surprised, innocent-looking good ole boy in the chest right as he was turning to flee from the room.

The man who had enticed so many girls off the streets collapsed dead. The Arab man drew his own gun, just in time to see Max pointing a gun at him, firing at the misty white apparition that stood between them. "Do not shoot, my friend!"

Max's snarled exclamation rang out, "You are fucking dead, bitch. Stay—"

The words stopped in mid-sentence and Kris looked over two bodies crumpling to the floor to see Dylan standing there, lowering the gun before he lifted his eyes to hers. "Kris…"

That was the last thing she remembered hearing.

Jerry and Luciano stood side by side, staring at the fading white lights as Dylan dove through them, catching his lady in his arms and easing her to the floor. "What the hell..."

"Don't think hell has anything to do with it," Luciano said as the white lights faded, swirling upward, the soft light sound of laughter fading, replaced by a quiet sighing as the white mist faded away completely.

"I don't believe in ghosts," Jerry said, shaking his head.

"What about angels?" Ethan offered as he moved past them, kneeling down to lay his fingers at the fallen man's throat. No pulse. Max's eyes stared straight up, wide and frozen, a look of abject horror on his face.

Standing, Ethan said quietly, "Burn in hell." Then he moved over and checked the bodies of the other two men, skirting Dylan as the man cradled his woman in his arms.

Luciano and Jerry met each other's eyes.

What about angels?

CRCBCRCB

Dylan brushed back her tangled red hair, studying her pale face. Tiny abrasions from her leap through the glass sunroof marred her milky skin. But she didn't have another mark on her.

"You feeling pretty tough now, babe?" he teased as he settled on the edge of the chair placed by her bed.

"Tough. Sure. I let that jackass Raintree drug me, fell asleep in the middle of the most important thing I've ever done in my life, and then I passed out as soon as it was over," she muttered.

"I don't think Ethan taking chloroform to you counts as you passing out," Dylan said. "And just so you know, that was his bright idea. Not mine."

She slid her eyes, cool and distant, to his face before going back to stroking the sheet. "I led you there. You couldn't have saved them without me," she said quietly.

Dylan blinked, his lashes hooding his eyes. "I know that. You risked your ass though, and I don't like to think how close you came to dying. Being hurt. They were going to grab you in the mall. Do you know that?"

Arching a brow, she said, "I'd rather that happen than them get another child." Kris lifted her chin. "Of course, if somebody was willing to *listen* to me, I could have probably stayed a little farther from this mess I landed in, and still done something worthwhile."

Dylan's face heated and the rage of emotions inside him reflected on his face. "I know that. I knew that before Shawn found your damn journal and told me what in the hell you were doing," he said, catching a lock of hair and twisting it around his fingers. "I fucked up. I admit that. Partners don't leave the other one behind, do they?"

"Partner? We aren't partners. I'm an editor, remember? I run names for you from time to time, tell you when one makes my belly itch. I have dreams from time to time and I tell you about those," she said, her fingers folding the blanket that lay across her lap.

"You're not happy with that," Dylan said gently, reaching out and tugging the blanket from her fingers, lacing her hands with his. "You left mundane behind a while ago. I should have seen that. Should have seen that you're not...ahhh..."

She lifted a brow at him. "I'm not what? Soft? Fragile? Helpless?"

He grinned. "Fill in the blank?" he suggested. "You found what you needed to be doing. You have to do something about the voices that whisper to you. I understand that now. So if it's partner in truth you want...?"

A smile trembled on her lips. "You mean that? You think I can handle myself?"

He laughed. "Hell. It's more like can I handle you." Sliding from the chair, Dylan lowered his face and buried it her lap, wrapping his arms around her waist. "I was so damned scared. I thought I'd lost you."

He wasn't talking about the capture of the kidnappers though. Her distance over the past few days was eating at him and holding her close just made him need to hold her even closer. To make sure she never left.

"I wasn't going to leave you," Kris whispered shakily, threading her hand through his hair. "I was just...giving you an eye opener."

Dylan laughed. "It worked. So are you going to make me feel better by marrying me?"

Kris's hands stilled in his hair. Then she started stroking through the short, tousled locks, and she said, "Why the hell not? I've been yours for years anyway. Might as well make it official."

About the Author

To learn more about Shiloh, please visit http://www.shilohwalker.com or

http://shilohwalker.wordpress.com. Send an email to Shiloh at Shiloh_@shilohwalker.com or join her Yahoo! group to join in the fun with other readers as well as Shiloh! http://groups.yahoo.com/group/SHI_nenigans/

Look for these titles

Now Available

The Huntress
Hunter's Pride
Malachi
Talking with the Dead

Coming Soon:

For the Love of Jazz
Beautiful Girl
Destiny Awaits
Hunter's Night

Surrounded by death, a man with a terrible gift reaches for life.

Talking with the Dead
© 2006 Shiloh Walker

A horrific tragedy blasted open a door in young Michael O'Rourke's mind—cursing him with the ability to talk with the Dead. Nearly two decades later, Michael has moved from victim to survivor, using his abilities to seek out those who would go unjudged.

With his gift, he talks to those who've died violently and seeks out their killers. Only once he's found the murderer, can the victims be at rest. After his last case, the only thing he wants is peace and he hopes to find it in the small town of Mitchell, Indiana.

But something is horribly wrong—the dead are waiting for him there, as well.

Small-town sheriff Daisy Crandall is frustrated. The murder investigation she's leading is going nowhere, the few leads she's had haven't panned out. She needs a break—this case is personal and when a stranger arrives, turning up where he shouldn't be, she's suspicious. Finding out that he is more than what he appears to be, should shock her but doesn't. The fact she's highly attracted to him at the worst possible time is a hindrance.

Unfortunately, teaming up with Michael is the only way.

Now it's a race against time before the killer destroys the life of his next victim...

Available now in ebook from Samhain Publishing.

Too late. He was always too late. This was the story of his life. He came in after the horrors happened and tried to piece things back together again.

It was destroying him.

The tiny chiming of a bell over the door intruded on his brooding and he glanced up automatically before returning his attention back to the plate in front of him. It held no appeal for him, but he knew if he didn't eat, he'd never rebuild the strength he had drained tracking down Watkins.

Energy crackled through the room as a cool breeze from the outdoors came gusting through the door just before it closed. Like static electricity, the energy danced down his skin, shocking him, sizzling under his flesh, bursting through his mind like fireworks on the Fourth of July.

Slowly, he raised his eyes from the unappetizing food and found himself staring at a snug little backside covered in khaki as a woman boosted herself onto a stool at the café counter. Her hair was golden brown, caught in a thick braid that hung more than half way down her back. As he watched she shrugged out of the rather official looking jacket, Michael cursed the blood that was suddenly running hot through his veins.

This was a distraction that he didn't want and didn't need.

First the dark cloud that had taken hold of his mind and now all he could smell was the faint tropical fragrance that drifted from the woman's hair and the soft vanilla of her skin.

And the purpose that filled her entire being. It was like she was walking around wrapped with neon, but only Mike could see it.

Anger.

Frustration.

Rage.

Bingo. The woman was all but a walking, talking cry for help and Mike just didn't know if he could take any more on right now. Then he blew out a breath and muttered, "You can handle it. You always do."

Rolling his eyes skyward, he thought silently, *But it would be so nice to actually be able to have a relaxing vacation.*

A soft, familiar voice echoed in his mind, *"Then maybe you should try some remote cabin in Alaska. Might be a few less unsolved murders out in the middle of nowhere."*

Years of practice had taught him not to flinch, not to jump, not to even look directly at the man speaking to him. Nobody else would see him. He had been dead for twenty years. *"How's the afterlife, Lucas?"* he asked dryly, arching a brow as he nonchalantly turned his gaze to stare at his brother.

"Ever the smart ass, Mikey." A slow smile tugged up Lucas' lips in a grin that haunted Michael's sleep. *"You know, you could move into one of those glacier caves. I bet not too many people have been murdered in one of those. You can get some peace there."*

Lucas' face was forever young. Some movies painted ghosts as grisly images, but it had been Michael's experience that a ghost was an echo of what the ghost remembered seeing in life. Lucas looked exactly as he had the last time he'd seen himself, standing in the bathroom, running his hands through his hair. Wavy brown hair, a little too long, blue eyes surrounded by spiky lashes that both of the brothers had inherited—and hated. Thin to the point of being bony, with big hands, big shoulders. Exactly as Michael had looked at that age. Mike had grown into his body—Lucas hadn't been given the chance.

Forever young. Forever handsome.

"You're becoming pretty damned moody, Mikey."

A tiny smile lit his face. Nobody but Lucas had ever called him Mikey. And even though he had most likely passed the age where Mikey was an acceptable name, hearing it from Lucas was oddly comforting. Just like seeing him was comforting. But at the same time, Mike hated seeing him.

He interacted with ghosts on a regular basis and they only hung around the living for as long as they had unfinished business. Once their business was finished, they passed on.

Lucas had been waiting for twenty years to finish his business and he didn't seem to be in any hurry to move on now, either.

"When are you going to move on, Luc?"

"When I make sure I keep a promise. Promise is a promise, Mike. I told you I'd make sure you were happy. That's when I'll move on."

With a sigh, Michael shoved a hand through his hair. This was an old conversation, one they'd had a hundred times. *"There is something wrong here."*

Lucas lifted one shoulder in a restless shrug. *"I know. I felt it this morning. Young people. A lot of blood. Some old. Some fresh. But something is definitely not right in Smalltown America."*

Michael suspected the lady sitting on the stool in front of him had answers. He could see it in her weary, bitter eyes and the way she sat. Although she sat tall and straight with her shoulders pulled back, there was an invisible weight bearing down on her.

He didn't need to see the shiny brass badge on her jacket to know what he was looking at.

Cop.

From under the fringe of his lashes, he sat back and studied her. It was there in the purposefulness of her walk, the way she held herself, in the tense frustration he felt rolling off of her. *"Go ask her,"* Lucas suggested.

"Stranger in town, asking if there's something odd going on in her town. Oh, yes, excellent way to not attract attention." Michael shot that idea down as he shoved the sandwich on his plate around.

"If you don't eat that, you're going to be sorry later."

Michael curled up his lip and slowly lifted the sandwich, trying to tune his brother out as he bit into the pile of meat, cheese and bread. It had about as much flavor and appeal as a sawdust sandwich would, but he knew he needed it.

"That's a good boy," Lucas teased, reaching out to pat Michael's head.

Michael felt the touch like a cool wind on his scalp. It didn't bother him anymore when the dead touched him. But he still slid Lucas a look and silently said, *"Fuck off, man."*

Lucas might be dead, but he was still Michael's brother.

Printed in the United States
91765LV00005B/27/A